THE

CUBIST'S HOUSE

A NOVEL BY

JEAN BONNIN

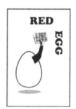

RED EGG

4 1 0255329 6

By the same author

A Certain Experience of the Impossible (2009)
Lines Within The Circle (2012)
Un-usual Muse-uals (2012)
Being and Somethingness (2015)

Jean Bonnin

Jean Bonnin was born in Lavaur, in the Tarn in France, in the year of the deep snows; he was brought up mainly in Wales and England. He took his first degree in government and politics at Birmingham, and his second in political philosophy at Hull; his doctoral research was on the theory of despotism. After university he lived and worked in France, Portugal, Ireland, and the former East Germany. On deciding to leave the underground and avant-garde music scenes of Berlin and northern France behind him – but not to abandon his music-making altogether – he returned to Wales where he now lives with his memories and his out-of-tune piano.

The Cubist's House

An Original Publication of Red Egg Publishing

An imprint of Red Egg International
First published in the UK by Red Egg Publishing

in 2015

www.redeggpublishing.com

Copyright © Jean Bonnin 2015

British Library Cataloguing-in-Publication Data
A catalogue record for this book is available upon

request from the British Library

ISBN: 978-0-9571258-5-8

THE

CUBIST'S HOUSE

A NOVEL BY

JEAN BONNIN

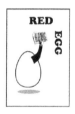

Without culture, and the relative freedom it implies, society, even when perfect, is but a jungle. This is why any authentic creation is a gift to the future. (Albert Camus)

The art world is now a slave of mass culture. We have a sound-bite culture and so we have sound-bite art. You look at it, you get it – it's as immediate and as superficial as that.

(Matthew Collings)

Whoever controls the media – the images – controls the culture. (Allen Ginsberg)

We have to continually be jumping off cliffs and developing our wings on the way down. (Kurt Vonnegut)

For Travelling Stanley, wherever he may be.

PART I

CHAPTER I

I haven't been well lately. If truth be told I haven't been well for some time. But while there are planets in the heavens and fish in the oceans I will not give in, I will not bow down. My feelings are my own, to be had or not to be had – but above all to be accepted and understood, not denied, denigrated or manipulated. And, yes, with all my lows and highs, and imperfections, this nevertheless is who I am. And that, I'm afraid, is just going to have to be accepted...

Now, as over the last year or so, I look better than I feel. That is luck I guess; luck, genetics and latterly a good suntan... I have dark brown hair, covering half my ears at the sides and falling half-way down my neck at the back. I have a solid jawline and my cheekbones, which were well-defined in my younger days, have been steadily disappearing with the ageing process and the filling out of my face. I have grey eyes, and silver flecked sideburns. My nose is somewhat pointed, with a slight kink in it where I flew over the handlebars of a friend's new bike when I was ten. I am five feet eleven-and-a-half inches tall and weigh about ten and a half stone.

But more importantly than any of that is how to begin to write about it all, how finally to write the definitive version of what happened? For me, for my unknown readers, and above all for you, my love.

I believe it was Sartre who said that a story should have a beginning, a middle and an end, but not necessarily in that order. Well, I wonder what he would have made of all this?

------ • • • ------

"Everyone has a story to tell..." I continued. "They say that, don't they? That *everyone* has a novel in him. But is that truly the case?

"It's like saying that everybody has a song in him or everybody has a great painting in him, or her. And then again... it's not like that at all, is it? For unlike with songs or pieces of art – where you have to be able to think in terms of rhythms and melodies, or pictures and perspective – with writing... well, everybody uses words.

"Maybe that's where *everybody has a novel in him* comes from. By virtue of everyone utilising words and everybody having a story to tell..."

I babbled on, excited I was finally leaving - until I got around to telling them what I'd wanted to tell them from the outset: "And right now, as I've mentioned to some of you in tutorials, I feel as though the time is right for me to begin my fourth novel. And for me to be able to do this successfully I require time; uninterrupted time... And this is why regrettably I won't be here next year.

"I apologise to those of you who may have been counting on me, but I'm sure that whoever is my replacement will be more than capable of supporting you in your final year of studies. It goes without saying I wish you all the best of luck, both for the forthcoming exams and for next year. Enjoy your studies, be diligent, and have a great summer...

"So, that's it really... Yes... if you have any queries or wish to see me about anything you'll be able to catch me either in my office or most probably loitering around the coffee machine for the next few hours."

This final sentence was greeted with a smattering of applause and five or six unconvincing laughs from the back of the lecture theatre. "Thank you all and goodbye," I added as the eighty or so of them shuffled their way towards the exits. But I didn't really care – not any longer. In my mind I had finished weeks ago. If the Dean of Faculty hadn't unexpectedly granted me the year's study leave I'd have just quit: taken my things and left.

London was no place for me any longer, not the way I was feeling. I'd attempted to shut myself off from as much of it as possible. But it was the end of the academic year and assignments had to be set and papers had to be marked. I couldn't have gone on for much longer, though.

Colleagues would ask me if everything was alright. I would nod or change the subject. I would try to remain as invisible as circumstances permitted. I'd hide away in my office and lock the door, pretending I wasn't there if anyone happened to knock.

The students appeared to like me, and respected me – as far as I could tell. There was a certain cachet to being a published author, and a good number of them would have wished the same for themselves. I assumed that, at least in part, this was the reason for my lectures' being so well attended. And somewhat immodestly, to be fair to myself, when I was enthusiastic about my subject matter, my two one-and-a-half hour weekly lectures with them were entertaining and, dare I say, thought-provoking affairs.

My plan was to get away, write, and attempt to piece together all that had transpired. I longed for peace;

peace and quiet and time. I needed somewhere with silence all around. A place where I wouldn't be disturbed, where a phone wouldn't ring and a passing car wouldn't pass. I needed to be able to indulge in my loneliness without feeling self-conscious about it: a place where I no longer had to put on an act.

This was to be my fourth book. My first had been published by chance. I completed it years before it ever went into print. I had written it as little more than 'one more thing to do before I die'. You know – see the Pyramids, learn to play the guitar, write a book… that kind of thing. Then I'd left it, forgotten about it, almost, until a friend of mine, Povol, was having a meal and several bottles of wine at my place. I believe we were celebrating something that he'd done, something minor, which escapes me for the time being. In any case, he was a literary agent and inevitably, we ended up discussing literature.

The conclusion to the evening – to my great reluctance I have to point out – was that he took my manuscript home with him. Two days later the phone rang. It was Povol. He couldn't contain himself, so full of praise was he for my writing. I was flattered, of course, and both somewhat embarrassed and disbelieving in equal measures. He wanted to take the manuscript on and told me that he'd do everything he could to find a publisher for me. I told him to do whatever he wanted with it, just so long as I didn't have to get involved.

And so it was. I heard nothing for over a year. Then one morning I went downstairs to find a package lying on my doormat. I took it into the kitchen and put some coffee on. I took a few moments to stare out into the garden at the day's gloomy beginnings, before tearing at the tightly sealed brown paper package. And there it was: my manuscript had miraculously been transformed into a novel. It was difficult to believe. I read and reread the name on the cover. The title at the top was also mine. The artwork wasn't something I would have chosen myself, but I didn't seriously consider that until much later.

So there I sat in my not-fully-awake-yet pre-coffee haze with a newly published novel on my kitchen table, one that just so happened to have been written by me. I saw my words neatly lined up in rows, separated by chapters, lined up and squared off on page after page. The smell of freshly printed pages filled my nostrils. And gradually I realised what a momentous day this was: a day that was to redefine my sense of worth.

That first novel had been autobiographical, or at least semi-autobiographical. Not that anyone would have been able to tell. I had securely hidden my life with sleight of hand and misdirection. I'd wanted to put onto paper the memories, events and people I believed had guided me, or jolted me, into the person I was. It was a cryptic diary in the form of a story; an account where I'd kept in only the most interesting episodes.

Consequently, then, I became an author. And as the incredulity turned to pride and a sense of achievement, and as the pride turned into all the possibilities this unexpected new twist in my life could open up, I nonetheless felt like an impostor. A sentiment I continued to feel right up until the publication of the second novel.

When the second one was published I finally saw myself as a legitimate writer. I had gone through the entire process of writing it, from the scribbling of the first word to the final full stop, with a mind to getting it onto the bookshelves of the bookstores up and down the land.

This second time there was little that I'd consciously put in about me – hidden or otherwise. It was a story, a story of fiction I'd expressly written with a view to selling. Since my late teens I'd sensed it was well within my capabilities to write an imaginative original story. Allowing my mind to wander unshackled, free to pluck stories from the sky, seemed like a blessed way of spending one's days. And that's how it felt sometimes, writing that second one – you reach out for one thing and something else unexpected appears. You feel like a deity in a faithless world. Creation is at your fingertips – as is death, as is history, as is every life-story waiting to be told.

A woman walks into the room – she is the devil, an angel, she has a secret she is guarding well... or quite possibly she is nothing more than a woman walking into a room. Infinity is a concept that it seems only writers can come close to comprehending. No limits, only possibilities: endless alternatives raining in from on high. With every stroke of the pen a million parallel universes present themselves. Nietzsche said God is dead. As far as it goes that's right. Yet with writing it is the writer who is omnipotent.

With my final lecture delivered I headed home. I took the underground and got off at Camden tube station. Summer in the city, even early summer, tended to bustle along in a claustrophobic haze. Oppressive heat and breezeless streets full of people seemingly going nowhere. The bars were crammed and spilling over onto the pavements, making you step out into the street to pass by. Crisp packets and half-eaten hotdogs awaited a non-existent street cleaner; music drifted out from doors and open windows, and the clatter of inebriated conversations all competed in a place where silence is as gold dust.

I felt as though my skin were loose, hanging off my body. Grey and torpid, blocked away from the sun: hours spent in lamp-lit rooms even during the hours of daylight. I stopped at Youssef's Mart for a bottle of whisky. He served me with a compassionate smile and a nod of the head. It was not the first bottle of whisky I'd bought from Youssef, but it would be the last for some time. I returned his smile. My brown paper bag and the manner in which I held it were conspicuous in their discretion. It was mid-afternoon. I walked up to Kentish Town. I walked slowly, unintentionally so. I was preoccupied with the day's beginnings and everything I had to do before the day's end.

As I crossed over the canal and looked down into the water I knew it didn't really matter what I was feeling. None of it mattered any longer. Soon I would be replacing these dull waters for waves and a fishing line and a desolate beach.

I turned the key in the lock of the main door that opened onto the street. I lived in a four-storey house that had been divided into flats in the mid-'sixties. Mine was the entire top floor, with a roof patio. It is said that Jimi Hendrix had a short-lived liaison with a woman who had a flat on the third floor at the time. I don't know – could be true.

I climbed the stairs and unlocked my front door. I slung my brown jacket over the back of a chair, poured myself a glass of whisky, sat down and turned the stereo on. Something exotic with beautiful voices, intriguing beats, feeling as though it originated from far away: consisting of ancient sounds from instruments I couldn't picture. I swilled the chestnut-coloured liquid around my glass. The flavour of wood and seedy clubs soothed me. I savoured the moment as I did the knowledge that this was the last evening in my apartment. I submitted to the music as it transported me to a more anonymous place.

And as the music floated around my head and I could picture a medina and brightly-coloured fabrics, and as I began to drift, the telephone rang. I groaned and turned the volume down on the stereo. I heaved myself over to my desk in the corner of the room. "Yes?" – I demanded… No reply. "Hello, who is it?" I enquired – this time less brusquely. Nothing – except for the faint sound of breathing followed by the click of the handset being replaced.

I returned to the settee. I plumped up a pillow behind my head and stretched my legs out. I turned the volume back up and considered who it might have been. Certainly no one from work – it was the end of term, I never socialised with them, and I'd managed to avoid most of them for several weeks in any case. No students had my home number, except for one, but she hadn't attended my lectures in ages. I hardly ever went out, apart from going for the occasional pint in a little backstreet Irish pub on my way home. And I had no friends to speak of – hadn't had any for quite some time… So I shrugged it off as a wrong number, for to do otherwise would have taken me down avenues I wished to avoid.

I noticed the clock on the wall and decided to get on. I pushed myself up to a sitting position and sat with my head bowed. After several moments of contemplation I got up and headed for the bedroom. I tracked down my passport and threw it along with everything else into a tan leather holdall somebody had once brought me back as a present from Tunis.

I didn't require much. All I really needed was solitude and pens and paper. Words would come easily there, fuelled by this new vocabulary of mine. I'd never written from the dark side before. I suppose that was the perverse upside to the smashed-plastic-snowstorm-reality that my life had become.

This book, I was certain, would turn out to be unlike any of the others. It was going to come from another place, a place hitherto I had only suspected existed. No, that's not quite correct. It was a place that I had no doubt existed, but up to that point it had been a place I'd been able to avoid. But *now* I understood the black dogs and the darker people. I had been there too and looked over the edge and it had scared me.

All of those writers and poets to whom previously I'd paid little attention, I now knew where they'd been. I could touch their distress. And I was happy in the knowledge that I was not alone. I was amongst friends. Crazed and mad – not all of whom had made it – but friends nonetheless.

CHAPTER II

Planes and plastic food, and cocktail waitresses with their hands flapping and their emergency doors…

I arrived to a sunny day. A friendly waiting bus driver approached me as I exited the building and offered to put my bag on board. It seemed as good an option as any.

The bus moved along at a village pace. People shopped or traded or talked on street corners. Three elderly gents sat at a café table drinking a morning drink, talking about the day, and the life, and the pace in these changing times. Three men who I imagined had sat at the same table as boys, then as teenagers, then as young men watching the women go by. Then as husbands and as fathers, carrying on a tradition they had begun as fresh-faced youths. And the women sat at home drinking tea together talking about the day, and the life, and the pace in these changing times. And the men talked as they had always talked, and talked about what they had always talked about; sitting in the same places drinking the same drinks they'd begun to drink as young men. Then the time would come when there would only be two. From one day to the next it would happen. And the vacant chair would serve as a reminder. And then eventually on one sad day there would be only one, and there'd be no purpose in going alone…

The mountains came first, followed by the sheer jagged descents into the diamond sheen expanse of the ocean. We wound upwards and people got off in little dormant goat hamlets glued onto the sides of cliffs by stilts and good fortune. As I looked out of the window and we dropped towards the ocean I had the feeling that soon I would arrive. The place that I found, wherever it happened to be, would represent the stone-scratched line in the rock-face which would signify both a beginning and an end. And I scoured for something that signalled I had arrived.

The heat rattled down into the metal bus as I felt every bump through my insufficiently padded seat. The boulders, the sea, the plunging cliffs and the solitary wooden farm dwellings passed before me as if on a roller backdrop like in the old films when they didn't bother with location shots. Briefly I wondered whether I was actually there at all; if I'd managed to escape or if shortly the backdrop would fall and the scene of the city would be revealed.

Then my mind drifted, as did the parched earth dust clouds thrown up by the wheels of the bus. Islands, I considered, as my mind jumped from one reflection to the next, had a special feel to them. They had a sense of freedom and power. The unyielding forces of nature and the cosmos seemed to me to be much more apparent than on greater landmasses; closer, somehow. Every evening the sun is extinguished by the ocean, which is controlled by the lunatic moon. It is the perfect marriage and the perfect union, and in turn the perfect separation. Played out on constant replay the two great powers are brought together, collide, die and are reborn…

I considered this thought for several moments. Then I noticed we were stationary. I shifted my gaze to the interior of the bus. Four passengers were seated, one of whom was peering at me: a hairy young man with bushy eyebrows and a split lip. I peered back and raised my well-groomed eyebrows in his direction. He quickly turned away. It was then that I saw the driver had inexplicably disappeared. I looked around and out of the windows. I couldn't see him anywhere. And since I had been lost in my thoughts I wasn't sure for how long we'd been stationary. As much by default then as anything else I decided this was as good a place as anywhere to get off.

No sooner had I stepped down onto the chalky surface than the driver reappeared from behind a tree. This reminded me of the shopkeeper from Mr Benn, who, as if by magic always appeared at the appropriate moment. I watched as he made his way over to me. He winked and slapped me amicably on the back and despite his four- or five-day growth looked a lot younger close up. He climbed back in and started the engine.

I watched as the bus spluttered slowly away and idly noted how it was of a different colour from the two other buses I'd seen on our route. Once it reached the end of this straight section of road it turned to the right, heading inland back towards the mountains. It puffed one last dirty-looking cloud of smoke from its exhaust as a final farewell and was gone. For a time I didn't move, staring vacantly at the corner of the road. All was still, save for a delicate breeze coming down from the mountains.

I dropped my bag at my feet and surveyed my new surroundings. Six buildings. On one side of the chalk and dirt road was a bar sandwiched between two two-storey square whitewashed dwellings with Roman roof-tiling. Opposite them were three buildings with only a couple of metres between each of them. One of them was also whitewashed while the other two had a daubed terracotta appearance to them.

I took my bag and went up the three stone steps into the bar. It was dark. A welcome breeze struck me as I stood in the doorway. A large fan was slowly revolving in the centre of the ceiling. It wobbled slightly and made a faint click on every second revolution. I waited until my eyes became accustomed to the sombre interior.

The dark turned to light. I saw two elderly gentlemen sitting by the window off to my right playing a board game I didn't recognise. Behind the counter observing me stood a man of a similar age to them. I placed my bag on a table to my left which was situated next to the one other open window and approached the bar.

I asked for a beer. Or rather, I said the word *beer* – banking on the internationality of the word to make me understood. After the smallest of affirmative nods I was waved away back to my table. I put my bag on the floor and pulled out a chair. I was soon served with a frothy glass of golden liquid, a bowl of mixed olives and a bowl of nuts that appeared to have been sprinkled with a red spice, possibly paprika or chilli, I thought. I indicated my gratitude with a smile, to which the gentleman grunted and headed back behind the bar.

It was a pleasant novelty being served with reluctance and the absence of false grace; a stark contrast to the London cafés from which I'd grab a cappuccino on the run. Instead of either the forced smiles on a servant's wage or the obsequiousness of a clawing owner, this was a man who didn't have to concern himself with competition and wouldn't have cared if he had.

During those latter days in the capital, as my mind and body had been longing to get away, I wonder why I hadn't left much earlier; just gone, run away, saved myself...

It just was the way it turned out I suppose. And then finally there I was in that little bar hoping that nearby I'd find somewhere to live. I didn't really care what I found so long as it was a place where I could live undisturbed, where I could write, and where I could – oh, I don't know – get happy again, I suppose.

The rattling of wood on wood and the waving of arms and exclamations told me that the two men had completed their game and were preparing to begin another. The owner occasionally wandered over to see how a particular game was progressing. He'd watch for a moment or two whilst drying a glass with a tea-towel. He'd tut and shake his head before sucking in breath between his clenched teeth and pursed lips. From his palpable displeasure one could be forgiven for assuming he was the true expert of this game; whatever the truth of the matter he clearly would have done things quite differently.

I had a third beer and considered ordering something to eat. To one side of the counter was a glass cabinet containing an assortment of different sized rectangular bowls of various mixtures of vegetables and diced meats in sauces. A large metal plate had a number of pastries on it, but I wasn't sure whether these were sweet or savoury. The bread was light brown in colour, knobbly and coarse. The four remaining slices were in a pile on a green ceramic plate whose surface was comprised of numerous coloured miniature tiles that formed a pattern of concentric circles.

I pointed at several of the bowls and the plate of bread. The owner nodded before he once again flicked his hand at me as a signal to return to my seat. Five minutes later he came over to my table carrying a large plate and a small square side plate. On the small plate were the four slices of bread, whilst the larger one consisted of eight dollops of assorted snacks. Some were oily, others were dry and coated in spices and herbs, and there was one small mound of saffron-coloured rice with green flecks.

I needed to find myself a little house made of stone. I would be a different person there bunkered away from the world, alone with my thoughts and my story. I expected time to expand and contract in unfamiliar ways in such a setting. I anticipated my thoughts and interpretations of events to flow in unfamiliar ways: therapeutically so, meditationally so. That would be a positive thing, I told myself, considering my state of mind; shake things up and appreciate that one form of existence was not the only form...

The owner came over, and as he stood clearing away my empty plates I pointed to a pencil drawing I'd done on a paper napkin of a building with a matchstick man in a bed next to it. As he bent to look at it I said the word *accommodation*. To which he nodded and with his index finger stabbed the air twice in the direction of the ceiling. He wrote a price for the room on its reverse side.

The proprietor indicated that I should follow him. We pushed our way through the heavy fibrous curtain. Behind this was a corridor and thick worn-by-age stone steps that curled around and up to the left. We reached the landing and walked along to the end. He unlocked a door and went in first. The room was dark and smelt musty, and I wasn't that enamoured of it. Possibly seeing the doubt in my eyes he once again raised his well-worked index finger, as if to say 'wait a moment'.

He scurried past the double bed and with one singular sweeping motion parted the curtains. This was done with such zeal that two curtain rings flew off the end of the rail.

The dazzling yellow sunlight engulfed the room. I saw the river that fell like glass into the sea. Suspended animation, caught motionless, the water almost floating in mid-air. Old man's beard, old man's hair, frothing white water into the turquoise-skinned diamond depths. From the mountains far off to the right like a glistening serpent it rolled around boulders and in between rocks.

The well-seasoned leather-lined face of the owner showed clear pleasure as he opened the window with a shove, leaned out and somewhat theatrically took in a deep breath. I got out some money to pay for the room, the meal and the beers, and to show my commitment. He indignantly waved it away, handed me the key and left.

For nearly ten minutes I stood gazing out of the bedroom window. I lay on the bed feeling lighter than I had done in some time. I closed my eyes and fell into a restful void…

When I opened my eyes again the summer sun was splicing the waves in two. I went over to the window again to enjoy a view that wasn't predominantly of cars and concrete. I watched until the final splashes of molten sunlight gave way and darkness began to slip over the sky.

A curtain made of the same rough material as the one behind the bar separated the bathroom from the bedroom. The shower, toilet and basin were functional and clean. The water was cold from the mountains – numbingly so. The first jet took my breath away.

After I'd finished my shower I dressed in my cotton clothes for hotter climes. They consisted of cactus green trousers and a long cream-coloured shirt with five large buttons which looked as though they were made from bone: remnants from a week's holiday in Sardinia two Christmases before.

I only just managed to sidestep the owner holding two glasses of overflowing beer as I slipped through the curtain into the bar. He placed one of the glasses on the counter and shook my hand. Then he swept his arm from left to right, a gesture I interpreted as meaning that I should make myself at home.

Five elderly men, four of whom were bearded, sat at the table where the two had been playing their board game earlier on. Two women and two men were sitting at the table next to where I'd chosen to sit on my arrival that afternoon. The two women were both red-headed: Uluru Rock sunset red; one with her hair beaded in tight plaits, the other with short spiky intentionally messed-up hair.

The woman with the longer hair was wearing a flowing gypsy dress, rusted red in colour and with intermittent miniature mirrors woven into the fabric. The short-haired woman had jungle green combat trousers on. One of the men had a knotted matted wire brush of a beard with grey flecks. The second man had oriental eyes, chestnut brown, with shoulder-length wavy stygian hair. They looked as if they were all in their early- to mid-thirties.

I returned to my window seat, watched people out of the corner of my eye, drank my beer and enjoyed the slight breeze that intermittently brushed against my face. I half listened to other peoples' conversations. They were of course indecipherable, sounding as they did like strange experimental chitter-clang music to my ears.

The group of four on the table next to me were speaking German or Dutch. The spiky-haired woman gave me a smile whenever our eyes met... I recollect fleetingly thinking that it was odd to come across other strangers in such a remote place. And possibly I should have let this thought develop further. But buoyed and distracted as I was with the novelty of finally being in an environment where I could allow the rhythms of my mind to flow freely, I did not.

The group of four got up to leave. They reached the door and stepped outside and then talked for the briefest of moments. One of the men nodded sagely before disappearing around the corner of the building. When he was nearly out of view I saw him lift up a black block. I caught only the briefest of glimpses and didn't give it much consideration at the time. Later, however, I queried whether it could have been a walkie-talkie or communication device of some kind.

The woman with the spiky hair looked at me from the top step of the entrance as her three friends headed into the darkness. She paused, which added to the intrigue, looked out after her disappearing friends then slowly headed towards me. She stood the other side of the table from me and asked if she could sit down. I nodded.

CHAPTER III

So she sat down.

"You know the shamans say that the dinosaurs never became extinct – they simply turned into the birds."

"That's hell of an introduction. You been saving that up?"

She grinned and we shook hands. "My name's Ilona."

"Pleased to meet you, Ilona. I'm... I'm *pleased* to meet you." I repeated rather clumsily: the result of a mid-sentence decision not to divulge my name. "You want a beer?"

"Please... So what are you doing out here on this little island in the middle of nowhere? We don't get many strangers round here." She reached over to the table she'd been sitting at only moments before and grabbed her empty froth-congealed glass. I filled her up from my jug and told her that it was a long story.

"What about you and your friends?" I asked, deflecting the question.

"Oh, they're not exactly my friends… I've only known them for a little while." She winked as she said this.

"I assumed you were all together," I said as I considered what her wink was supposed to signify.

"No, they live in a… I don't know really, a sort of fundamentalist hippy commune I guess you could call it, in one of the secluded coves." She waved her hand loosely over her shoulder, I assumed to indicate the general direction of the commune.

"Right."

"I don't really talk to them about it… But, you know, they're Dutch and I'm from East Germany." She shrugged. "It's nice to have the company… We can understand each other easily enough, especially if we speak more slowly."

"Uh huh… The commune sounds mysterious."

"Um, maybe. I haven't been there myself… it sounds all a bit freaky Ran Dieky to me. No," she shook her head, "the four of us, sometimes six or eight, all meet up for beers and a chat once in a while. As far as I'm aware we're the only non-islanders on this part of the island. It's just pleasant to get together sometimes. Especially for me since I live on my own."

"What was it you just said…" I interrupted, "about freaky something or other?"

"Sorry? Oh well, you know – I'm just sort of here on a long holiday, well, a bit more than that actually, but that'll do for the moment. Whereas they're, I don't know, trying to live some rigid utopian removed-from-it-all…"

"No, I mean the freaky Ron something," I interrupted again.

"Oh right," she chuckled "you don't know who Mr, or maybe it was Professor, Ran Dieky was?"

"Never heard of him."

"Oh, well he… possibly he was a Doctor." She thought for a moment. "Doctor Ran Dieky? Professor Ran

Dieky? Doctor Ran Dieky? Oh, I don't know. Anyway, he came up with the *Thousandth Monkey Syndrome* and everything that goes with that."

"Which is?"

"Oh, OK… you know I'm doing most of the talking here, don't you?"

"Well… I…"

"It's fine. But soon it'll be your turn."

"Yes, of course… Another beer?"

"Thank you… OK then, so *Mr* Ran Dieky – or whatever his title was – said that if you teach a monkey a new skill, and then you teach another monkey and another, until you've taught about one thousand of them the same thing, then afterwards the whole species will be able to perform the new skill. Even if the thousand or so of them has been constantly isolated from all other monkeys."

"Wow, is that true?" I asked incredulously.

"Well, apparently so. But that's not all. Ran Dieky goes on to state that this proves that every species has what he calls a *Grand Consciousness*. So that if a certain number of a given species learns new patterns of behaviour they all learn it. They don't question it or find it strange in any way, and very soon, possibly even instantaneously, they can't even remember a time when they didn't know what they now know… Does that make sense?"

"Oh yes. Well the words do, anyway."

"Good," Ilona said somewhat doubtfully.

"So then…"

"Yes," Ilona interrupted.

"Yes, what?"

"I'm anticipating what you're about to say."

"Really? *What* am I going to say?"

"I think you're about to say something about human beings."

"I was, yes… Look, if he implies that this is the same for all species, well then, that means us also, doesn't it?"

"Absolutely," she grinned. "You want to hear what else he says?"

"Go on then."

"OK, but then it's your turn. "

"I'll be happy to tell you a little about myself, it's just that, well, since you've started…"

"I know, it's interesting isn't it? If maybe a bit far out."

"Yes, it's always interesting hearing about what people believe."

"…So then," she continued, after taking a long swig of her beer, "Ran Dieky said war and man's disposition towards conflict was learned and is not instinctive. At some point, he states, a certain percentage of mankind learned, or was taught, to fight. So we all did. Or, at least, if we didn't fight, we all gained that new skill which from that moment on gave us the option to fight – which we hadn't previously had."

"Hold on, I'm just going to get this jug refilled."

"Here, let me do it." She took the jug, held it above her head and waggled it from side to side. The proprietor signalled that he'd seen her, and she placed it back on the table.

Then she stared at me, into my eyes, a faraway stare I interpreted as being the visible manifestation of an inward search to regain a foothold back into a previous passage of thought.

There were other signals she was giving off as well, subtle and subliminal – signals she was probably not aware of. I was certain however that something on a near subconscious level was being conveyed. What I was unsure of was what it meant: a sideways look at an inopportune moment, a nervous smile, an uneasy rub of the neck, an unnatural delivery, an inappropriate over-familiarity (which admittedly could have been mere friendliness – something that living in London you learned to mistrust).

Some of it was definitely there; some of it, I recognise, may not have been there at all. I had essentially been, for want of a better description, very ill. And part of that illness, part of any mental health issue, involves interpretations, assumptions and feelings about things that most people wouldn't spend time even considering...

She looked me directly in the eye, clearly trying to regain her thread. Before she managed to remember where she'd got to, however, I asked her how Ran Dieky thought man had learnt this new skill.

"Well, the whole thing is..." She paused and tilted her head gently up to the left. She peered through the window and focused seemingly on nothing at all. I in turn directed my gaze towards her partially open mouth and her thin powder-pale-pink lips. I thought about her mouth for a moment, then almost immediately afterwards I thought about how this wasn't my kind of conversation. Her company was nevertheless beneficial: preventing me from spending my first night in that bar alone and probably mentally drifting back to the place I was there to forget.

"Fine," she continued as her eyes and thoughts re-emerged from a faraway place, and her lips came together and smiled. "Monkeys learn their new trick from man. Fair enough, but who teaches man? That's the thing."

"Exactly," I exclaimed, sounding more exultant than I'd wished. "Don't tell me it's the monkeys."

"No. Better than that. He says there are eleven dimensions. And there are entanglements or... erm... disruptions... disruptions is maybe a better word, coming from these other dimensions."

"You mean," I began, but then changed my mind and inquired instead: "How do you know so much about all this anyway?"

"Oh," she blushed slightly and looked up at the ceiling above my right shoulder. "Er... just put it down to a combination of reading and er..." she smiled at me, got a handkerchief out of her bag and wiped her nose, "the fault of an ex-boyfriend."

I don't know why, but I didn't believe her. Sometimes the difference between believing someone and not is very slight. Something wasn't quite right; despite how unembroidered she came across she was nevertheless hiding something.

"Sorry, I shouldn't have asked," I said.

"No, that's fine." Then after a moment's pause she added: "Why shouldn't you ask?"

"No reason, I guess... So?"

"So, yes... You know how when you're in a room that's devoid of ventilation and somebody's smoking a cigarette, and they're holding the cigarette perfectly still?"

"Yes."

"Well, the smoke rises perfectly straight at first. Then, inexplicably, after half a metre or so it continues its journey towards the ceiling by curling and spiralling upwards. Science has as yet been unable to explain this. Ran Dieky states that it's interference or what he calls *overlaps* from one of these other dimensions."

"Umm... that's one hell of a theory."

"Isn't it just."

"This guy he's... well, he's just..." I grappled for an appropriate expression.

"Freaky Ran Dieky," she offered.

"Exactly that..." I held up my glass towards her and taking my cue she held hers up and we clinked them together. She seemed pleased with this gesture. "So", I resumed after a few moments, "what about the whole aggression thing then?"

"Well, Ran Dieky believes that because of these overlaps Beings from these other dimensions can affect our behaviour..." She paused, but before she had a chance to continue I interrupted by asking if she believed in all of it herself. "Look, I'm not saying I believe it, am I?" She sounded indignant. "You asked me," she continued, "where the expression came from? And... you know... I'm telling you what I think these hippies from the bay believe, aren't I? *Not*"- she accentuated the word 'not' – "what *I* believe in."

"No, fine... I was only wondering what your take on all of this was, that's all."

"Humph..."

I watched Ilona as she spoke to me with her slight Teutonic lisp, with her electric hair and her lively eyes. I wondered if she was wearing a small amount of lip gloss, for her lips would occasionally catch the light and glisten. I wondered why she was talking the way she was. And I considered whether any of what she was telling me could serve as inspiration for my next story.

I drifted from concentrating on her bizarre story. My mind jumped as her mouth silently – at least seemingly silently to me at that precise moment – continued to move. I considered Western towns, for this place felt like a bar where cowboys might meet. I speculated as to why a piano was sometimes referred to as a Joanna. But then almost instantly guessed it was most probably rhyming slang, and nothing to do with the Wild West. I grabbed as many snatched glances of Ilona's mouth as I could without her noticing.

Then I saw spurs and cowboy boots, Clint Eastwood, and Cleavon Little, the black sheriff from Mel Brooks' film *Blazing Saddles*. I peered out of the window expecting a horse to be tethered up to a post. My reflections jumped again as I pictured the day I found out Rosio's father was a multi-millionaire Argentinian beef magnate. It was at least a year and a half into our relationship and I recall secretly thinking how he could prove to be a 'helpful' father-in-law. But I grew to realise that she never took a penny from him – so he could have been a pauper as far as having any effect on our lives was concerned. That said, I did once briefly come across some trust fund or something or other. But before I'd had time to grasp the significance of the papers Rosio had returned home. And the next time I'd looked, weeks later, they were gone.

I slowly tuned back into what Ilona was saying. "This is all very…"

"Yes, yes, I know," she interrupted. "But what *I'm* fascinated with, more than purely the idea itself, is the *person* who can arrive at such a theory in the first place… There's a study right there, right?"

"Well, I guess."

A man of about twenty-eight or so with a mandolin strapped to his back stuck his head round the door. He scanned the room, his eyes working their way around from right to left… I continued to float between listening to Ilona and retreating into my own world of reflections, of regrets and of hope.

Eventually his gaze rested upon where we were sitting. For the most fleeting of moments our eyes met. He promptly looked away, and then pretended (I say 'pretended' because that's what it felt like) to continue scouring the room. But it didn't feel real. After his gaze had rested upon Ilona and me, his continued air of looking for something or someone seemed contrived. He had already found what he was looking for; the rest was merely to cover up that fact.

Could I have been mistaken? Yes, quite possibly. Did I think I was? No… It was true that I'd been in a fragile state of mind for quite some time. I'd seen things that hadn't been there and on other occasions I'd completely missed the obvious. Nonetheless, I wasn't stupid. That young man seemed to me to be looking for Ilona or looking for both of us. And this only added to my doubts that Ilona wasn't exactly who she appeared to be.

It seemed opportune then that a Groucho Marx quote should pop into my head at that moment: *Who are you going to believe, me or your own eyes?* And somewhat inveigled by that thought I persuaded myself to discard such meditations.

"...Imagine", Ilona was saying, "you are a creature living in two dimensions and you want to make contact with us. How would you do it?" I shook my head as she reached down into her Soviet Army duffel bag. She produced a crumpled piece of paper and a pen. Holding the corner of the paper with one hand she brushed it as flat as it would go.

While she was doing this I noticed a painting on the far wall above the heads of the now six elderly gentlemen. Appropriately enough the painting was of a bearded man. He had an aquiline nose and a dark complexion, and was standing on steps to a building that was off to the left and all but out of view.

The man was gazing into the middle distance looking majestic and sagacious. Sitting on the bottom step was a woman with wavy auburn hair; appearing tranquil and at ease she was also staring at something of which we were given no clue. In the background near the horizon were hills, luscious green valleys and an emerald sea. The hills and valleys were strewn with towers and buildings of spiralled white granite.

It was dusk in the painting and a brushed crimson tinge was washing over the scenery. I surmised it was purporting to be a portrayal of mysticism and ancient times: idyllic and idealised. Possibly it was supposed to be of Atlantis in the distance (before the flood), or possibly it was a depiction of the gods.

"So," she finally pronounced, "a flat piece of paper."

"Flattish," I smiled.

"Yes, flattish. But for these purposes let's imagine it's perfectly flat."

"Alright."

"So, Ran Dieky states that this, for example, is how creatures living in two-dimensional worlds make contact with us." She stabbed the piece of paper from underneath with the pen. "Because they have no other choice."

"What? They take a…"

"Hold on! You're not a very patient man, are you?" she snapped. And in that small instant I saw a nastiness I wouldn't have expected. She caught herself almost immediately, however, and reverted to the amicable storyteller.

"What I'm illustrating – incidentally, in the same way my former boyfriend showed me – is how two-dimensional creatures contact those of us who exist in three dimensions. What I'm saying is they have no way of letting us know they're there apart from 'punching' holes through to us."

"You mean…" I began.

"I mean", she continued, "crop circles."

I laughed. "But, they're…"

"They're what? They're fake, hoaxes, cons?" She said this whilst moving her head sarcastically from side to side, skewing her mouth slightly, and adopting a mocking tone.

"Well?"

"OK, a lot of them are. But", she went on, "Ran Dieky gives very good examples of ones that simply can't be explained away."

Her mannerisms and easy intonation for the majority of the time corresponded to someone who was merely imparting knowledge to an interested party. Her eyes, however, conveyed something more. They were the eyes I thought of the doorstep witness selling the word of God.

"Uh huh," I mumbled as I considered what she'd just said. "Well," I said, "it's certainly the most imaginative explanation of crop circles I've come across."

"Isn't it? That's exactly what I thought... even if a lot of it *is* rubbish," she added as an afterthought. "I mean, there are so many crop circles each year that at least one of them has to be the real thing. And, if only one of them is authentic where does it come from, right?"

"Umm" I said, as I pictured some of the beautiful patterns I'd once seen in a friend's book about crop circles.

"As for the war stuff... well, the creatures from the higher dimensions are either good or bad – depending upon which dimension they're from. Some of the bad ones started coming to earth hundreds of thousands of years ago. Ran Dieky says he's not sure what their motives were...

"He does, however, hypothesise, stating that in his opinion either they wished to colonise Earth but needed us to destroy ourselves first, or they wanted us as their slaves, or it's simply a cruel game they've created.

"Whatever it is: they instilled in our brains an aggressive warlike tendency. We're very peaceful, harmonious creatures at heart. We've just been made to forget who we really are. Aggression and a competitive nature have been instilled into us. As with the monkey example we are unable to remember a time when we didn't have to compete and fight for our survival. The thing is though..." she paused, I later presumed for emphasis, "it's not strong."

"What's not strong?"

"I mean they don't have a strong enough power to make us aggressive, they're only able to make us think we're aggressive."

"I think, therefore...". The end of my sentence petered out, slurred, lost the punch of its beginnings. Possibly due to a change of mind, lack of confidence, or most likely due to loss of interest, either in what I was saying or what *we* were discussing.

Ilona hadn't noticed. "Exactly," she said enthusiastically. "I think I'm aggressive therefore I am aggressive."

"Umm..."

People came and people went – never too many one way or the other to make much difference to the atmosphere in the bar. The lights in their stone wall recesses and the candles on the tables, lit shortly prior to sunset, added to a sense of intimacy, exclusivity, even.

Aliens and exhaustion could easily have led me to concoct innumerable underlying mysteries for the reasons behind each person's presence in that room. For with so few buildings around I wondered where the dozen or more people could have come from.

Imperceptibly, I expect, I grinned to myself at the thought of all the intrigue and subterfuge I could invent if I chose this bar to be at the centre of my next novel. I could make it into a secret club or a place where members of a religious cult might meet. A place where, despite impressions to the contrary, everybody knew each other and were all observing me. Or possibly they were gun runners and drug smugglers disguised as fishermen. The possibilities were endless.

Days come and days go and some of the most intriguing experiences I have had have been by chance. A missed train or a late night bus, a busker with a guitar or a hitched ride in a stranger's car... Somebody once told me on one of these serendipitous meetings (if that is what it was) that coincidence is merely coincidence, but once a string of unexplained 'coincidences' occurs one has to look a little deeper.

As a consequence I intentionally altered the manner in which I interpreted events. Namely, when several unusual incidents occur more or less one after another, I allow myself to perceive them as being more than simply chance occurrences in a random universe.

This I do to amuse my mind and allow it to diverge and create interesting scenarios. I don't think I ever really believed haphazardness to be anything other than how it seemed. All I did was orchestrate a method, an approach, which enabled me to consider a series of apparently unconnected events. Much more fun, you see, to join dots rather than leaving them isolated.

Everything in any event was reduced (or augmented) to interpretation. So why not? Why not postulate an approach through which to evaluate the bizarre coincidences of existence? Certainly, as a writer, why not? Why not be more creative in one's dealings with the everyday happenstances of life? Create links where there most probably were none. Invent stories and make up spiralling tales from what an outsider would see as nothing at all. A chance chat, a screeching car, a still smoking cigarette butt with a lipstick-stained filter and no sight of the owner, a forgotten scarf – all insignificant events if left in isolation. Yet strung together, they form the basis of a mystery.

CHAPTER IV

CHAPTER V

So then it was my turn... *This* was going to be the real beginning, the true beginning, my true beginning. To hear my words out loud, how my brain translated my circumstances into a form that could easily be relayed to another person, could only be helpful. Therapeutic blah blah blah...

I began by telling Ilona I was a writer. She found that exciting and asked me what my name was. I told her that she could call me Zaccariah, Zach for short.

------• • •------

Zaccariah wasn't my real name, but it was the name I had chosen for myself. I hadn't wished to use my real name: Jethro Carmichael. Something to do with anonymity and creating a symbolic break from the past; it had seemed sensible at the time. I'd dallied with the idea on the plane – the name, I mean.

Zaccariah had been my grandfather's name; my mother's father. My mother had died during childbirth with my younger brother. And due to this, coupled with our father not being around, it became my grandparents' responsibility to take charge of their daughter's two offspring: me and my brother Ruben.

My grandfather was an eccentric man, prone to tantrums and great insight. He was a loner by nature who, due to circumstances, had been forced to spend most of his life in the company of others. He had never had the space to truly develop into the person he could have become, which I think could have been quite brilliant.

This summer marked ten years since I last heard from my brother. He went off travelling shortly prior to his twenty-fifth birthday. Cambodia was the last place anyone had heard of his whereabouts. The assumption was that he was dead; the hope was that he was happily living out his days on a paradise island somewhere.

Reuben had been a difficult child. We'd both been difficult children in our own ways. But whereas I was merely jam-packed with unabated energy, Reuben experienced sudden and acute mood swings. One minute he was happy, the next he was storming upstairs and locking himself in his room for hours on end. When it was really bad he could be up there for days, only coming down for the occasional bite to eat.

Sadly, nobody ever established what Reuben's problem was. My own view was that it was a combination of three elements. His having been born prematurely I think could have contributed to his psychological problems; his belief he was responsible for our mother's death was a constant source of distress for him; and the tendency our family has towards introspection and internalisation cannot, I think, have helped his mental health.

In later years as I got to know my musical history, I realised how similar, at least to my mind, Reuben was to Nick Drake. And once I'd stumbled upon this similarity I was struck by how remarkable not only, as far as I understood them, their inner universes seemed to be, but also how physically alike they were.

Our grandfather was by no means a good role model, either, and certainly not for somebody who was clearly a troubled individual. Grandpa Zach was too unpredictable, too scatty, too much of a whirlwind. Reuben wisely kept his distance, requiring peace and to be left to his own secret contemplations.

To me, my grandfather resembled a rather fantastic wizened old sage from a child's fairy tale. When he was angry, however, he was best avoided. This was easy enough since on such occasions he would take himself off to his shed-cum-workroom. He would rant and bang around until whatever it was that needed to pass had passed.

When Grandpa Zach was fun he was great fun. Full of crazy plans and half-baked inventions, tinkering around with coloured powders and pungent chemicals. Exhilarating noises and colourful smoky explosions were commonplace in his garden shed. I would be up a tree or scrumping in next door's orchard when there would be an almighty bang. I would peer through the gap in the fence or down from my crow's-nest tree-house vantage point. I would see my grandfather stumbling out of the shed door, looking dazed in the billow of green smoke that accompanied him.

As I reached my teens Grandpa Zach allowed me to help with his experiments. He would talk to me as an equal, as an adult, which you seldom find as a child and appreciate wholeheartedly. He would ask me for my opinion on such and such an idea, or to help out with whatever new experiment he had concocted. And I suppose in later life if I hadn't loved English literature so much I would probably have become a scientist, following somewhat in my grandfather's footsteps. I did get an 'A' Grade in my Chemistry A Level, after all.

Either way, I believe I had an upbringing that cannot be faulted. Ruben, though, would have significantly benefited from the stability a more traditional home life could have provided. None of this was down to my grandparents, who did the best they could. It can't have been easy for them, either, having to look after two young whippersnappers whilst coping with the loss of their only child.

So, *Zaccariah* was the name I chose for myself. Not because I especially saw my grandfather in me. It was more that it represented where I came from; and despite what had happened to my mother and the inner turmoil of my brother, it was a time when I was happy.

I chose this pseudonym to create the illusion that I was somebody else; for myself almost as much as anything else...

------• • •------

CHAPTER VI

The story I told her…

The months rolled on and we were happy, Rosio and I. She was Argentinean. Originally from Mendoza, a pretty little town situated in the valley below the Aconcagua Mountains. I had met her at the Glastonbury Festival one summer.

Her name – Rosio (pronounced *Ross-ee-oh*) – meant 'dew' in Spanish, which was appropriate since we'd met as dawn was rising. We found ourselves standing next to each other at the entrance of a jam-packed marquee listening to a group called Channel Light Vessel Automatic. She was there, so it turned out, by chance: the result of a momentary pause in an otherwise fruitless night-time meander to find her tent.

I was there by design. I had seen the group play at my old University several years before. I'd liked them on that one previous occasion. Not to the extent of chasing them up or attempting to track down any of their music on vinyl, but they'd stuck in my mind all the same.

When I first saw them they were a three-piece. The singer-cum-lead-guitarist had been gowned as a medieval fire and brimstone preacher. Everything he wore was black – all the way down to his exaggeratedly pointed black leather shoes. The only part of his outfit that had not been the colour of night was his whiter-than-white diamond-encrusted cross hanging around his neck. The bass player was dressed in the traditional, what probably could be described as 'gothic', garb of an undertaker, including a dented top hat perched precariously on his rhythmically bobbing head.

The conclusion of their set consisted of them, in a three-minute guitar-wielding frenzy, mercilessly smashing up several Sgt. Pepper style dummies to within an inch of their plastic lives. By the time Rosio and I saw them, which was seven years after they'd played at my University, they'd become a ten-person outfit. Visually, they were still interesting, dressed up as surgeons and vicars and World War I fighter pilots, but for me they had lost their bite.

Eventually, we found Ilona's tent pitched in the left-hand corner of the Green Fields. Not that we slept. We spent the rest of the night and the dawn-light hours sitting wrapped in a blanket in front of her tent on her blow-up mattress. We talked and smoked. We talked about music and ourselves. She was wonderful and natural and completely unaffected. In the morning, the true morning, I went off to track down some breakfast.

The track was dusty; it had been a hot June. Early morning activities were commencing. Blurry-eyed people, jugglers, soft sweet wafts of marijuana, coffee drunk out of coconut shells, a bearded man with a blanket on the grass verge selling Peruvian hats made from llama wool, a naked couple, skinny, hairy and well hung, walked by smiling to everyone they passed. A guy with a guitar was strumming a Neil Young song, and a woman without a bra was eating a pasty, a shack on the right was selling didgeridoos, to the left was a small shop covered in hand-carved suns and moons with strong clouds of nag champa incense emanating from its dark candle-lit interior. I faintly heard a short blast of the chorus of The Waterboys' song *Old England* coming from a tent off to my left; then it, as did my thoughts, drifted away.

Next to the head-shop, which was playing a track that appeared exclusively to consist of the repetition of the mantra 'Toadstool soup, toadstool soup, drink it singularly or in a group...', was a Wild West style log cabin with a semi-circular arrangement of benches. It was selling veggie fry-ups from a hatch. I went over and waited patiently behind a group of three people indecisive about what to order. Behind the counter coming from a mono cassette player was The Clash's version of *Armagideon Time*, and I began to sway to its gentle rhythm.

When it was my turn I leaned on the kiosk's serving shelf and ordered a couple of pancakes with homemade strawberry jam, a couple of orange juices and two milky sugary coffees. I left a deposit for the tray and ambled back up the slope, spilling coffee as I went. I spotted the naked couple in one of the 'quiet spaces' doing yoga: an intricate set of moves I believe was called Greeting the Sun. Ironically, whilst greeting the sun they were partially obscuring it with a moon.

Several splashes of coffee bounced out of their cardboard cups as I negotiated the uneven ground and the maze of guy ropes and tent pegs. On my return I found Rosio curled up asleep on her blanket. I placed her breakfast next to the entrance of her tent and began to tuck into mine. I sat there in the increasing warmth of the morning sun looking down over the immenseness of the festival site. I could see large colourfully striped marquees and languidly rising fire smoke. From left to right and back again I scanned the city of tents: the temporary sprawled community that once a year lived together and then was gone.

I contemplated a story a long-since-lost friend had once imparted. It concerned where he came from, which was somewhere near the Lake District. He told me that in the estuary near his home there was – due to the mud banks and residue and silt – a rock that looked like a standing stone and could be seen only once every few years. It was called the Seldom-seen rock. And like the disappearing rock, I thought, this was a city for a moment in time, then as if a great magical spell had been cast it vanishes.

Rosio stirred and turned over as I drank my sweet coffee. Once I had finished my breakfast I headed back to return the tray. Drowsiness and a semblance of alertness were alternating in waves inside me. I strolled back lost in thoughts of life-stories and connections between people.

I had always appreciated momentous or at least memorable beginnings – memorable beginnings and the marking of time. Life was a long procession of forgotten memories. If something happened (a meeting or a conversation) and the surroundings, or what was said or done, were somehow extraordinary or unusual there was more of a chance the memory would last. That it would be remembered.

And I knew then that irrespective of what happened between us in the future it was a time that would remain with me… How often does one see a crazy band, meet a captivating woman, stay up all night and watch the sun rise?

Life very quickly became normal. The years passed…
On a Friday I would stop off at my sombre little Irish local for a couple of pints before returning home to Rosio for a glass or two of wine. After this we'd often go out for a meal to a small Italian restaurant we knew just around the corner. Occasionally, usually on a Saturday, but sometimes in the week, we would go out to see a film. There was a

backstreet cinema only two Tube stops away, which played mainly foreign, especially South American, films. After the film we would pop into the wine-bar across the road for a couple of glasses of red. I wasn't really a wine bar sort of person, but Rosio seemed to like the place.

None of it was exceptional, or remarkable, or challenged the status quo in any way – but it was life. It was our life. We probably didn't talk as much as we could have. If anything, I'd have said that was a positive thing. We talked or we didn't. Surely that's a much healthier state than feeling obliged to communicate when really there's nothing much to say.

I certainly believed we had no big issues to contend with, no obvious psychological problems to deal with, no jealousy and no laying down of rules by one of us for the other. Possibly, subconsciously, we were both biding our time until the next big adventure came along... I don't know.

Our relationship had certainly begun in a haze of non-conformity and excitement. We had embarked upon a journey where the thrill had been our desire to do things differently. In our own small way we had been adamant we were going to break the mould; we certainly weren't going to fall into the pasta on Tuesdays and His-and-Hers towels syndrome. But that was then.

It must have been about three and a half or four months prior to arriving on the island that I began considering a story for my fourth book...

I went to work and I returned home. We stayed in or we went out – together or separately. And all the while, well, not all the while, but a lot of the time, I was trying to come up with an idea for my novel. I would listen in to people's conversations on the Underground. I would pay closer attention to the mannerisms and idiosyncrasies of the people I passed in the street. I found that fliers and street hoardings became more interesting. I listened to the radio with increased concentration. The minutiae of life began to acquire almost scriptural significance instead of remaining the barely noticed details of everyday existence. Everything felt heightened as everything became a potential source of inspiration. And yet, no matter by which avenue I endeavoured to access a way into a new story, I found myself frustrated.

I became increasingly exasperated. The more this feeling emerged, the more I realised how devoid of ideas I was. And the conclusion I eventually arrived at was that I had dried up. I had nothing left.

I was no real writer. For, I figured, *true* writers evidently had a font of imagination that was limitless. For me, so it seemed, the sum of my creativity equated to the three novels I had penned. That was it! Three books that felt to me as though they'd been written by somebody else. Three books, of which the first one had been a fluke…

I was a fraud and I had nothing to write about. My life was boring. And I had no inspiration because I was uninspired. Possibly, *I* was also uninspiring (but that was another matter). Routine and mediocrity, like zombies taking over bodies, had replaced living and feeling. Unannounced and unnoticed they had arrived. One minute life was fun, exhilarating and full of crazy dreams, the next it had been replaced with a *Doppelgänger* devoid of emotion. It looked like the real thing, it smelt like the real thing, but once you scratched beneath the surface you realised the soul of your friend had been stolen.

I relayed this to Rosio – not the part about life being boring, not in so many words, more to do with my worries concerning my inability to come up with anything for my next novel. I suppose in retrospect I did hint that maybe our lives had become predictable, samey. And I remember saying something along the lines of not having anything to write about. At the time I thought this was vague enough, but possibly it wasn't.

But as I tumbled into my self-absorption, what had once been our pleasant city life became my dark wide-eyed metropolitan perdition.

Rosio was very supportive... at first. One of the things Rosio *was* encouraging about was my writing. For which I was extremely grateful. Where I had doubts she had none. When I no longer saw the point she re-energised me. When I lacked confidence she built me up. When I thought something was badly written she would tell me that it wasn't – or that it was, if it was, but in a nice way.

I was certainly a more interesting person because of my writing. Despite her having come from a wealthy family and being spoilt as a child, she was nonetheless a pretty sassy woman. She wasn't shallow or superficial; nonetheless, I feared that without the writing I could easily have ended up being an average Joe.

I became more and more difficult to live with. I would storm out of one room into another at the slightest thing. I would slam doors – whether Rosio was at home or not. Most of the time I would go and lie on our bed and listen to music on my headphones, sometimes for hours on end.

Why I became so affected is unclear to me. Possibly I had wished to be considered a writer to a greater extent than I had admitted to myself. Or possibly I saw being able to write as the only area of my life where I had the potential to raise myself out of the gutter of ordinariness. Or possibly I had more in common with my brother than I liked to admit. I don't know. What I can say is that over this period I bizarrely experienced an overwhelming sense of loss.

And it was around this time Rosio began to go out more frequently. Who could have blamed her? A small number of her Argentinian friends had formed a small group, so she told me, and had begun their own cultural soirées together. These, I gathered, were conducted at one or other of the participants' homes – but never ours.

I, by comparison, ceased going out. I shut myself away. I listened to music on my headphones. I would sleep for two or three hours in the afternoon. My head was filled with worries and strange and dark surreal half-thoughts.

Intermittently, I would sit at my desk and attempt to force myself to write. The floor in that part of the living room became littered with scrunched-up pieces of paper. Rosio said that that corner of the room was looking like an art project. She'd meant it as a joke to lighten things up a bit. But I'd been offended and stormed off to my room, telling her to 'piss off' as I went.

Despite my malaise, or depression, or spiralling self-analysis or whatever it was I was still able to spot a boring sentence when I saw one. And my writing was boring because I was boring, or we were boring; and that was because our lives had become boring. We had changed from who we had been, and who we had promised ourselves we would become. At least I had. Possibly Rosio was happy and it had all been a game and she had never meant the early talk.

I spent many perturbed hours contemplating us and my writing during this time... and the conclusion I came to was that I didn't really like me very much. Not then, not at that moment, and certainly not without my writing. Without my writing I was but another bod hanging onto a shirt and tie riding the Metro towards a tomorrow that would never arrive.

CHAPTER VII

It escapes me now how it all came about. For what particular reason, that is, I decided to leave the disquieting comfort of the apartment. Whatever it was, whatever train of thought eventually led me to believe it was a good idea finally to venture out into the unforgiving bombardment of flimsy street-life insignificance, I can no longer remember.

It is also beyond my recollection at this juncture as to whether any words were exchanged between Rosio and me prior to my closing the flat door behind me. Or indeed if she was even there at all...

There are many blanks. Whatever the details may have been, I know that I eventually found myself at a bus stop staring intently into the depths of the rain-splashed puddles.

I recall sitting there gazing out as if hypnotised, as if searching for answers in the rain. And the more I scrutinised the puddles and the water and my spinning thoughts the more removed I became from... from everything; from the street, the seat, from the grim daytime clatter of city hopelessness, and from *me*.

Four or five other people were either waiting for the bus or taking momentary shelter from the downpour. An elderly gentleman with a white fluffy moustache, who must have been in his late sixties, turned to me without warning and said: "In the States it used to be the case that you were innocent until proven guilty, nowadays you're guilty until proven rich." I nodded from behind a veil, which I suppose he took as a signal to continue. And for the next ten minutes or so he chatted away.

At first I was only vaguely aware of the near-constant hum his words were producing. Gradually, however, his utterances began to penetrate my self-absorption and reluctantly I found myself tuning into his story.

He told me he was seventy-five. His snowflake white Einstein-style hair, his slightly squinting left eye, his unruly eyebrows and his thin, marginally upturned lips took nothing away from the fact he looked good for his age.

With a wink, a clenching of the mouth and an amiable nod he proceeded to recount the story of his life. He announced that contrary to how it may appear he was not of these islands. This raised a slight smile in me, for although he could pass for an eccentrically dapper English gent on the outside, his accent was nonetheless an inescapably strong Manhattan slur. And later, much later, when I looked back at that moment I realised how he must have been fooling with me. But joke or no joke I was aware it was the first occasion I had smiled in a long while.

Fernando Parsons was his name, so he told me as I turned to look at him, but everybody called him 'The Parson'. He was born near the railroad tracks, and from an early age he had snuck rides up and down the country. Most of his early years were spent begging or playing the harmonica for a dime or two. He'd throw his cap down at the entrance to railroad stations, or outside bars as the men were about to get kicked out. Fridays were best: Fridays were payday. If they hadn't spent all their hard-earned dough on strong liquor and floozies he could survive a whole week on what he made on a good Friday. On a bad Friday he'd get nothing apart from abuse and being told to move on.

So it was. He migrated from one town to the next and to the next. When he was thirteen, in some god-forsaken mid-West hick town, in the middle of January and feeling down on his luck, he was invited back by a scarlet and flouncy woman for a hot meal and a glass of ginger ale. The Parson, although I'm not sure whether he had already acquired this reverential tag, jumped at the chance of hot food and getting in from the cold.

It took a little time before he realised she was a swish Madam from a high-class bordello. He simply wolfed down his meal in what was, as far as he was concerned, the swankiest hotel he had ever seen. Four of the other women who lolloped across the plush sofas watched agog as Fernando devoured his plateful in the fastest time they had seen that side of Maine.

They approached Maggie, who had brought him in, and after the five of them had spoken for several moments Fernando was offered a job. He accepted without hesitation, and soon learned how everything worked... Within a couple of days he was cleaning up the rooms after the women and their tricks were finished. By the end of the week he had lost any cherries he'd had, and by the end of the year he'd been given more responsibilities: it became his duty to keep the bar stocked up, he arranged for all the laundry, and checked all the deliveries.

The women treated him like a surrogate son as much as anything else. It was the first time he'd experienced anything remotely resembling a loving environment. This was his home, and the women were his friends and his sisters and his mothers and teachers – and his lovers – all mixed into one; and he was spoiled rotten.

"It couldn't have lasted though", the Parson told me with a sigh as he sat down beside me.

Due to an altercation with one of the women's boyfriends – which he didn't elaborate upon, presumably because even after all this time it still upset him – by the age of fifteen and a half The Parson was working the fairs and carnivals. He became what he told me was known as a 'Carnie'.

Over the years he did a variety of jobs. From manning the coconut shy to tending the hoopla stand, to helping the psychic make objects float and spectres appear. Finally, he ended up, until three years before I met him, when he came to Britain, as a weight and age guesser.

By that point the other three at the bus stop – the elderly woman with her string shopping bag, the Punk with his *The Clash* t-shirt, and the power-dressed Asian city woman – had all begun eavesdropping in on The Parson's extraordinary adventures. With only a little coaxing he was persuaded to put on a show for his newly acquired audience.

As soon as he began skipping lightly from one foot to the other and elaborately examining people's hands and teeth and necks you could immediately tell he was a natural born showman. That aside, he was awful. Apart from *my* age, he didn't guess anyone else's to within five years – and he was four years out with my age. At the time this amused me greatly… in truth it amused me more than perhaps it merited. But I suppose that was due in part to some kind of relief or release.

In the short space of time I had been listening to Fernando's life story I had been completely transported. His tales of dusty mid-Western towns, brash women in cumbersome velvet dresses and tight bodices, whisky-rattling poker games and dodgy deals had enthralled me. And these evocative accounts of the days before the car was king and when the railroad still called all the shots set me thinking about my writing.

The mid-thirties Asian woman in the fawn-coloured mackintosh had left moments earlier for the café across the street. When the bus finally arrived The Parson and I were the only ones left under the cover of the shelter. "You see," he said with a wink, "at the Carnivals the people would pay their money. If I guessed their age correctly that was that. If I guessed wrongly they'd get a prize." I nodded up to him as he quizzically observed me to see if I'd understood. He bent down, looked conspiratorially from left to right, and then said: "You see, the prizes", he threw his head back and guffawed, "were always worth less than they paid. A win-win situation." He slapped me on the back, guffawed some more, turned and as unexpectedly as he'd arrived left me alone once again with the rain and my thoughts.

As he strode off confidently into the damp city, I sensed that I was feeling the onset of some lighter sense of self. More: I was finally feeling the emergence of a modicum of enthusiasm. For it was slowly dawning on me that I had found my story.

Yes, I thought. The Parson's story would become my story. That was it. Simple. And it was brilliant; both the idea and the story. It had everything: whores, destitution, a grubby orphan kid who learns how to play a good hand of poker, *and* it had humour. And what it didn't have I would provide, and where there were gaps I would fill them... His story would be the carcass, I would provide the meat.

I had finally found the first domino. It was very exciting as the story began clarifying inside my head. And in truth so rapidly did it shoot on ahead of me that I couldn't keep up. I had to get it down on paper *immediately*, before some of it was lost...

I got up and hurried in what I was pretty sure was the direction of home. Excitement and adrenalin fuelled my steps. I was on the brink of spending deliciously endless hours at my desk writing. It was all laid out in front of me. I had not lost it. I damn well was a writer…

At last I had found my fourth book.

CHAPTER VIII

I strode with the footsteps of a hurried man. I was desperate to reach the sanctuary of home and the sanctity of the blank page – the page that I was about to fill.

In my dark fug of malaise I'd wandered further from home than I'd realised. I'd been oblivious to the city's décor and the rolling concrete. I was better now, though. I felt different. I felt alive.

After more than an hour's walking I finally found myself at the corner of my road where I popped into Youssef's for a bottle of whisky and a bottle of red wine. For tonight we would celebrate.

I arrived at my main front door – the one that opened onto the street. I rang the doorbell with rhythmic playfulness. I pressed out the chimes so as to recreate a well-known if untraceable musical jingle. I wanted to hear Rosio's crackled voice over the intercom, to which I would say, "It's me, and everything's OK now, darling."

But there was no reply. This I seem to remember explaining away as a toilet visit, a bath, or her not wishing to answer to strangers. I got my keys out and unlocked the door. I allowed it to slam behind me, finally shutting out the gloomy town and the emotions that had all too comfortably befitted the weather conditions. I went up the staircase firstly with energy swiftly followed by a shortness of breath.

I knocked on our door – tradition dictated I must. But without waiting for the sound of footsteps or the cursory call of "Who is it?" I turned the key slowly in the Yale lock. As I did so I considered what appropriately momentous phrase I could muster up to mark such an occasion.

Time held itself weightless and just out of reach, as phrases both celebrated and of my own invention passed through my sensors for deliberation. With arm outstretched and key inserted, both were frozen awaiting my next move.

I contemplated great speeches, witty asides and succinct one-liners from men of letters. I thought of Ustinov and Wilde and Fawlty Towers. I racked my brain for something appropriate to mark the verge of this new beginning. Something poignant by a favourite author of hers about creativity or being blocked would have done the job.

Reluctantly, I decided to settle upon either the somewhat uninspired announcement I had arrived at downstairs, or possibly: "Honey, I have my fourth book, and it's going to be my best!" Neither phrase, however, I considered, would adequately reflect such a pivotal moment. Nonetheless, I bore in mind that spontaneity is often the great mother of originality. And hence I hoped that something inspired would pop out of my mouth at the precise moment I saw her; or more accurately at the precise moment I saw her noticing my expression of glee, smugness, relief… whatever.

I turned the key in the lock. The door slowly swung open, wide, to its full extent, on well-greased hinges, without a sound. And instantly, as the door fully exposed the room, I became a disbelieving voyeur studying a freeze-frame scene of destruction.

From this fleeting sense of cinematographic slow-motion, suddenly everything speeded up. I struggled for breath. I felt hot, flushed, and was aware of my blood rushing and heart pumping. Heart pumping faster; I could feel it coming through my skin, in my chest and in my neck. Maybe I turned red the way people do; cracked veins showing on a sot's face.

Ransacked, burgled chaos; shelves toppled and tables overturned, chairs broken and wires hanging loose. Food on the floor and a limply hanging fridge door. Tape cassettes, eggs and coffee beans made up an unappetising omelette on the kitchen tiles. The taps were turned on, albeit to a very slow drizzle, and fortunately the plug wasn't in. The TV was face down on the floor and our old video recorder had been stamped on by a vicious heel. It was of little cheer that it had not worked in a long time. The mirror in the bathroom was cracked... that was unlucky.

My home was a war zone, and whichever treaty of peace or neutrality I may have signed, it had not been adhered to. My enemy had lied, and whatever I believed had been agreed to had been little more than a cynical ploy. It was no more than a worthless piece of paper to keep me quiet until the time came when it served my antagonist's purposes to have me annexed.

Thoughts of stories and writing and romantic ideals bulleted from my rotating mind. I had nothing to say: nothing wise nor witty, tragic nor appropriate came to my lips. This was no longer a time for clever asides and memorable remarks; this was a time to shout out Rosio's name at the top of my voice. Where the hell was she?

I stormed through the apartment calling her name. Tears dampened my cheeks as I prepared myself for a crime scene splatter pattern round every corner. I entered the final room, our bedroom. I looked in the wardrobes and under the bed, even in the dirty linen basket. Then, when I was sure she wasn't in that room either, I went back into the hall and began looking for her all over again. I even looked in the shower cubicle to eliminate even the wildest of horror film scenarios.

Once I was satisfied there really was no way she could be anywhere in the apartment I slowed down. A sense of extreme relief and joy enveloped me when I realised she had been out when all of this mayhem and destruction was occurring.

I stood for a moment in the middle of the sitting-room observing the devastation. What do you do when you have been violated, when your space has been invaded? Start cleaning up immediately or go out and gather your thoughts? Before considering anything else the first thing to do was to phone the police. Closely followed by phoning around to see if anyone knew where Rosio was.

I trampled over debris to the phone on my desk. As I was about to pick up the receiver I spotted a folded note with my name on it written in large capital letters. Perplexed, I opened and read it:

> *Don't phone the police.*
> *I did all this.*
> *I couldn't take it any longer!*
> *Don't try to find me because*
> *you won't be able to.*
> *I've gone away.*
> *I'll be in touch some time…*
> *Bye!*
> *Rosio*

I stood there silent… Crushed, squashed into a cube as if just a car in a junkyard.

------ ● ● ● ------

Thoughts of writing flew from me like birds scattering from a farmer's gun. I found myself flapping in panic. I found myself flapping in panic at this madness launched in my direction. It had come from nowhere. It was completely unlike her. Cruel and unpredictable were two things she was not.

OK, I suppose I was at least partly culpable. Well, she had said as much hadn't she? *I couldn't take it any longer!* But take what exactly? What kind of a note was that anyway? Take me, I guess; she couldn't take my spiralling moods – that's what she meant.

It had all come from nowhere, though. There had been no hint, no suggestion that she would not stand by me, not that I could recall. If anything, over the days preceding this madness she had been even more supportive than usual. She'd even been planning a summer holiday for us. She'd said that getting away would do me good. She'd even bought the tickets. She waved them in front of me one evening. Not that I'd paid much attention.

And it was over the couple of months or so leading up to this period that she had repeatedly coaxed me to keep at it. She had *always* been encouraging when it came to my writing, insisting I had at least one great work in me. That my magnum opus was yet to come; my *1984*, or *Catch 22*, or *The Trial*, or even my *Hitchhiker's Guide to the Galaxy* might only be one novel away. Kind words indeed. Not that I believed her.

The point was that she believed in me. When I was down, really down, she would sit outside the bedroom door and read to me... She never knew whether I heard her or not. The door was locked and a lot of the time I was listening to music on my headphones. Sometimes I *would* hear her, though: crisply yet gently, with that slight Spanish lilt of hers, she would read extracts from my previous novels. It was sweet of her. I do not think it really helped, but I suppose somewhere in me there was an appreciation that I was not entirely alone.

Despite all of that, then, and more, she left. It didn't make sense. She could have talked to me about it first, surely. Maybe she tried, I don't know. I suppose she must have just cracked.

And so, a book-burning fascist hopelessness had once again swooped down and taken me in its iconoclastic claws. It was as if the bus stop happiness had never happened. I had cynically been re-immersed into a world I believed I had finally eschewed.

This was my new norm. The old norm was the new norm, and any chink of light that may have alluded to there at last being some hope was gone…

It took me five days to return everything to some semblance of order. I threw away anything that was irredeemably broken, I reordered papers that had been tossed to the floor, and I got the chair covers cleaned which had either been smeared with food or had had bottles of ink tipped over them. And I indulged in many heavy bouts of remedy-drinking.

I lay down, I got up, I drank (a lot); I slept, I watched TV, I thought about Rosio, and then – after having taken two weeks off saying I had a glandular complaint – I returned to work. And I coped as best as I could, and I acted – again, as best as I could. I went through the motions, doing my utmost to survive without crying or screaming or losing it completely.

Providentially, a University lecturer's lot, especially during the summer term, is not overly demanding. I thought it would not be too much of a conjuring trick to go for the remaining weeks without having to engage for any length of time with another member of staff. I told myself that so long as I was able to tough it out until the end of term I'd be fine. My timetable was sparse and the end of year exams were close enough.

But it was far more complicated than I had anticipated. I should have left for sunnier climes immediately. It's difficult to function properly when you're being stalked by a black shadow that you know wants to wrestle you to the ground. Probably something honourable and boring such as job-security had made finishing the year seem like the right course. Ridiculous, really, that I had become so part of the machine that spontaneity even in a time of crisis was beyond me.

Then came the wonderful news that my request for a year's sabbatical had been agreed to. That news provided me with the escape plan I required and made my remaining weeks more manageable. As soon as summer term was over I could be off. I could just shut everything down and go.

Time went on and I was unable to prevent myself from dwelling upon the weeks and months that had preceded. I felt betrayed and lonely, and could not comprehend how the situation had got to where it had. Where was she and why was she not there? It was all too bizarre. Sure, things had been difficult. I had been difficult – but I needed help, not rejection… I did consider whether she had used my state of mind as an excuse to leave; whether there had been something else going on. I was not sure. One thing I was sure of was that I would not have done it to her. No way.

So then, all of this was going on in my head. Yet gradually it was beginning to take on a lighter hue. Time did that, I guess. Time and the knowledge that blue skies, green opal seas and a house on its own were all within reach. Oh, how the thoughts of the warm sun on my body, coffee and freshly baked bread on a porch and reclining in a hammock in the afternoon kept me going…

The students were friendly and concerned (about themselves) and had more and more questions as the exams approached. I tried to care, but their futures were their own business and they mattered little to me any more. The answers were in their lecture notes or in their text books, or in both – go off and look at them instead of bothering me. This is what I thought, but naturally I never said a thing. My best tactic was evasion; try to remain as unreachable as possible. Sometimes they would catch me in my office or immediately after class. For the most part I remained off campus unless absolutely necessary.

Then finally it was time to leave. I switched everything off and cleaned the apartment. I reconciled myself to the fact that the plants would die. There was no one I could think of who would look after them. A couple of them, a yucca and a spider plant, Rosio had been tenderly nurturing since we'd first got together. They, along with three or four on the windowsill, I left to wilt away into nothingness.

My more poetic self told me that there was some justice in that, or, if not exactly justice, poignancy. It was yet another indicator of finality. Things were coming to an end; her plants would cease to be a consideration, as would she. Then when I returned, I believed, fresher and happier after a year's break and with my new manuscript in my hand I would throw out those dead weeds from, what by then would have been, my all-but-forgotten past.

It felt wrong, though, sad even, I remember thinking, on my day of departure as I carried my two travel bags on the Underground for my last day at work, that Rosio wasn't coming with me. It was, after all, she who had first thought it such a good idea for *us* to get away. And it was she who had found the destination.

I stared at my blurred double image in the glass opposite me. She had been quite insistent, I recollected. Pushy even. "It'll do you – us – good to have a break in the sun... It'll help you calm down and regain some perspective," she'd said. "And it'll help your writing no end!"

As I sat there listening to the rhythm of the train on the tracks, with my eyes inadvertently resting on the legs of a woman standing by the door, someone I would have said was of Nigerian descent, I thought how ludicrous it all was...

As well as my holdall I had a shoulder bag. Rosio had changed money into the local currency of the region prior to all of this madness. This foreign cash, along with my passport, the plane tickets and some photocopies she'd made about the beauty of the region, Rosio had left in a Chinese ceramic bowl she kept on the sideboard just outside our bedroom. Prior to leaving I'd scooped up the contents of the bowl and put them all into the outside zip-up compartment of my shoulder bag.

Once my work was over for the day I had a leisurely lunch in the University canteen before heading for the airport. I'd booked myself onto an evening flight. This left me with several hours to kill at the airport. I wanted to play it safe. Experience told me that you never got away on time on the last day of term. Something always cropped up. Not this time, though. I deposited my tray on the trolley and walked out of the University without even the hint of a possible delay. No colleague, no student, no tripping over my bag as I got up from the table; nothing – I was on my way.

I arrived at the airport without a hitch. I drank a coffee. I strolled around and looked in the shops. I bought three magazines: one was a music magazine, pleasingly thicker than normal because it was a special edition; one was a scientific magazine and the final one was a political journal.

Whilst I was in the mood for purchasing reading matter – since I was not sure of when I would next find English-language material – I browsed around the bookshop. After at least forty minutes of reading blurbs and the first few pages of the books with the more interesting-sounding titles, I bought four novels: one by a Russian author and one by a Czechoslovakian writer, both of whom I'd been meaning to read for a long time. One was a posthumously published autobiography of a Japanese avant-garde musician whom I recalled Rosio mentioning on more than one occasion. And the forth I have to admit was a copy of my own first chef-d'œuvre: which, I decided at the time, would provide me with tangible proof that I could do it… proof that I *had* done it.

I changed planes in the capital, onto a smaller aircraft more suitable for internal flights. I arrived at the tiny airport at a little before ten in the evening. The warmth of the night air hit me, as did the sweet aroma of warmer climes' vegetation.

Two others got off the plane with me, but they had only hand luggage and soon disappeared. I waited as my bag was lowered onto the runway next to the aircraft. I carried my two bags across to the wooden terminal building. As I entered a man with a black peaked cap with a shiny emblem on its front greeted me with an out-stretched hand.

"Hello, yes?" I said.

He looked at me and then looked around the room that was badly in need of a lick of paint. "Welcome… We always greet new visitors to our island," he said nervously, as he squinted and rubbed his face up and down several times.

"Uh-huh."

"Yes..." I thought his accent consisted of hints of American mixed with something else. The American pronunciation probably came from watching Hollywood films or US TV shows. "Regrettably, I have to inform you that there are no taxis or buses at this time of night." I twisted up my face. "I am really sorry," he said, looking truly remorseful – rather too much so. His expression, I felt was far too sad for the information he was imparting. His tristesse it seemed to me was more suitable for, I don't know, the announcement of a death possibly. And I fleetingly wondered if he had girlfriend troubles.

"Umm, what about a hotel?"

"It is most unfortunate, but you'll have to stay here the night..." He had a darkness under his eyes, a tired look. His left eye, I noticed was slightly bloodshot, which added to his look of fatigue. Apart from the cap, which appeared to be new, he looked dishevelled. He was probably in his late twenties. He had a thin, long face, was unshaven, but his stubble was light in colour and therefore looked less than it probably was.

"There must be a guesthouse or..." As I said this my gaze was distracted by a small cuboid earring in his left ear. He must have had an idea of where my new line of vision had settled since he raised his hand up to his ear. He fiddled with it for a moment. Not wishing to make him feel uneasy, I looked back into his eyes.

"Not here, I'm afraid." He was saying. "But there'll be a bus at about eight or eight-thirty in the morning..." And with that and several backward steps away from me and with a flicked goodbye wave, he went and sat in the corner of the room and picked up a newspaper.

There was no cafeteria inside the building. There was a drinks dispensing machine from which I bought myself a coffee. I sat down and began to look at my Czechoslovakian novel. My mind was elsewhere, though. Uneasy and uncomfortable thoughts made me question whether I'd made the right decision: whether I should have used the ticket Rosio had bought instead of finding a destination for myself. But possibly all I needed was a good night's sleep in a comfortable bed.

Apart from the man who'd greeted me, the only other person in the waiting room was a stout gentleman with a bulbous, crimson-coloured pock-marked nose. He was wearing a lopsided navy blue peaked cap with golden coloured rope braiding and a navy blue blazer with a stain down its front. The top buttons on his shirt were undone, revealing a white string vest.

I looked back at my book. Then I turned as discreetly as I could to look at the twitchy young man who'd welcomed me. He was sitting with his head against the wall and his eyes closed. I untwisted myself to face the front again, but before I'd completely turned back I did one of those double-takes. I looked again at the chap, whose cap was now sloping down over his eyebrows and noticed that he'd taken out his earring. I remember regretting having been responsible for making him feel so uneasy.

I put my bags on the seat two removed from mine. I lifted my legs up onto the adjacent seat and lowered my head onto my bags. I looked up to the ceiling, exhaled a long deep breath and closed my eyes.

PART II

CHAPTER IX

Once I'd recounted the fragments of my life that I was happy for Ilona to hear we chatted for a while about her. I found her to be more forthcoming about her less recent past than anything to do with her motivations for being on the island. As the people were thinning and the stars began to dance we exchanged a look.

She got up and bent down and brushed my cheek with her lips. We gently said that it would be good to meet again. I don't think she really meant it. As it turned out we never did see each other again. Possibly she'd only been a ghost; and all this most likely is but a memory of a ghost or a ghost of a memory. Huh.

I ended up spending my first three nights in the room above the bar. It was a good place to begin my adventure. Everyone appeared friendly, and I was happy to be an unknown in an unknown land.

And in this world of mine, of self-imposed exile and counter-Warholian anonymity, I could be whoever I wished to be. I didn't have to answer questions nor ask any.

It felt as if I'd travelled back in time. To a land that lies forgot. I was being romantic, of course, because I *had* finally escaped. I felt calm, calmer and comfortable in this small bar on the northwest edge of this island. No more duplicitous doublespeak from the money-makers and the money lovers, and the... the former lovers. Especially the former lover.

But this was only part of the change I required. For I wasn't looking for company, I was looking for solitude. I wanted a place of my own. I wanted to write. I wanted to switch off. Ultimately, I wanted to be alone.

I was sitting in the empty bar on what turned out to be my last evening there. I held in front of me an open book and sipped at a glass of cold beer. I was not paying any great attention to what I was reading. The book was merely a prop: something to hold up to prevent me from staring emptily into space.

As I sat there alone save for my thoughts in strode a determined looking young man. He headed directly for the bar. He was wearing immaculate pine-green cotton trousers and a cardinal red t-shirt on which was the naïf representation of the human form painted in white. It had two arms and two legs (one of which was much shorter than the other), a thin body and a big round head with a solid circle in its centre. And surrounding the whole symbol was a square that was clearly hand painted.

It was an image I recognised from one of Rosio's many art books. It was, I recalled, either an ancient Toltec or Olmec petroglyph from Mexico. I remembered it because when I'd returned to our ransacked home, which I'd spent the subsequent days straightening up, there had been several of Rosio's art books that had been left open on top of each other on the dressing table. I'd left them where they were for some time. Then I'd looked at them for possible messages, signs and explanations. None of which was forthcoming. Anyway, one of the books was open at this rather striking Mexican image, which I'd ended up reading a little about before discarding it as another fruitless exercise.

At the counter the young man tapped a coin on its surface to summon attention. The proprietor stuck his head around the corner of the curtains and indicated he would be out shortly. The young man affected a less than convincing impression of patiently waiting. Betrayed, he was, by the constant jerky motions of his head as he looked around the room. Despite glancing at the walls, and the counter, and the pictures hanging around the room, and the food, and the bottles on the shelves, he never once turned in my direction.

The elderly owner served him a bottle of beer which the young man exchanged for his coin before turning and making a bee-line straight for me.

"Hello, I'm… well, I'm pleased to meet you", he declared as he thrust his outstretched arm under my nose. His English was of the public school variety, clipped, and I did not much care for his introduction. As I was about to tell him as much he continued: "I'm sorry, may I sit down? I am reliably informed that you're on the lookout for permanent accommodation."

"Er, for a few months, yes, I am."

He plonked himself down and took a long swig from his bottle of beer. He proceeded to tell me that Renney, his employer, had heard about my plight and had sent him down to see if I would be interested in renting accommodation from him.

Renney owned two dwellings, apparently: the one he lived in, and the other which had until three weeks ago been let to an American artist and his wife and was now vacant. When he finally got around to introducing himself properly this perfunctory young gent told me his name was Stefano. He told me that if I were interested he could pick me up at nine the following morning to show me the premises. I thanked him and said that I would be ready. He finished his drink in two final gulps, inclined his head and left.

I awoke at seven the following morning. I could see the clouds skimming the mountains and the birds dancing on the warm currents of air. I showered, got dressed and packed my shoulder bag with a bottle of water and a warm jumper just in case. I went down into the bar and ordered a coffee.

Nine o'clock came and went, as did a quarter past and half past. As I was beginning to invent stories in my head of how I had not trusted him from the outset, at nearly twenty to ten he turned up. What had been his neat and orderly side-parted brown hair the previous day appeared a lot more out of control and unruly, and at least to my mind much more befitting of someone called Stefano.

"I'm most awfully sorry. Really, it's terribly bad manners to make you wait like this."

"Oh, that's..." I began, noticing that his accent had lapsed somewhat, and now had a more non-descript Home Counties feel to it

"No no, I really am sorry. A bit of a mix up you see. Renney thought he'd told me – said that he'd told me – but, of course he hadn't, um, to clean up a bit, you know, the house. Clean it up before you arrived, you see?"

"Don't worry, it really doesn't matter."

This was a completely different person and a vast improvement on the one I had encountered the day before. It was the regimented unflappable types I could not abide.

He had a motorbike and a spare helmet, so off we went. It didn't take more than fifteen minutes. It would have taken over an hour on foot. Once out of the bar we travelled in the same direction the bus had taken after it had dropped me off. Where it had turned right and subsequently out of view, we sloped off to the left over rough terrain.

The track was rubble and holes, loose and untended. We snaked around boulders and over hillocks, heading vaguely in the direction of the coast. As the road rose and fell and we bumped along with the contours of the ground I would catch ephemeral glimpses of the iridescent waters. Only for split seconds then they were gone, replaced by the blue sky and the barren ground.

Finally, we climbed for approximately fifty yards, bouncing along as we went. At the brow of the incline we stopped and Stefano pointed. "That's it", he shouted.

At the bottom of the slope was the farmhouse. The Roman-style guttering and tegula roof tiling looked authentic to me. The whitewashed façade was very bright, newly done, reflecting the mid-morning light. It was a cottage, a farmhouse cottage, quaint and homely looking. Instantly I decided that so long as the interior lived up to the promise of its exterior, it would be perfect for me.

"Do you like the look of it?"

"Well, from here it looks lovely."

"Alright then, this is where I must leave you."

"Sorry?"

"I'll return for you in an hour."

"Well, why don't you at least take me to the front door?" I found it odd to be left at the top of the incline.

"Renney wants you to have the full effect of the beauty of the place…" He looked from me to the farmhouse and back again. "You'll absorb more if you have to walk the last part."

"Uh-huh. And you'll definitely be back in an hour?"

"Absolutely," Stefano reassured me. "Probably less… I'm only off to buy some groceries."

With that and a rev of his engine he left in a blown-about twirl of chalky dust and the rattle of loose surface. I held my hand over my nose and squinted until the air had settled.

The light fluttered and shimmered as I made my way down the incline. The pastel yellow sun shone down its heat from just beyond the house. The water glistened its reflection, turning pools of turquoise into white silver. The slight breeze created a patchwork of a thousand tiny mirrors which in turn reflected and then concealed the sparkling light of the sun's rays. The cloud wisps that daubed great swathes of the morning sky ensured that the sun's heat was not yet at full strength.

The track expanded into a wide parabolic gravel surface in front of the farmhouse. I watched as Stefano's boss put two glasses of a brightly-coloured drink onto the table. He went back inside, reappearing moments later with a glass jug containing the same incandescent liquid. I caught the briefest glimpse of a flame, and then it was gone. I walked slowly to give me time to observe the man who had appeared on the porch… He was rotund, with a full beard, dressed in white. From where I was I thought he looked a little like how one might imagine Moses to look.

Renney pulled out one of the chairs. Just as he was about to sit down he went back over to the front door and glanced inside. When he finally sat down he took out a walkie-talkie and spoke into it while nodding his head. He put his walkie-talkie away and waved as soon as he spotted me.

"Hello, hello, hello… Renney van der Straten at your service," he said, his hand held out as he descended the two porch steps to greet me. Renney had tightly curly dark brown hair with minute silver flecks. His nose was slightly pointed, but not enough to make him look mean. His face exuded a certain air of wisdom, I thought, and, lined though it was, he was not un-handsome. He had a belly on him, although I had the impression it was more muscle than fat. He was probably about 6ft 2ins in height since I was 5ft 8ins and he had a considerable advantage over me.

"Greetings and welcome," he continued. "Please come and sit down. Can I offer you a mid-morning fruit juice? I made it myself from some of the fruits to be found on the island, with crushed ice. It's delectable, please try." He was a boisterous fellow, oozing charm, and I couldn't help but take to him.

I introduced myself once I could get a word in. But he already knew my name and a little about me. This was, after all, a small community and no doubt word got around fast.

We sat and chatted and drank his delicious fruit juice, which I was convinced must have had food colouring added to it for it to be that vivid. It was a glorious morning, with the sun and the gentle breeze and the mountains in the distance. He told me that there were only a few people still alive who spoke the local dialect. And in that tongue the tallest peaked mountain, he pointed inland, is known as the 'place of the monster's final descent into hell'. He winked at me after saying this, to which I smiled.

Renney seemed content to sit and chat. I suppose I wasn't in a hurry either. But so much of my time had already been spent waiting. I wanted to get inside close the door and cry, or laugh, or shout out loud, or begin to write. Whatever I chose to do didn't really matter; the point was finally to be settled in the place that would make me strong, strong and creative again.

Renney told me he lived in a white three-storey house a little further along the coast. It had been constructed before the war and was a little-known gem. It was built by a *barking mad* (his words, not mine) artist-cum-architect originally from Prague. It was apparently one of the only examples in the world of Cubist architecture. He told me that sporadically – no more than once or twice every couple of years – he would be visited by a young artist or pilgrim wishing to see the building for him- or herself.

According to Renney it was quite magnificently eccentric, but still hardly worth someone's trekking all the way out there into the middle of nowhere to take a look at it, in his view. Especially when studying a photograph in an old text book would have done just as well. He recounted all of this with a glint in his eye, which suggested that it probably was well worth seeing.

This was the reason the previous tenants had come to the area, suggested Renney. That and the exceptional quality of light and the general beauty of the place. He told me they'd been there for a year and had the idea of starting an artists' colony. The problem was that nobody else came. They had had several visitors, over Christmas, mainly, but that was that.

Eventually, Renney took a pause from recounting everything that popped into his mind and showed me the inside. Some of the American couple's paintings were still on the wall. He saw me looking at them and told me that they were going to return for them at some stage… or, he added quickly, he'd simply get Stefano to post them. They were Surrealist and Abstract pieces, in the main: 'pictures of the mind' is what he called them, with a dismissive wave of the hand. Whatever they were they weren't anything I would have assumed required good light or tranquillity. Maybe that wasn't quite fair; but in such breathtaking surroundings paint the bloody mountains… or the sea, or the clouds! Not a goddamn orange square on a blue background of two squares with electrodes plugged in and overlapping each other.

The farmhouse was a one-storey building consisting of two rooms and an outdoor toilet at the back not far from the cliff's edge. The room in which I stood would in Estate Agents' parlance be called the kitchen-diner, most probably prefixed with the term 'rustic'.

A smack of melancholia struck me as I thought of Rosio. We could have been there together. This is where we should have been – looking over this accommodation together. I knew she would have loved it. She'd tried to get me to look at her photocopies of the region often enough, after all.

A table and four chairs, a settee and a rocking chair, paintings and a North African rug on the walls. To the right was the kitchen, separated from the main room by a wooden counter attached to a chest-high wall. There was a rudimentary cooker consisting of two rings and a small oven, run from a large gas bottle beneath the sink. Cups hung from hooks. The bedroom's window was wide open. Sheets and covers were all neatly folded at the bottom of the double bed and everything smelt fresh and clean. And the *pièce de résistance* was a vase of fresh flowers on the dressing table, which I presumed Stefano had hurriedly placed before coming to collect me.

We went back outside and I asked him how much he wanted for it. He said that he was going to let me have it for a very reasonable price. One, because he knew I wanted a place, but also because he wanted a tenant as quickly as possible. Fair enough.

"So, how much then?" I asked.

"You can have it all for exactly the same price as you are paying in the bar for your one bedroom."

"Yes, that does sound reasonable."

"But…" Here it comes, I thought. "Since this is a very good deal I need some form of a guarantee you're going to stay for a while." He winked.

"Uh-huh?"

"I know you're looking for a long-term place to stay… So at this price I'd like you to commit to a minimum of four months."

I could not quite place his accent. Dutch or Flemish or possibly South African would have been my guess on that first meeting.

"OK, so?"

"Yes, so," he continued. "I want you to pay for all four months upfront. You get a cheap and beautiful place to live and I get someone permanent."

"OK... and if I want to stay for longer than four months?" I enquired, wishing to make everything absolutely clear from the outset.

"No problem. I need a minimum of four months' rent so I can forget all about it, then you can pay me every month if you like. Alright?"

"Um..."

He paused for a moment before asking me what I thought.

"Well," I began, "I think it's a lot of money all in one go like that... but"

"Yes, yes, but the actual rent's cheap, isn't it?" Renney interrupted and gave me a jovial slap on the back.

"Yes, I was about to say – but, it *is* cheap."

"So, you'll take it?" He prompted with his undulating intonation and expectant eyes.

I briefly considered delaying my decision so as not to appear too eager. What was the point, though? The farmhouse was exactly what I wanted. The thought of not revealing my hand was a ridiculous way of thinking – a city wheeler-dealer way of thinking, which was not really me. It is an approach that infects you if you mix with the wrong people, or live in the wrong place for too long. And there was no longer any need of it here. Honesty, simplicity and openness would become my new approaches to interacting with others.

"I'll take it," I announced.

"Excellent, excellent! You will love it here and we shall become good friends. And you will have a most *beneficial* stay. Yes – I promise you that… A most beneficial stay indeed."

I was not so sure about the good friends part. But I overlooked that detail when he told me I could move in as soon as I wanted.

"Today, if that's alright with you," I said with an ill-concealed smile.

"Alright? Of course it is alright. It is fine and wonderful."

"Great. Thank you."

"Please – this is your home now", he said accompanied by a sweeping gesture of his arm.

I went around the back of the house to the toilet. I stood staring over the cliff's edge at the golden beach and the shimmering sea that were just below. It was now all mine. The sense of relief mixed with joy made my eyes fill up with tears. It was as though I finally knew I could relax and be myself.

Unfortunately, these feelings of optimism were not about to last. Little did I know it at the time, but everything was about to go dreadfully wrong.

CHAPTER X

The days passed. I cried. I sang to myself. I danced around with no clothes on. I tried to repair the beaten-up old guitar I found in the built-in wardrobe in the bedroom. I couldn't really play; just a few chords and a couple of sing-along tunes. But I figured if I was ever going to learn here was the place to do it. I bought fruit and vegetables, tins of things and packets of things, and booze and juice from the local store across the road from the bar. I bought enough to last me for ages and paid the shopkeeper to give me a lift back to the house. I ate on the veranda, stared at the sky, got drunk and tried to empty my head.

On day six I decided to do some exploring. I filled my bag with fruit and a bottle of water. At the back of the house was a path that led down to the sea. I stood at the top of the winding track gazing out from the place I believed would restore my sense of worth. After a few moments and several deep satisfied breaths I began my descent, eager as I was to go for a swim. Occasionally I slipped on the loose shale. I never fell, however. I'd merely lose my balance for an instant before steadying myself.

After half an hour I reached the beach. I jumped the final step onto the sand with both feet together. Half an hour from my secluded house to this crescent moon-shaped biscuit-coloured bay was all it had taken me.

I ran towards the clear waters stripping off and laughing and whooping as I went, throwing my clothes high up into the air behind me. And though I didn't realise it I was enacting an amalgamation of scenes that had rested dormant in my psyche for years: running sexually charged towards an exotic looking Bond girl, showing off to bikini-clad beauties, or possibly, hence more pointedly, if somewhat darkly risible, subconsciously maybe I was dredging up the opening titles from *The Fall and Rise of Reginald Perrin.*

I careered into the waves, lifting my legs up high so as to maintain my momentum. As soon as I was deep enough I dived in. The crack and the pain were like thunder inside my brain. White pain like a sledgehammer concrete slab car crash – crack bang teeth-rattling white light. I stumbled up clasping my hands to my head. I fell. I rose again… Blood streamed down my forearms. I forced myself towards the edge; fighting against the tide and the weakness and the overwhelming feeling of nausea. I reached where the dark sand stopped, where the damp of the waters hadn't touched. I passed out.

CHAPTER XI

"Bloody idiot!" exclaimed Renney, and slammed his fist down on his desk.

CHAPTER XII

When I regained consciousness I was lying in an unfamiliar bed. At the end of the bed was a table with scented candles flickering in the gentle breeze. It was dark outside. I attempted to lift my head from the pillow but immediately felt sick.

I sluggishly raised my hand up to my head. It had some kind of material around it. I wished I had a mirror. Without turning my head I reached out to my left then to my right. On what felt like a small cabinet I could feel my bag. I pulled it on top of me and got out my bottle of water. I needed to drink. I poured nearly half of it into my mouth. It tasted stale and plasticky. I replaced the cap and left it lying on top of me. Several moments later I leaned over the side of the bed and vomited.

When I finished heaving, wiping the last puke-strings with the back of my hand, I plonked my head back down and drifted back off into unconsciousness. At some point I came round and saw a young woman with auburn hair walk over and draw the curtains. I tried to say something, but she signalled for me to remain quiet by putting her finger up to her lips.

I drifted in and out of consciousness for what must have been several days, maybe more. I don't recall being awake for more than fifteen or twenty minutes at a time. On one occasion I woke with a cold damp flannel across my forehead. Another time the woman with the auburn hair had the bedclothes pulled back and was wiping my chest and arms with the same wet flannel.

One time I was awoken from a deep sleep by a gentle shaking of my arm. She was sitting on the edge of the bed. It took me several moments to focus. She had an angelic glow around her head, which once I had fully regained consciousness I was relieved to see was merely the sun shining through the window behind her. She held her finger to her lips once again indicating that I shouldn't attempt to speak.

She gently held my head up to enable her to put another pillow behind me. Once propped up she took a bowl of clear broth from the night table and delicately spooned small amounts of the liquid into my mouth. It was salty with a hint of vegetable. On tasting it I realised how thirsty I was and how much my body craved salt. I drank eagerly.

My auburn-haired nurse slowed me down, fearful, no doubt, that my stomach would again expel its contents onto the floor. She placed the bowl back on the cabinet, gave me a warm smile, and left.

Sitting more upright in bed I could at last begin to evaluate my surroundings. I was in a square room, made – rather bizarrely, I thought – entirely from bamboo. The door was directly in front of me, but closed. To the left of the door was a large wardrobe with a full-length mirror. Due to the angle of my head in relation to the mirror I could see there was a large brightly-coloured painting on the wall above my head.

On the periphery of my vision I could see the gently billowing curtain to my right – but not enough to see out of the window. In the right-hand corner of the room next to the door was a low rectangular – once again bamboo – glass-topped coffee table. On top of this was a mug, a small self-standing mirror and several items of makeup.

The days and nights drifted indistinguishably by. The tossing and turning came and went. My head was propped up and pills were swallowed with tilted-back glasses of water. Identity intertwined with fever-fuelled dreams. Dark memories and hopelessness spilled over into regret and incomprehension.

Once my sleeping patterns finally began to resemble something more closely recognisable as normal, my carer introduced herself.

"Hi, I'm Sabina…" she said as she pulled back the curtains. It was morning and the sun was still low.

"Now then," she uttered with a playful harrumph, "how are you feeling?"

"A bit better, thanks," I croaked.

"Good. You're certainly looking a lot better." She said this as she began plumping up my pillows.

"Yes? That's good to hear."

"Look, I'll go and prepare you a light breakfast, shall I? See how you cope with that, huh?" I nodded. "And," she turned back around on reaching the door. "You want to tell me your name?" she coaxed with a flutter of her eyelashes.

"Jethro, I volunteered. She raised an eyebrow. "Jethro Carmichael…" It was only later I realised how dreadful I'd be at espionage. Forgetting completely, as I had, at the first opportunity, to give my chosen alias.

Sabina with her long, straight black hair, her nose ring, her twenty or so pinprick-sized birthmarks on her cheeks and her mole just above the left-hand side of her mouth would pop in four or five times a day with food and plenty of liquids: water, soup, and herbal teas mainly.

Occasionally, she would stop and sit on the side of the bed and talk away, perfectly at ease both with herself and in my company. She would absent-mindedly take hold of my wrist or place her flat palm on my forehead. Once when birthmarks came up in one of our conversations she told me that in Iranian folklore a birthmark is said to appear on a child when a pregnant mother touches that particular part of her own body during a solar eclipse.

Also, quite frequently, she would ask me questions related to literature. What book I was reading, or what the book I was reading was about. Or even what my favourite books were and why, or indeed what my favourite films were.

One evening she entered the room, and feeling a great deal stronger I said, "Well, Doctor, how do I look?"

She laughed. "You definitely look on the mend... But, Doctor?" She giggled to herself before continuing, "I used to be a nurse in a previous life, but not a Doctor."

This explained a lot, I thought. "And in this life?" I asked.

She squinted her eyes and put her hand up to her mouth and pinched her lips between her thumb and index finger. "Umm, good question. In this life? ...In this life I'm an *ex*-nurse I suppose." She smiled once again, but her expression told me she knew her answer was inadequate.

She came over and sat next to me on the bed. Without thinking she reached over and took my wrist. I suppose she was checking my pulse. It appeared as much to be an instinctive habit as anything else – something a nurse automatically did without thinking.

"So what happened to me after I banged my head?"

"Well, after you hit your head on the rocks me and some friends brought you back here."

"Friends?"

This was the first mention she'd made of there being anyone else around. I do not know why, but it was a bit of a shock. She told me that if I felt up to it I could join them all for a light lunch the following day.

The next day I awoke mid-morning excited at the prospect of finally getting out of that room. My clothes had been neatly folded and left on the coffee table. As I was pushing the bedclothes aside I heard tentative knocking at the door.

"Come in," I said whilst pulling the covers back over me. There in the doorway stood a tall, lithe man who was probably in his early forties. Any thinner and he would have been underweight. He smoothed away a strand of his long brown hair from in front of his eyes before addressing me.

"Hi, I'm Theo," he began with a discernibly lowlands lilt. "Sabi asked me to accompany you on your first morning up and about."

"Oh… OK," I said, without even making a token effort to conceal my disappointment.

"She felt really bad because she forgot that today's Sunday." He announced with the misguided assumption I would understand what he was talking about.

With my eyebrows raised accompanied by a vacant stare he could see that I had no clue of what he was going on about. "Sunday is market day… They've all gone to the market."

"I see," I said, although I did not really see at all.

He looked at me and smiled, and I warily smiled back. Then he nodded and said he'd wait outside while I got dressed.

I felt sad as I lowered my feet slowly to the floor. To be leaving my sickroom without Sabina present didn't seem right. I'd grown attached to her, and stupidly hoped she saw me as more than just a pathetic patient.

I pushed myself up into a standing position. My legs trembled as I made my way over to the full-length mirror. I gazed at the cut-out cardboard figure in the mirror. My head was neatly bandaged. My skin possessed a translucent quality, and my eyes were large shadowy skull sockets.

Theo returned and I followed him out of the door. The first thing I noted was how the surrounding forest was denser than I'd imagined. Then as I descended the ten or so steps I saw that there were four other bamboo cabins. They had been built so that together they formed a gentle semi-circle. Behind my cabin, a little deeper into the forest, were three tree-houses with rope ladders leading up to them.

With Theo's arm around my waist and my arm around his shoulder he led me through the clearing. The clearing was the communal area. There were tables and chairs crudely made out of logs and tree trunks. There was a large circular hearth containing a stone barbecue with the charred remains of what I presumed was the previous evening's fire. There were several guitars leaning against tables and tree-stump stools. I also spotted a mandolin and several bongos and djembes.

The sunlight seeped and oozed and flowed over and on and in between the obstructions that contrived to hinder its direct path to the forest floor. In places an entire shaft reached the ground uninterrupted, creating an amber rod of light inside which dust particles and forest debris lighter than air lethargically wafted around. The carpet of leaves and twigs and the multitude of other things green and brown were mottled by this morning light. The result was warm and cool, shade and light. As we walked the beams created pools of illumination, spotlights on a stage.

We reached the other side of the clearing. I saw that in between the trees were layer upon layer of twigs and undergrowth that had been placed there as a concealing barrier. There was a thoroughfare, but unless you knew exactly where it was and which branches to push aside you would never have found it.

Theo made a gap and we edged our way between the trees and brush until the wonderful moment when I got to see the sea again. I was sweating profusely and feeling dizzy. I told Theo that I needed to sit down. I sat with my back against a tree, ensuring that I remained in the shade.

As I regained my strength I cast my eye over the bay. I realised I was now at the opposite end from the path that led down from my house. And I remember thinking that I must be where the alien-believers live.

Theo asked if I would be alright for several minutes while he went for a swim. I told him to be careful of the rocks. He laughed and then explained that at this end of the cove there were virtually none. It was only at the other end that there were lots concealed just beneath the surface.

A deliciously cool breeze gently rustled the leaves against each other and allowed my sweat-drenched body to dry. I watched as Theo stripped naked and ran into the waves.

After half an hour we walked back through the maze of undergrowth and sat at the table in the clearing. Theo said that he would prepare some soup and bread and cheese for us. I asked him how long his friends usually spent at the market. For a split second he looked blank. As though I had asked him a question from nowhere about Dadaism or the importance of mirrors in art, or something equally á propos of nothing.

Almost as instantly as this air of befuddlement had crossed his face, it disappeared. I put any confusion then down to his not having understood my question. His eyes registered meaning and his mouth clicked into gear and he told me that almost invariably it took them the whole day. On market day, so he told me, they would get up early and take two buses to the other side of the island, usually returning after dark.

Theo told me it was a way for them to make some extra money. One of them made drums, while the others made dresses, skirts or jewellery. They didn't yet earn much, but they hoped to supply one or two shops on the mainland in the future. He shrugged as he said this, which I interpreted as meaning that he didn't hold out much hope.

After the meal I told him I was feeling tired and wished to lie down. He escorted me back to the cabin to ensure that I was alright. I had only been intending to have a short afternoon snooze. As it turned out I slept virtually uninterrupted all the way through till the following morning.

I was awoken by the sound of the wardrobe door creaking. Sabina was choosing some clothes to wear. She took out some clean knickers and a bra, and a long rusty-coloured cotton dress. She did not notice me watching her. As she began to turn I closed my eyes pretending to still be asleep. A moment later I squinted them open from behind clenched eyelids only to see her take her makeup bag from the table. And with a lightness of foot she crept slowly out.

I stretched and was aware that I felt markedly better. You could always feel when the bug had gone, or the stiffness was less, or the numbness had dissipated... I got out of bed and looked at myself in the mirror. My cheeks had more colour to them. I put on my T-Shirt, shorts and trainers and opened the cabin door. Over in the clearing six people were sitting at the table drinking coffee. One was Theo, one was Sabina and one was a young man I recognised from my first evening in the bar. But the other three I'd never seen before.

One of them spotted me standing there, he whispered a few words to the others and then they all turned towards me. On seeing me they began to clap. Then the two men stood up and began to cheer and whistle. "Hooray! Hooray!" they shouted. I suppose it was sweet of them. I felt uncomfortable though, embarrassed, it was too sugary-sweet for me. That said, I also felt, rightly or wrongly, that for the first time in a long time people gave a damn.

"Come over and join us," one of them shouted.

Theo ran over to me with long bouncy strides. "How are you feeling?"

"A lot better, thanks."

"That *is* good, very good. As you see they are all very happy to see you up."

"Yes, you're all very kind."

"Nonsense, it is normal, no? Everybody has been very worried about you. You know, Sabi gave us daily reports on how you were doing."

"I didn't, no..." I was beginning to realise how much my presence had affected these people's lives.

"Yes. And, I don't know, over the first few days you were checked on regularly at night too – by wonderful Sabi of course. She told us you had many bad dreams... and shouted loudly sometimes."

"Really?"

"Oh yes – you were a very sick man."

We approached the table where they were all sitting. I was reminded of an article I had read in one of the magazines I'd purchased at the airport. It told of the relatively new phenomenon of laughter classes. Apparently, laughter classes were springing up throughout India. A group of people would meet once a week in a public park, they would all stand in a circle, and the tutor or leader or whatever he was would begin to laugh. Others in the circle would follow suit until they would all be laughing. Essentially, they were laughing at nothing in particular, or rather they were laughing at laughing and probably also at the ridiculousness of it all.

So as I stood there with them all grinning up at me expectantly, I felt as if I was in some strange hippy toothpaste advert. If I'd initiated a laughter class they'd all have happily joined in and we could have been laughing there for ages.

There was a bench either side of the table. Sabina sat on the end of the bench to the left, next to where I had come to a standstill. She rubbed her hand up and down my back whilst gazing reassuringly up at me. Theo went and sat back down at the far end of the opposite bench. I felt like a long-lost friend, or a soldier boy coming back from the wars.

"So, Theo you know. This is Carolina, and Phoenix," said Sabina. "That's Zap," Sabina pointed. "Hans and Olaf." I smiled and nodded to each of them as I was told their names. "And this, everybody, is Jethro."

They said their respective *Hellos* and *Welcomes*. But before anyone could begin to say anything else I thought it was an apt moment for me to address them while they were all together.

"I'd just like to say," I began, "thank you all... although thank you seems inadequate, but, you know, thank you all so very much. You saved my life, because if you hadn't found me and looked after me I daren't think what might have happened."

They began to clap, but I held my hand up to indicate that I hadn't quite finished. "Now obviously I don't know everything that's been going on... well, hardly anything in fact. What I do know is that I owe all of you an immeasurable debt of gratitude." More claps ensued. "Wait a minute," I said "– and the other thing I know is that above anything else I know that I owe more than I can express to Sabina."

She gave me a friendly little shove. "I've taken her room and her bed, and so very much of her time and, by the sound of it, a lot of her sleep as well. So, well, if you do wish to applaud me now I thank you for your warmth and generosity. But in applauding me please also be applauding Sabina, for it is to a great extent down to her that I am still alive."

They were all smiling at this and a couple of them, I could tell, were moved by my speech. They had fallen silent. "OK, I've finished – now you can clap!" Smiles at first quickly followed by laughter and applause greeted these final words. Sabina moved along and I sat down. I was given mint tea and some bread and jam. They talked to me for a short time before gradually reverting to talking amongst themselves. I think they realised that after my speech I would prefer be left alone to eat my breakfast, and to cease being the centre of attention.

One morning Sabina leaned across the table to tell me that after my shower she wanted to change my bandages and have a look at how the wound was coming along.

Once that was decided I asked her how the market had gone the other day. I was instantly struck by how flustered she looked by my question. She inhaled deeply and pinched her cheeks between thumb and forefinger with her left hand. "Oh god, I'm really sorry... I meant to tell you," she said.

"What's the matter?"

"Oh... how stupid of me!"

"What?"

"Oh, I forgot to tell you." She shook her head.

"What did you forget to tell me?" I demanded, more gruffly than I had intended.

"Well, when we went to the market I took the key to your house out of your bag."

"Oh, really. Why?"

"Um... Well, you were still asleep. I thought I'd get some clean clothes for you. You know... since I was passing... I was only trying to be... you know... and then I forgot to..."

"Don't worry," I interrupted. "It was a kind thought. Thanks."

"If I'd have thought about it before I could have asked you. But of course you were asleep."

"Forget it. It was a kind thought."

"Are you sure?"

"Yes. Don't give it another thought. It's fine, really." Then I paused to allow her to add something more if she wanted. But she didn't say anything, she merely smiled, nodded and looked down. "I think I'll go and take that shower now..." I said. To which she nodded once again, while, I thought, closely scrutinising my expression for any signal I may have involuntarily been giving that indicated I was more irritated by her actions than I was saying... That's what I thought anyway.

The shower cubicle consisted of three walls of bamboo above which a watering can was suspended on a pivot with a string hanging down. Sabina reminded me to be vigilant about not getting any water near my head. I nearly slipped a couple of times – and once nearly brought the bamboo walls of the cubicle down as I scrabbled for grip. Otherwise, I was pleased to be clean, felt refreshed and was ready, I thought, for what the day had in store for me.

I returned to the cabin with a towel wrapped around my waist. There was a knock at the door. Sabina came in with a bag of my things. In addition to my clothes she'd picked up some of my toiletries, my pad and pens, and the novels I'd bought at the airport.

She checked my wound and left. I sat on the edge of the bed staring at the picture that had been chosen for the cover of my novel. I wondered if she had noticed my name on the spine, and, if she had, what difference it might make.

CHAPTER XIII

Up on the cliff a large black cloud was forming. This was both meteorologically and metaphorically accurate.

------ ● ● ● ------

The Cubist's House consisted of three cubes, one of which was underground, built into the rock. The two which were visible were painted white. The upper cube – which had a small circular Roman-tiled sun-roof perched on three white concrete trunks and was topped off with a giant white egg-shaped spire – had been positioned so that only half of it was touching the cube underneath. Its overlap made it appear that it was suspended in mid-air.

The construction resembled a pair of dice, one die balanced on top of the other as far as it could possibly go without toppling over. Apart from creating a bizarre optical impression the overlap also created a canopy under which stylish tables and chairs stood.

It looked dangerous. This was part of its attraction. It was certainly an oddity, no doubt an oddity wherever it happened to be built. As it was, in a rock, shrub and sand landscape with little more than the occasional dilapidated farmhouse to break up the scenery, it was absurd.

------ • • • ------

Renney had already read Jethro's first and second novels and was now steadily working his way through his third.

The monitor attached to the wall above Renney's desk flickered. He had become too engrossed in his reading to want to be distracted by the feed of fuzzy images. Hence, he'd turned his back on the monitor which, along with all of his surveillance equipment, he'd purchased from an East German secret service chappie.

The loud knock at the door gave Renney a start. Marcus, Stefano's half-brother, stuck his head around. Renney reminded him that he didn't want to be disturbed. Marcus apologised before telling him that the Americans were demanding more paint.

"Um, how do they seem?"

"Well, they appear to be coming to the end of their manic phase and well... appear to be getting down to more, I don't know, probably what you'd call more considered, introspective stuff now, I guess."

"Right," said Renney thoughtfully. "Tell them they'll get some more in the morning." With that he waved Marcus away.

Renney watched the door close behind Marcus and looked down at his book for several seconds. He glanced at the door before swivelling around to look at the screen.

He placed the novel face down on his desk and observed how the American couple were mixing their paint with more water than usual. Probably, he thought, to eke it out until they were supplied with a new batch.

Renney reflected upon how they had been producing some excellent work recently. This in turn led him to recall how imperative it was that he remind Stefano to collect the remaining paintings from Jethro's house. It was an oversight to have left them there; he grimaced as the thought shot through his mind.

Renney zoomed in one of the cameras to see how Sam's painting was coming along. It looked good, he thought, a large 12-footer this time. He took out his notes from the filing cabinet. He wanted to go over them again just to ensure that nothing had been overlooked...

Sam and Diane were from Portland, Oregon. They were thirty-six and thirty-two, respectively. They had met nearly seven years earlier in Paris; Sam was in his final year of architectural studies while Diane had just completed her fine art degree and had subsequently been working in a bar in a back street near the Georges Pompidou Centre. They fell in love and moved into a tiny two-roomed apartment in the vibrant melting pot that is the *16ème Arrondissement*.

They lived off the paltry sums she earned from her bar work. He had become disenchanted with architecture, and although he completed his course to ensure he graduated, as soon as he had finished he decided to focus his attention on his first love – painting. Times were hard, yet despite Diane's long hours for little pay they were happy.

Two minor exhibitions brought him a degree of success. His breakthrough, however, at least temporarily, was when someone Diane had been talking to at work went round to visit Sam. He was from a Parisian-based two-man music group called Panel Feçtoon. It turned out that they had only just completed their fourth album and were looking for artwork for their cover. One of Sam's older pieces, on the floor of the living room leaning against the wall, caught the musician's eye. Not long after it became the album sleeve. The album was a minor European-wide hit; on the back of it Sam got a few commissions. When the group made their fifth, and what turned out to be their final, album Sam was again asked to do the artwork.

By then Diane had taken the bold step of giving up her work at the bar. It was about time, so she felt, that she set about her own career in art. That's the way it was, with Sam now earning just enough for them both to eat and pay the rent, that Diane tentatively embarked upon producing her own body of work.

Things were certainly still difficult for them, but in a different way from before. Previously, although they had little to live on they at least knew how much they had from one week to the next. Once Diane gave up her job, even though she would from time to time sell one or two small pieces, it was essentially Sam who was now the breadwinner. The problem with that was that it provided an irregular source of income. Sam would sell something and with money from the sale they would be able to live for several weeks, or sometimes a couple of months, depending upon the size of the piece. But then, as the money was coming to an end, they would begin to get concerned.

Diane hated the idea of having to get another crummy job as a waitress or barmaid. If the money ran out it was she who would have to go out and get a job. Luckily, with sometimes only days to spare, it always seemed to sort itself out. Either Sam would sell something or he would get an advance on a commissioned piece.

Over the previous year everything had become more difficult. A combination of two seemingly contradictory factors contributed to their dwindling fortunes. Firstly, there was a lot less money being invested in the unknown artist; and secondly, there was a glut of up-and-coming in-vogue artists. For them to survive they knew something drastic would have to change. They were aware of this, discussed it frequently, and sometimes shouted and banged doors and stormed off to different corners of their apartment as if they were in an obscure French film *noir*.

It was at this juncture that Sam's brother offered to pay for them to take an extended break.

Brian, Sam's brother, was the proprietor of his own law firm in New York. He offered to pay for Sam and Diane to have four months travelling around in the sun. Sam was initially reticent about taking money from his brother. He did not want hand-outs, especially hand-outs, as he saw them, to fund their bohemian lifestyle, but Brian was insistent. That, coupled with Diane's enthusiasm for the idea, resulted in Sam's reluctant acceptance of his brother's offer.

It took six weeks for them to return their apartment keys and sort out their belongings. The only condition Brian had was that one of their first destinations had to be a visit to the Cubist's House. Brian, so he told Sam, saw a piece about the bizarre house on an Arts programme and he'd thought of his brother. It was exactly the kind of strange artistic anomaly he knew would intrigue Sam.

In addition to discussing the architect's life and work the television programme had also, according to Brian, shown the area around the Cubist's House. The area, he told Sam, appeared to be very tranquil and remote and ideal for Sam to begin reinvigorating his creative juices.

Brian was not in the slightest bit artistic, but he adored his brother. He admired his individuality, and wanted him to be a success, even if he found him somewhat flaky.

Renney looked up from his file. Sam was still painting. Diane was getting ready to take a shower. They were well fed, had comfortable accommodation, and were producing good work.

He put the file away, picked up Jethro's book and continued to read.

CHAPTER XIV

The gavel was banged down loudly twice.

- Order! Order!

I put it to the court that this man cannot write.

- It's not true! – I protested.

- Silence! I will have silence in my court.

My advocate, a ferret of a man, tried to pacify me by gently holding my shoulder back and forming a shush shape with his lips but without actually emitting a sound.

- The defendant, the judge continued, is sitting here before us having been accused of promulgating the fabrications that not only does he have the ability to write competently, even imaginatively, but also, as a result of this deeply held falsehood, the defendant believes he has been published.

The court burst into laughter; feet were stamped and tables slapped. In amongst the din I could make out some of the comments coming from behind me and above me in the gallery.

- - How ridiculous!
- - Of course, he's completely mad you know.
- - Poor chap, it's really an illness... we should be curing him, not punishing him.

- - It's not true, I have been published! – I stood up and shouted at them.

This set them off again. It took several bangs of the gavel, and Order! Order!s, and demands for silence before the courtroom began to calm down.

- - How do you plead?
- - Not guilty, Your Honour – I said defiantly.

Once again, the courtroom dissolved into mirth. This perplexed me... So, tentatively I offered:

- - Umm... guilty?

And once again I, for some reason unbeknownst to me, caused tears to roll and sides to ache.

- - This is the best trial I've been to in ages.
- - Marvellous, isn't it? He's certainly on the ropes, poor fellow.

I began unequivocally to tell the Judge that I could be expected to plead either 'guilty' or 'not guilty' only if he informed me of what I was being accused. I was silenced, and my advocate (who, I was beginning to realise, I didn't like very much) had been of no help whatsoever up until that point.

- How, ladies and gentlemen of the jury, can we be expected to pay any heed to the defendant's assertions that he has an insightful knack when it comes to the written word, when he is clearly incapable of distinguishing the not so subtle differences between the terms 'guilty' and 'not guilty'?

The Judge looked like a toad, all warty and slimy green with a throat which vibrated when he spoke. He sported a wig which hung down in braids either side of his bulging eyes.

- I put it to the jury that at the very least the accused is greatly deceiving himself and, at worst – and this is the conclusion I lean towards myself – he is a liar, ladies and gentleman. Yes, a liar a liar a liar and his pants are on fire.

As the repulsive little creature was giving his speech he enthusiastically bounced up and down on his seat with his wig flailing around and beads of sweat running down his forehead. Once he'd finally come to rest again he was puffy and out of breath and his judicial hairpiece was lopsided. It now hung down over one eye.

- What's going to happen now? – I whispered to my advocate.
- I'm not quite sure – he began, which didn't exactly fill me with confidence. Either – he continued – the jury will go off to deliberate, or there'll be a pause for entertainment.
- ENTERTAINMENT? – I squawked incredulously.

- Oh yes. It's traditional. Sort of symbolic, if you like. Been with us for hundreds of years... with these types of cases.
- Uh-huh! And what exactly are *these* types of cases? – He rapidly turned his head towards me, looking at me as though I had just cracked a joke. When he saw that I wasn't joking he said
- What do you mean?
- Just that! What are these types of cases?
- Well, this case... *your* case.
- Yes?

He closely inspected my expression so as to be doubly sure I wasn't pulling his leg. Satisfied that I wasn't, and that I really did have no idea what he was talking about, his expression towards me completely changed. From being one of whimsy and vague curiosity, it altered to being one of utmost distain.

- Your category of case, which you haven't in the slightest tried to help me to win with your selfish continual outbursts, is what in legal parlance is known as 'Irredeemable Artistic Delusion'.
- Oh, right, this is complete rubbish! – I shouted at him as I jumped to my feet. He pulled me back down and said
- Hold on! Here comes the entertainment, you'll enjoy this.

From the right of the courtroom, through the double doors, came a procession of powder-pink pigs in bright pink tutus. They skipped along, evidently quite pleased with themselves, doing the Can-Can from one side of the room to the other and then twice around. This line of nine or ten pigs – I noticed as my eyes followed them around – had exaggeratedly long eye-lashes. Oddly enough, this inappropriate pause in the proceedings was led by a stocking-footed Black Rod. The pigs completed their two laps and headed for the door opposite the one they'd entered. Black Rod was business-like throughout, taking everything in his stride, giving not even the slightest hint of a deep-rooted desire to lift up one of his legs in a Can-Can-esque fashion.

He solemnly raised his hand and the pigs stopped. Two or three of the pigs, it has to be said, were less disciplined than the others. Instead of following the script's directions as the others were doing and gazing majestically forwards along the line, they had their heads turned towards us and were grinning and fluttering their eyelashes coquettishly.

This was not the behaviour of the well-brought-up pig, and certainly not in a courtroom environment. Black Rod tapped what can only be described as his 'black rod' thrice against the solid panelled door. He waited for a moment then tapped again. Whatever was supposed to happen – presumably, the opening of the door – did not happen, and so he tried again more insistently than the previous times. Still nothing.

I floundered my way through that indefinable state between sleeping and waking. Sabina's insistent knocking finally forced its way into my thoughts. "Are you decent?" came Sabina's voice from outside my cabin door.

"Umm... yes, yes – come in."

She placed a cup of coffee next to my bed. Once I was fully awake she told me that when I was dressed she'd like to talk to me outside and check how my head was coming along.

Fifteen minutes later she took my bandages off, inspected my head and wiped it with a damp flannel. She told me that everything looked fine and I should see how I went for a while with my head uncovered. We were sitting alone at one of the tables in the clearing.

Her look changed, rather rapidly I thought. "I have something to tell you," she began. "There was something I omitted from my account the other day."

"Oh, yes?"

"About the day we went to the market."

"Umm?"

The others, so she told me, had gone on ahead. She'd gone to the farmhouse and grabbed the possessions she thought I might want. All of which I knew – for apart from anything else she'd already given me my things. So naturally then I was wondering what she could be leading up to.

She continued by telling me that she'd taken the path down to the beach and walked a little way before sitting down to enjoy a little time on her own. "I suppose I was curious to see what you were reading," she said. "You know… we're so short of reading matter around here. I just… without thinking really… I just reached into my bag and, well… one by one took out the four books, and… well…"

So, that was it: she'd seen my book and now knew that I was (or at least *had been*) a writer; and felt bad for having invaded my privacy. She assured me that she hadn't divulged anything to the others since she wanted first to hear what I thought about it. She told me she felt really sorry about what she'd done, and knew that really she should have asked me.

I gave Sabina a brief explanation of how I found myself to be on the island. Nothing to do with Rosio and my madness at the time, only that I was there for a bit of peace and quiet to write my fourth novel. It was true, I divulged, that I'd initially had the idea of keeping that I was a writer to myself. It was not a law of the Medes and Persians as far as I was concerned, and I told her to forget it. In any case, if I'd really wanted nobody to know I wouldn't have brought my own book along with me, or I'd have hidden it. That's what I told her, anyway.

She smiled, winked and gave me a kiss on the cheek. We talked about how my head was feeling for a few moments. She said that the weekend after next there was going to be a party to celebrate the fifth anniversary of their community. Theo and Boudewijn were going to perform a song they had secretly been practising. The girls, according to Sabina, had prepared one or two surprises of their own. To my dismay, Sabina wondered if I would like to contribute to the evening's activities by reading something I'd written. Just as I was about to shake my head – both because I had nothing new to read and because I didn't feel I was ready for that kind of exposure – she delivered her *coup de grâce*: the evening, she said, was also to celebrate my recovery… I told her I'd think about it.

CHAPTER XV

Renney pushed some buttons on his second-hand East German surveillance equipment. The pictures were grainy, in black and white and prone to jumping – but they did the job. He'd get himself a better device once he was convinced he was going to make some money out of all of this.

Renney decided to look over the footage of the beach once again. He pressed the *Play* button. The distant figure of Jethro emerged from the bottom of the cliff path. He dropped his bag at his feet and looked around. Then with fervour he ran towards the water, throwing his clothes off as he went. Renney saw him run into the waves and dive under. Then there was a lot of splashing before Renney saw Jethro stumble to his feet holding his head. He staggered back onto the shore, where he collapsed.

Renney sighed to himself as he pressed the *Fast Forward* button. He watched as a young man and young woman ran into shot. Renney halted the speeded-up action by pressing Play again. They bent over him, but not for long. The man picked him up and slung him over his shoulder. They scurried back off in the direction they had come, and disappeared from Renney's screen.

"Bloody idiot!" Renney exclaimed as he watched the original recording of the accident. He'd watched it on three previous occasions and on each occasion he'd barked *bloody idiot* at Jethro's stupidity. A bird squawked outside; momentarily, Renney was distracted. He peered through the window in front of his desk, but couldn't see what kind of bird it was.

He shook his head slightly and refocused back on the screen. He left the picture running for several seconds longer, but nothing more happened. Nothing more ever happened. The only movement was that of the waves. As he stabbed the *Stop* button he thought he might get Marcus to erect a warning sign on the beach, immediately shook his head again as his tongue clicked against the roof of his mouth twice.

The purring of a motorbike caught Renney's attention. He picked his nose before switching to the camera fixed to the front of the house. On the screen he saw Stefano turn off the engine and alight from his bike. His wooden trailer was attached to the back to enable him to transport the Americans' paintings from Jethro's house.

Renney pressed the intercom button and tapped the microphone a couple of times. A crackly tap-tap boomed across the forecourt. This was something Renney always did. It was a procedure Stefano found both immeasurably irritating and completely unnecessary in almost equal measures. "Put the paintings in the shed," Renney said. "And did you get the paints?"

"Yes," shouted Stefano with his head tilted slightly up towards the skies as if addressing a voice from the heavens.

Stefano entered Renney's office and handed him the paints. After a short chat, in which Stefano wasn't really engaged, he left to put the paintings away. Renney watched him start his bike back up through the window and went along the corridor to descend the flight of stairs to what had almost instantly become known as the American Sector.

At the bottom of the stairs was a large and completely superfluous bullet-proof door. Renney'd bought it from the same Berliner who had sold him the surveillance equipment. He'd liked the look of it. Its intimidating nature would, he thought, concentrate the mind. But in the main he'd bought it because it had been cheap.

The door had a combination lock, the code for which only Renney knew. It also had a rather clever, a little too clever by half, possibly, time-lock release system – that was faulty. Through the bulletproof door was an enclosed fortified-glass space more or less the size of four telephone kiosks. Beyond this was another sturdy door, which wasn't bullet-proof, though.

This second door could also only be opened by tapping in the correct combination, but for this door both Renney and the Americans knew the release code. The doors together worked similarly to how many mainland European banks' entrances operated: you could open only one door at a time; the inner door, for example, could be released only when the bulletproof one was locked.

Once through the outer door Renney placed the paints on the floor. As he turned to leave he heard Sam's voice crackling through the intercom.

"Er, excuse me, Sir…"

"Yes, yes. I've brought you the paints you wanted," said Renney distractedly.

"Yes, thanks. No, it's not that."

"What then?"

"Erm, well… you haven't told us what's going on…" Sam paused as he deliberated over the correct words to use so as not to irritate Renney. "Er…" he continued "…my brother has lots of money if…"

"Just make sure that you keep painting and no harm will come to you," Renney interrupted. He shut the door behind him and made his way towards the stairs before Sam had a chance to say anything more.

Renney returned to his office and plonked himself down in his battered-looking black leather and chrome executive swivel chair. He swivelled around, kicking a spin off his desk every couple of times he completed a turn. And reflected upon how everything was progressing…

The Americans were doing fine – he would finish re-reading their file later. He was not in the mood right then. It was Jethro who concerned him. Jethro was a different proposition altogether. There was no immediate rush, but if the situation did not ameliorate pretty sharpish he would have to hurry things along.

He buzzed Stefano.

"Yes?"

"Where's Marcus?" asked Renney.

"At the new house."

"How much longer till it's finished?"

"Well, last I heard it should be ready in a couple of weeks."

"Didn't Marcus say that a couple of weeks ago?"

"Well…"

"Never mind. Bring the car round to the front, will you?"

"OK."

Renney switched the intercom off. He placed the torn piece of paper he'd been using as a bookmark back into Jethro's novel and left it on his desk. He raised himself with a groan and headed for the front of the house.

He had an old Willys cj2a roofless camouflage painted jeep. He'd been meaning to change it for some time fearing it might make him stand out. The trouble was he was so fond of it.

Ten minutes' drive along the coastal road and Renney arrived at the house he was having constructed. Marcus was doing most of the work himself, with an occasional trusted friend being flown in for any of the more difficult specialist jobs. When it came to construction Marcus was good, very good, but he had neither the skill nor the courage to attempt to replicate the Cubist's House.

The new building was a white rectangle, unlike the two defiantly balanced dice of the Cubist's House. To Renney's mind, however, the new building also consisted of two dice, only this time with one directly on top of the other... To everybody else it didn't look in the remotest bit like one die on top of the other. It looked exactly like what it was: a white rectangular building.

Nevertheless, it had been well thought out and certainly mirrored the style of the Cubist's House. At its best the construction was somewhat minimalist and possibly mildly Bauhaus-esque with a nod to the Constructivist utilitarian structures of the east. At its worst it was a boring white block.

A dusty grimy Marcus with a bare torso and wearing green combat shorts came round the corner of the house. He spied Renney and quickly turned around and scurried back out of sight.

Renney pushed the front door open, walked in and turned through the door to his left, into the office. The office was situated in the same position in both houses. But that was where the similarities ended. There would be three underground accommodation suites in this construction, as opposed to the two in the Cubist's House. This second house would eventually become the main building, with the Cubist's House used solely as Renney's accommodation, storage, and for administrative purposes.

Once activities had been fully transferred to the second house, Renney would happily give a tour to any art student or random visitor who periodically happened to

116

turn up to see Vladimir Putchkiov's architectural wonder. He might even give them a potted history of how the Cubist's House came to be built.

He believed that the project he'd embarked upon on this little inconsequential island could be revolutionary. Whether everything produced the results he envisaged remained to be seen. Indeed, whether the artistic and psychological world ended up believing he had augmented the ground-breaking experiment he believed he had was far less likely than he imagined. Nonetheless, he thought he was on the verge of making an impact at least equivalent to that of Duchamp's *Fountain* upon the eventual direction of the art world.

Once his contribution to art, and indeed his genius, was recognised there could be organised tours, accommodation, even a hotel and a restaurant. Art students, he thought, could come and enjoy the superb light. Architectural students could come on working holidays. There could be a complex of studios where students could come as part of their courses. Renney considered it to be perfectly feasible for an entire facility to be constructed, one that ideally would have a close connection to a university department somewhere.

Students and tourists would come to see the place where Renney changed the manner by which people perceived the capabilities of art. He would appear on cultural timelines as being the instigator of a moment when the understanding of what artists were capable of significantly shifted. He would appear alongside the likes of Dali, Da Vinci, Michael Angelo and *Les Demoiselles d'Avignon* by Pablo Picasso.

The revolution, Renney wrote that evening in capital letters at the top of a clean page in his diary, *will* be televised. Renney, who sometimes liked to see himself as a cross between the 7th Marquess of Bath and the self-

appointed King Richard Booth of Hay-on-Wye, on occasion
got carried away...

CHAPTER XVI

Renney owned nearly five kilometres of coastline – or more accurately cliff-line. The width of his land, at its widest 1.54kms, varied by up to forty-five meters from one point to another. This was due both to the raggedy Mandelbrot-like folding inwards and outwards of the cliff's edge and because of the comparatively straight line of his inland border.

It is in the Auvetian Treaty of 1206 where Renney's land is first mentioned as being separate from the adjacent common land. The Treaty came about after the four-day marriage celebrations between Constantine of Venice and the island's Prince Leopold III. It enshrines the rights of those who reside within the borders of the territory, giving them a significant degree of self-determination and law-making rights. This was significant since in the fourteenth century this part of the island was relatively highly populated.

At the time the Treaty was drawn up the territory included the beach and waters as well as the land. After the First World War however, the central mainland government passed laws preventing beaches and coastlines from being privately owned. In most of the country this wasn't a problem. However, for the new *diktat* after the First World War to apply equally to this five-kilometre stretch of coastline, they had to amend the Treaty of 1206. To achieve this required the agreement of those residing on the land at that time.

An addendum had been made to the original Treaty stating that only those who'd resided on the land for at least a year were permitted to vote on issues concerning the land itself. This provision had been added to the original document for fear the former landowner might one day want his land back. Also, this requirement prevented anyone from attempting to flood the area with his own supporters on the day of a ballot...

Another of Renney's imprecise ideas was to build a museum in honour of the Treaty and the history of this small strip of land. Fascinating though all of the region's history undoubtedly was, far more interesting was how Renney came by the land in the first place: a story that, if there was ever going to be a museum dedicated to the hundreds of years of often peculiar occurrences in that area, would have a whole section to itself.

------• • •------

Renney Van der Stratten wasn't his real name. Although his accent was at least partially contrived he had nonetheless spent several years in Holland and Belgium on and off. He was from an old Bostonian family originally and his real name was Lawrence Howton.

He hated returning home. He hated his mother. He went home only for the sake of his father, who he felt sorry for, and possibly because of some mistaken loyalty or connection to his younger self. Even this was hardly ever reason enough.

His mother found him to be an embarrassment and the way he looked she didn't want anyone to see her with him. She always made him meet her on the outskirts of town, far away from where she lived. She'd meet him in a teahouse, bringing him a navy blue blazer with a crest on the breast pocket, a pair of baggy cream pleated slacks with tiny turn-ups and a hideous pair of shiny brogues. When he'd changed, she'd take him to the nearby barber's to get his hair cut into a short side-parting and to get his unruly beard shorn off. In those days Renney used to have long wavy hair; these days it was rather bushy and unkempt, with grey flecks.

He'd then have to spend the next ten days or so pretending to her awful friends how well he was doing. It wasn't as though he'd not objected: he had, on numerous occasions. The conclusion, however, to these contretemps was that if he didn't like it he didn't have to come home. Those were his choices: either do it her way or not at all. For many years he chose the 'not at all' option. For long periods he simply got on with his life and more or less ignored the fact that he even had such a thing as a mother.

As his parents got older he realised if he didn't do it their way – essentially, his mother's way – it would be too late. Consequently, he decided to make the effort to visit his parents a couple of times a year. Soon after arriving at this decision, he heard that his father had suddenly become seriously ill; within ten days, he died.

His mother became even worse than before. Renney tried his best but he couldn't really bear to be in her company. He'd felt a vague twinge of duty somewhere deep down in his belly when his father was still alive. This no longer meant a thing, especially when, on what turned out to be his final visit, a couple of events occurred that altered the course of his life.

On that final visit to his mother's house she told him she was going to be extremely busy and would be unable to meet him. She arranged to have his 'acceptable' clothes taxied over to the barber she always took him to. He could change there or in his car, she didn't really care which, so long as he didn't look like some lowlife recipient of food stamps.

He returned home on a Saturday afternoon. He knocked at the door in his navy blue blazer one size too small. His mother came to the door holding an embroidered handkerchief to her nose. She didn't say a word to him. She simply opened the door, turned, and returned to where she'd been sitting in the living room. Nine people not counting him and his mother were present. Like an irritating piece of fluff one has difficulty flicking off one's clothes Renney was brusquely waved towards the chair in the corner. He crossed the room giving an occasional nod as he did so. He knew four or five of those present. He'd grown up with some of their nauseating children: yacht-owning country club-member types.

They were gathered there for a neighbourhood meeting. His mother had been crying. She had red eyes and a runny nose. "What are we going to do?" she snuffled. The ensuing sighs, tuts and doleful shaking of heads indicated they were all at a loss as to how to proceed. Even though Renney had arrived at the tail end of their discussions he picked up all he needed to: the problem, as they saw it, was that a family of colour had moved into the street.

The obvious and rational response to his mother's question was that they should get to know the family, make them welcome. But *getting to know them* was not an option for these people. Their perfectly shorn bushes and precision-mown lawns reflected their inner selves.

This was the tidy face of fascism, the cordial well-kept side of prejudice. These were tupperware racists – but they were racists nonetheless. Not that their views were based on ideology or beliefs; they had no coherent thoughts or reasoning. They neither questioned nor justified what they said and thought. In a sense, Renney concluded, their stupidity protected them.

He sat there observing their mean faces and antediluvian expressions. These types, he reflected, would all die out soon enough. It was the other ones, the ones who considered they had a historical argument and a justification for their warped ideas, who were the most dangerous. More dangerous than those who had been brought up to think in a certain way and had consequently never questioned the nature of their beliefs.

Renney watched as they discussed their good-natured witch-hunt and where to plant their invisible burning crosses. He scrutinised one face after another. How he despised each of them. And what was he to think of his mother? He'd never seen this side of her. Why would he? This had always been a nice rich white area, and, of course, that was the point: if these narrow-minded throwbacks had their say it always would be.

With disbelief Renney listened as their opinions developed into a tangible plan: they would politely ask to purchase the black family's house, offering them a very generous price considerably above the value of the property. That, they believed, should get rid of them...

By the end of their discussions and cups of tea Renney vowed never to see any of these people ever again, his mother included. He was repulsed by the men's smug round reddened faces and the women's tidily crossed legs, pinched nostrils and prim self-importance. He'd stay for the few days as planned and he'd be as pleasant as he could for one last time. Then he would never return. His mother probably wouldn't even notice.

It was on the evening before the morning of his departure that the second event occurred that was to alter the future course of his life.

Renney's mother told him that before his father died he would frequently go up to the attic to spend several hours amongst his things. She never used to go up there because of her back. She wasn't certain how he occupied himself, but she did know that he had a large train set up there. She told Renney that she'd been meaning to get somebody to clear away all of his belongings. If he wanted to go up there and sort through some of his father's things before she got them all thrown out, he could.

Renney climbed the ladder to the attic and with an uneasy twist at the top managed to squeeze through the small trap door. He looked around, half-heartedly poking around at odd things, for a little under ten minutes, but he couldn't see anything that interested him. He was turning to leave when he realised that nowhere in the loft could he see his father's train set.

He turned back and allowed his eyes to scan the room with its inverted V-shaped beams. He found it odd. If his father played with his train set every time he went into the attic, where was it? Surely he wouldn't have packed it away in one of the numerous cardboard boxes up there. Renney went over to the opposite side of the attic from the trapdoor. He looked from left to right briefly, hoping that something might catch his eye and direct his search. Nothing did, so he began by rooting around in the box nearest to him.

It wasn't that he especially wanted the train set, but his father had been such a bland nonentity of a man that Renney was merely curious to see what must have been the solitary element of fun in his life. Renney believed that living with Renney's mother for so long must have battered any spirit out of the poor man.

Renney moved from one cardboard box to another, flapping cobwebs away with the back of his hand and then wiping his hand on his trousers. He thought that his father's hobby probably represented a tiny piece of defiance. It was something frivolous he could enjoy independently of his wife. But where was the damn thing?

Renney searched in box after box to no avail. As he was beginning to consider the possibility of having to create an imaginary memory of train and father together, he spied a small table in the corner of the attic. On the table was a tape recorder. He went over and pressed the play button. And there, out of the single speaker came the sound of an electric train: choo-choo.

Renney turned the volume down, nodded, cupped his beard in his hand and smiled to himself. His father had been spending all that time in the attic lying to his wife. Good for him, possibly he wasn't such a jellyfish after all. But, Renney reflected, if his father felt he wasn't able to admit the truth about how he was really spending his time what *had* he been doing up there?

Renney lowered himself gingerly to the floor with a groan and sat with his back against one of the vertical beams. One after another he reached into more of the nearest boxes and randomly began scrutinising some of his father's documents and scraps of paper. Whatever he'd been doing up there for all that time it must have been important; otherwise, why *so* much time?

He soon realised that whatever the answer to the mystery he was unlikely to solve it at that moment up there in the attic. He would need time to assess the significance of his father's papers. But which pieces of paper contained his father's secrets? He hoped that good fortune would guide his hand for he knew that the ones he left behind would all soon be dust. Renney stuffed as much as he could into the four large black plastic bags he'd found in the corner of the attic.

When the bags were so full he could hardly tie them up he stood at the top of the ladder and looked around. Quite possibly, he thought, this was the only place his father had experienced a modicum of peace.

CHAPTER XVII

...*He'd moved away from the slick city slickers and the pot-noodle pedestrians. Away from the smoke and the grey lights, the smell of tarmac and the clunks and scrapes of these machine times. The boy from the chippie on the corner married the girl from potato paraphernalia – they'll be having their second in June.*

He'd moved out of the land of the skyscraper stacks with their haphazard occasional lights left on overnight. He'd moved away 'cos of the ever-enveloping bandaged tableau of the bland and the uniform and the apparent acceptance of the predominant hue – given to, or chosen by, the multitude. The wisdom of the multitude... And then there was the rumble, the continual rumble with no obvious off switch: a lever of contentment. For the noise throbs and pounds as an underlying swirl – even in sleep the noise becomes a dream. And the concrete gets inside your brain after a while, seeping and creeping like grey goo.

To the countryside. To the countryside, away from the angles; away from the hordes and the sordid tales... purity without dust; a vocabulary of difference – based upon greenness and curves, and the silence and the nothingness.

Green, they say, is the colour of imagination, the colour of hope, the colour that soothes. Grey is dreary and wet and stains easily. Green invites you in. Grey is invariably cracked, frequently oozing its city pus; a secretion best left ignored for the fear of retching at the knowledge. Down in the subway... down in the subway the creatures crawl to their daily grind. Above ground the march is on.

The middle of nowhere, the middle of nothingness – being in the middle of something with nothing all around. Green is the colour of everything; curved and curvaceous, haphazard with no diktat: *sexy.*

He'd go to the train station every day, briefcase in hand, briefcase in hand – with briefcase in his hand. Leather with a shiny buckle it was – clip-clasp fastener with combination lock. It had been a gift from his girlfriend – she'd become a cheese quaver raver and moved to Amsterdam... The station was in the middle of nowhere, not near a village, not near anything at all. As far as he could see it served little purpose, apart from the purpose of serving, that is. No, that wasn't quite fair – it had served, and would serve again, the trap-cart communities and the isolated hillside families. It was just that he never saw anyone else at the station; at the train station.

He'd find himself a spot where he felt comfortable some way along the platform, which had some degree of equidistance to something or other about it. He'd take a long, measured gaze forwards into the forested horizon, then with mechanical precision he'd look left then right then left again... So was his morning ritual.

The old man seemed to appear as if from nowhere, so unannounced was his arrival. The truth was that he'd silently approached from a blind direction that not even a rear view mirror would have caught. He spoke in respectfully hushed tones with a strong, what I took to be, West Country accent: "Do 'ee believe in God?" he enquired. The man waiting for his train told him that he didn't.

"Aaarrr," he nodded, bestowing a far greater sense of sapience into that breathy one syllable than one might have imagined possible. The man edged himself forwards in the false hope that he might be able to see further up the line. The old man

shuffled himself back alongside. "There be an astral plane, y'know."

"I'm sorry?"

"An astral plane! An astral plane – where lots of truth can be found out." He doffed his cap and winked up at the man.

"I see."

"Yes yes. I goes there most nights. 'Tis strange and fun..." The elderly man paused to follow the man's gaze up along the track. "There's not many a train comes by this way n'more."

"Yes, thank you, I'm well aware of that."

"'Ee comes here every morning to wait for the train, i'n't that right?"

"Indeed I do," replied the neatly dressed man with unintended conviction as he gave his briefcase a little swing backwards and forth.

"Much luck?"

As he peered down into the old man's eyes he began to realise something. But before he was able to marry up this realisation with a cogent progression of thoughts however, the elderly man continued. "On the plane there's balls... spheres. Everything is white, dull white, and there's mist floats around your feet."

"Really?"

"Aaarrr! These balls they're dotted all over the plane. One's here, nother's over there – not next to each other; well, most aren't next to each other. It's quite a walk, y'know, from the one you're at to one o' the other five or six you sees in the distance... 'Ee can't see through 'em, mind! Well, you sees through 'em, but not 'see' see. 'Ee sees the shadows 'n' all, and the light, colours sometimes, but y'can't see inside like I sees you there. Got it?"

"I'm... well..."

"Course 'ee's got it, 'ee be an intelligent man. I sees that. Now then, let me ask 'ee again: Do 'ee believe in anything after this yer life?"

"I..."

"I knows 'ee said 'no' at first, who wouldn't? I could've been some kind o' nut or something."

"Quite."

"Well?"

"Sorry? ...Oh... Yes, well... um, I go to church every so often. Sing a hymn or two, heaven and hell and the Almighty... You know – Christmas Carols. Usual stuff, but it's not really..."

"Be your train coming yet?"

"Erm... no, not quite yet."

"Is that right? ...Now then, in these balls there's people. You sees their outline, their shadows. One person in each most usually. You hears 'em too, sometimes.

"There's this one ball I sees on the plane and it's completely black inside. Only close up can you make out this figure helplessly groping around blindly in the dark... He was an atheist when he was a living presence."

"What on earth are you talking about?"

"Don't you mind me – you just keep looking out for that train of yours ... Then there's these other ones – I won't go up to those no more. You sees the bright flames from far off. The screaming makes you sweat and shudder in your bones. Piercing it is – from unending pain. These are the only ones that are in a row. Light up the whole horizon they does. Full of flames and the silhouette of some poor soul in the most terrible of pain. There's those who live semi-permanent like, on the plane, who call this row of balls 'The Sinner Men'. One ball be a permanently boiling orange prison. All God-fearing he'd been in his living presence; believed in hell and damnation and all the rest of it. Convinced he was, silly bugger, that he was righteous, had done good – you know, one o' those types who thinks he's doing God's work. Course, he hadn't; he wuz a cruel blighter."

"I don't think I..."

"Now, the one in the sphere next to him had all the flames and the excruciating burning torture as well, but, difference is he really was a good man. Done good things, helped people and that. Still believed he was sinful right up until the end, mind. Now then, his flames stop every so often – not long enough for his body to heal or anything, but long enough for him to have occasional respite. Long enough some o' the time, perhaps, for him to be able to think about his predicament; you know, question it 'n' all.

"You see, there are these people on the plane – called 'helpers', they are. They don't go to all the balls, all the types of balls I means. But, I sees 'em sometimes – shouting and knocking at one or other of the balls. Trying to get through … trying to get the message through, 'bout where they is and the reasons and all that. Far as I can tell they'm ignored; largely ignored at any rate. Put it this way, I en't seen no success as yet. Dun't mean there en't bin, I's just saying – seems a waste o' time to me."

"Arr-ha! At last, here comes my train."

"You sure?"

"Well, of course! I can hear the… the rattling of the… track… Or, well… I thought I… umm… oh, well, er, possibly not. Maybe it was… I was sure I heard it… um, the wind or something…"

"Aaii!" said the old man as he nodded sagely.

"I'm sure it will be along in a moment."

"Aaii… I'm sure it will."

I looked up from my scrawled pieces of paper. A pause… and then they all clapped. They clapped in a manner that conveyed politeness more than enthusiasm. And as far as my self-doubt permitted, my perception was that it was only Sabina who was clapping with any real enthusiasm.

I'd wanted to write a new piece for the occasion. To read from my old novel would have been the easy option. But I was a different person now, and I'd come to this island to write. To write new words on new lines that conveyed new thoughts.

The way they applauded indicated, to my mind, that they didn't really know what to make of my reading. Maybe they didn't quite get it. Nonetheless, it was writing and I had written it; and it was a marked departure from anything I'd written in the past. It was different and I was different. But the main thing was I'd begun to write again.

As I was climbing down from the small stage Boudewijn stepped up with his guitar in his hand. He was wearing orange overalls with no t-shirt underneath. He had tightly curly, spring-loaded, shoulder length coffee-coloured hair, and a longish face with a chiselled chin. His eyes were brown and peered mouse-like from behind his round bi-focal lenses.

Our eyes met briefly. The instant they did, he looked away. Then, as if to say he'd appreciated my story, he gently patted me on the back as we passed. A gesture that for someone like him was most probably more significant than the action itself might have suggested.

Boudewijn was the quietest of them all. At first I put this down to shyness, and later thought he might even be a bit developmentally disabled or marginally autistic, as much as anything else. Later still, all of that notwithstanding, I realised that in fact he was attempting to be as pure as he possibly could be. Essentially, he was trying to maintain a childlike naivety uncluttered by the glitz, glamour and harshness of the modern age, as he saw it.

Boudewijn's persona was based upon an ideological premise. By living there in the forest by the bay he was rejecting modern life, at least that was how I took it. They were all doing that to a certain degree, but Boudewijn was going further. He was also rejecting how the modern age covertly affects one's *being*. He, for example, hardly ever engaged in small talk; he limited his interaction to what he deemed necessary. He walked slowly, measuredly, almost Buddist-like, as if his mind was contemplating the greater questions of life.

He had a uniqueness about him. He exemplified both beauty and tragedy in my mind. He had an awkward philosophy he was stumbling along to realise; a philosophy which was, I thought, ultimately destined to fail. The tragedy for me was that even if he succeeded in his own terms he'd affect nothing whatsoever. And his beauty derived from the unwavering belief that, in his own clumsy and misguided way, he had to take a stand.

I wasn't sure why the others were there; they gave me the impression they were all ordinary enough (I never heard any mention of aliens the whole time I was there, for example). Normal enough, not in a pin-stripe and commuter sense, but in a young people growing their hair long and wearing beards sense, momentarily living out their hippy dreams. Yet I sensed something inconsistent or perfunctory about the way they went about their lives. It was nothing tangible, merely a feeling I had that these people were two-dimensional – boring, I suppose. But who was I to make such judgements?

Clearly, then, I found Boudewijn and Sabina to be by far the most interesting characters there. Boudewijn I watched from a distance. My discourse with him had consisted of no more than a few short chats. But on each occasion he'd looked uncomfortable and hadn't contributed much, and consequently I'd let him escape at the earliest opportunity.

Sabina and I, by contrast, were getting to know each other as more than merely patient and carer – to the extent that though I didn't wish to appear pushy I did want to establish if there was anything more to our friendship. Or if it was just some form of sick man's emotional Stockholm Syndrome that had kicked in?

The more I considered it the more I thought that I could base a character on Boudewijn; I could base a character on Sabina too. And soon, I believed, I would be able to return to my mission. Soon I would be ready to cast aside my demons, forget about my history, take God by the hand

and make people dance. Soon I would write, fish, enjoy the sun and the grape, and with a bit of luck make love upon the beach.

PART III

CHAPTER XVIII

The forest looked dark. A circle of torches had been skewered into the ground, marking out the perimeter of the communal area. Candles and tea lights flickered on tables and blocks of wood. The moon made intermittent appearances. The music came from guitar playing and tribal drumming. When there was no music the dominant sound was the chattering and laughing of those generously helping themselves to the homemade punch.

I stood around at the side of the stage, watching the guitar playing and not really knowing what to do next. Realising I was still tightly holding onto my scribbled text I folded up the pieces of paper and put them in my pocket.

I felt myself slowly coming down after the adrenalin rush of my public reading. I thought I should mingle, grab a drink and enjoy myself. I'd been too wound up to talk to anyone beforehand.

There were about twenty-five or thirty people at the party. They were standing in small groups or sitting cross-legged on matting laid down on the forest floor. They all appeared to be in their mid-twenties to mid-thirties. Almost all of the men had long or shoulder-length hair. They wore straggly cut-off jeans or brightly-coloured cotton trousers. Some were bare chested, while others wore t-shirts of what I surmised were either long-since-forgotten or obscure rock and roll groups. And I spotted a handful of men huddled together at the edge of the site who were wearing either vest tops or normal t-shirts with German or Dutch writing on them. The ones I could read from where I was standing meant nothing to me. From the accompanying imagery, however, I guessed that they were political slogans.

The women wore simple clothes, smock dresses or worn, scraggly flared blue jeans and two were wearing baggy striped medieval-looking pantaloon-style shorts. A few, probably about five or six, had flowing dresses and braided hair. A woman I liked the look of, who I thought noticed me without wishing to be noticed herself, was wearing tight frayed khaki cut-offs and had spiky saffron bleached hair. She had large black square earrings and a pierced nose.

I had the feeling she'd have an interesting personal story to tell, and had half a mind to go and say hello. But at the instant I was contemplating going over to introduce myself a recollection flashed through my mind. A friend and I were sitting outside a Manchester pub happily enjoying our ale and the buzzing courtyard atmosphere. My friend, who noticed me observing a striking young Asian woman with a chain from her ear to her nose and wearing a t-shirt with a picture of naked breasts on it, said: "She'd eat you alive…". Unfortunately, the re-emergence of this memory at that time filled me with self-doubt. So I turned away from the woman and fleetingly recalled another episode: when Rosio and I had visited university friends in Manchester. But this new divergence didn't interest me and so I reverted to discreetly observing those present.

As I turned my head around to face the other way I saw the bizarre, somewhat disconcerting sight, of three people sitting on wooden chairs wearing masks. They were sitting in front of a large bush on the perimeter of the proceedings. One was a woman in her underwear, and the other two were men, one of whom was wearing a toga while the other only had shorts on. One of the men's masks was similar to a Venetian half-face mask with a long pointed nose. The other had on a blotchily coloured monkey face. Whereas the woman was sporting a Japanese emotionless delicately painted ceramic mask. As I observed them they remained perfectly motionless. It was a strange sight, that, to make myself feel less uncomfortable, I put down to baroque performers awaiting their turn on stage… I turned away and looked somewhere else.

As far as I could tell no one was watching me watching them. Almost all were engrossed in their conversations or concentrating upon the music being played. I got myself a cup of punch from a full bowl that had slices of fruit floating on its garnet-coloured surface and went to stand by the fire. Four men were sitting on the floor to my right. I warmed myself and drank what tasted like a potent concoction. I was happy to be left alone, at least until I settled down or until Sabina showed up. The flames crackled and swirled and soon began to soothe me.

I stood and stared into the fire. Gradually, I became absorbed. I saw the blazing orange shimmering ribbons like heraldic oriflammes dancing their primordial patterns. The pirouetting of the glowing light together with the heady brew and the marijuana plumes floating up to my nostrils from the group sitting on the ground transformed into the opening titles of *The Tales of the Unexpected*. The emergence of these swaying women from this happy, sexy, fiery Anglia television hell was followed by the title music, briefly but surely.

I looked around in a cartoon double-take way, unintentionally, but that was what happened. So real-sounding was the music I wanted to see if it existed anywhere other than in my head. As soon as I did so, though, the sound disappeared. Then I looked into my cup of punch, for no other reason than that it seemed to be an appropriate thing to do… I turned and turned again to see if anyone was paying me any attention, and probably subconsciously hoping for reassurance that I was not acting out-of-the-ordinary. I cast my eye cautiously once more into the nucleus of the fire and considered what had just occurred. I was glad when my attention was drawn by the conversation underway amongst a circle of people sitting on the floor close by.

"…Yes, I was born on the day Khrushchev gave his famous speech."

What a bizarre thing to say, I thought. I realised that I was getting too hot standing so close to the fire and took a couple of steps back. I wanted to see who had enunciated such a sentence. And as I stepped back I briefly glanced down. In the middle of the group sat an odd-looking fellow who was easily the oldest person at the event.

The gent in question was wearing a safari suit under which was a white shirt with the top button done up, and on his feet were sandals and black socks. The thick-rimmed round spectacles perched on the end of his nose added to his aura of eccentricity. His cross-legged entourage were no doubt as stunned as I was in the presence of such a guru of oddness and inappropriate footwear; and were hanging on his every utterance.

"Um… 1956, it was. Yes, yes, I know; hard to believe that someone with such boyish good looks was born so long ago." He punctuated this with the combination of a dry echoey cough and a mockingly embarrassed laugh.

"Yes, 1956, one of the three best years in modern times… You know what the other two were, don't you?" One of them gently shook his head while the others remained   immobile,   engrossed   and   somewhat disbelieving. "1969 – the year of the moon landing; and 1977 – the year that the pop music combo *The Clash* released their first eponymous album."

The expression 'curiouser and curiouser' inserted itself into my brain, producing a grin that I attempted to stifle.

"You, Sir! Yes, *you*, Sir… warming your nuts by the fire." I cautiously turned, hoping he wasn't addressing me yet rather suspecting that he was. He was.

"Hello?" I said.

"Yes, indeed, hello to you, good fellow. Do correct me if I'm mistaken, but I believe I caught you smiling at my choice of years…"

"Er, no, I wasn't… I…"

"No matter," he interrupted. "If you have no objection I'd be greatly interested to hear which three years you would consider the most momentous in recent history."

I stared at him for a moment, stunned. "Erm," I began. "Well…" I continued feebly.

"Yes?"

"Well…"

"Yes?" he repeated.

"Well, I don't really…"

"Come, come, old chap, it's only for fun."

"Well… I suppose… off the top of my head, erm, I suppose… 1945. And, um… whichever year it was in the 1450s that the Gutenberg Bible was printed."

"Interesting… but hardly *modern* history that. No matter, though… And?" he prompted.

"Umm…" I was annoyed with myself for not paying close attention, giving the 1450s as an example made me look a little stupid, I thought. "And, I guess…" I went on, "off the top of my head…"

"Understood."

"Probably 1928."

"Because?"

"It was the year Alexander Fleming is credited with discovering penicillin."

"Good, good."

"And if I were allowed a fourth," I went on, finally warming to his little game, and wanting to give at least one interesting and fun example: "since you chose a music-related year, I'd have to say 1969 – the year *Sgt. Pepper's* was released."

"Excellent answers; thought-provoking indeed. An entire evening's discussion could be based upon your answers alone," he enthused.

"I don't know about that… I'd have to think for a bit longer to give you a better-considered response."

"Indeed so. I thoroughly enjoyed your recital by the way."

"Oh, thank you."

"Yes, I've read three of your four novels, you know."

"Really?" I exclaimed. And probably for the first time in my life was I able to accurately apply the term flabbergasted to a way I was feeling. "…Wow, thank you… but there *are* only three of them."

He laughed, nodded and gave me a sly little wink – which I didn't see the significance of, before saying, "In that case I shall amend my previous divulgence to: I've read all of your novels… All of your novels up to this point." And he gave another knowing wink.

I smiled. "I shall refer the gentleman to the answer I gave a few moments ago, namely: thank you."

"Splendid. I would be deeply honoured if we could chew some full-bodied fat together during the course of the evening. I have an idea that may possibly interest you."

"Of course, when you like," I replied.

"Excellent. I shall come and track you down... For the moment, though..." He left this last sentence hanging as he turned back towards his adoring listeners.

Behind me was a thick cross-section from a sawn off tree trunk. It had a candle on it. I placed the candle on the ground and dragged the log to where I had been standing. I sat down, drank from my beaker, allowing my gaze to penetrate deep into the flames once more, and listened to the man's story.

"Now where was I?" he enquired of his entourage.

"1956," ventured one.

"Indeed so. 1956, yes yes. The year I was born. A momentous year... My mother is screaming whilst Khrushchev is addressing the Twentieth Party Congress. Communist speeches and having babies – both concerned with labour. Both, at least for me, inextricably linked forever more. As Khrushchev is giving birth to new ideas my mother is following a more literal path. The revolution, so to speak, is between her thighs...

"So there he is, standing before the multitude of Party officials. He looks majestic in his role as flag-bearer for the anti-imperialist model. Alongside him on the podium are all the big-wigs and integral cogs of the Party apparatus. Now then," he stated emphatically, after having spent a moment to observe those around him, "what mustn't be forgotten is that Stalin has died three years earlier. Stalin – the great victorious war-time leader; the defender of Communism against Hitler's invading army. Apotheosis is what we're talking about, my friends... The cult of personality compounded, since his death, into folkloric memories of a sunny childhood summer that never was."

I looked around at the faces with their opened mouths and expectant expressions. The cultish awe was strange to watch. They hardly moved, they watched, listened and took in. Not one got up and walked away, or went to the toilet, or even, as far as I had seen, took a sip of his drink.

One of them had a shaven head, was tanned, in his late thirties with mean lips and a slight split to his left nostril. He had a tattoo of a Celtic cross on his forearm and I surveyed him for longer than intended; or at least for longer than etiquette would deem polite. He turned to me with the rapidity of a camera shutter, glared and stuck his tongue out as his eyes appeared to bulge slightly out of his skull.

I jolted back a pace, blinked and rubbed my eyes with the palms of my hands. It was a cliché reaction to a bizarre occurrence. The funny thing is that when one is struck by the outlandish or anomalous one acts unoriginally, without thought, as one considers the incident and not one's reaction to it.

I felt droplets of perspiration spring out over my body: hot then cold damp sweat oozing from my pores. I slowly opened my eyes and cast my gaze back in the direction of the bald man. I caught him as he was in the process of turning back to listen to the storyteller. And I wondered what, if anything, I had just seen… Then, at the final possible instant before his eyes would no longer have been visible to me, and as *I* myself was once again also turning away to consider… I don't know – alcohol, drugs and sanity I suppose – I was sure he gave me a wink. And then as if nothing had occurred it was over – the event, everything. The whole thing had come and gone and I was left shaken wondering what had happened.

"You can see the problem Khrushchev had," our fireside raconteur was declaring. "Stalin had to be denounced, you see. It was time… it was time for the Soviet Union to disassociate itself from the previous régime and all its gulags and mass murders.

"It was a big thing, the successor reviling his predecessor. The idea had been mooted for quite some time behind the scenes. You know, that this was going to be the moment when the slate was sponged down and made to appear new again. Scrape off the permanent marker, paint over it and make everything shiny again... Er, have I mixed my... you know? Humph, no matter...

"Anyway, naturally not all were in favour of the plan. Quite the contrary: there was widespread opposition from behind the scenes."

"Why? Surely it was obvious that Stalin had been as atrocious as Hitler," said an afroed young black man smoking a roll-up.

"That may well have been the case *in reality*. But I think Hitler was always seen as being worse than Stalin. Rightly or wrongly – in my view, wrongly – Nazism was considered to be far worse than Stalinism. And I don't just mean in the USSR, but everywhere... The world over Hitler's régime was and still is seen as being more atrocious than Russia under Stalin.

"But the point is that if Khrushchev were to criticise Stalin he'd also be criticising the higher echelons of the Party. In other words he'd be criticising those who still wielded the power: namely, his colleagues."

"Uh-huh."

"Just because Stalin was dead didn't mean that anything else had changed."

"So by condemning Stalin..." began a long-haired man, who marginally resembled the actor Anthony Valentine, his left eye faintly twitching as he spoke.

"Yes, by condemning Stalin", he went on, "he was also condemning the great and the good who had inevitably kept their positions within the hierarchy.

"You see, nothing had changed personnel-wise except for Stalin. And this – and here's the meat on the bone – was true of Khrushchev himself. He didn't simply arrive on the scene from nowhere. No bright red alien space vessel had materialised to beam down the planet's new Socialist leader."

Clearly pleased with himself, he paused and peered above his glasses. He pushed them deliberately back up his nose, smiled briefly and continued. "After all," he said. "He wouldn't have become the new leader if he hadn't been one of the main protagonists in the previous régime. And right there, my friends, is the crux of the matter."

A man with a wiry goatee beard and short, tightly curled ginger hair, who I'd felt had been grinning at me as I was talking to safari-suit man, was sitting down again after putting some more logs on the fire. He coughed to draw attention to himself, then nervously twiddled with his beard before saying: "By criticising Stalin he would be criticising himself."

"Exactly!" exclaimed our peculiar-looking storyteller. "But the decision had been made – it had to be done," he said. "And we shouldn't underestimate the courage of Khrushchev to make such a stand either... Mikojan had paved the way by criticising many aspects of Stalin's leadership earlier in the week. Nonetheless, the anticipation was palpable.

"Khrushchev stood up. And while I was covered in blood many hundreds of kilometres away, so Khrushchev was surrounded by a lake of red flags... His speech", he said, "was extremely powerful. He reproached the cult of personality and stated that never again should it be permitted to play any part in the Soviet Union. More than this, most strikingly, he unequivocally condemned the actions and policies of the previous administration...

"And as he was doing this, emphasising his words with a pounded fist, a folded piece of paper was passed along the line to him. Khrushchev halted mid-flow and read it. Written on it were the words: 'And what did you do during that period, Khrushchev?' He looked around at those on the platform with him and demanded to know who'd written it. Everyone remained still and didn't say a word... He paused for a moment, before hollering: 'That's exactly what I did... I said nothing!'"

CHAPTER XIX

An arm reached over my shoulder and refilled my empty cup. As I was turning to establish its owner Sabina bent over and kissed me on the cheek. Later that evening we made love. Afterwards she asked me not to tell anyone. She prevaricated when I asked her for a reason. She looked furtive – but, thankfully, not regretful. Her cheeks were flushed and her eyes had that watery, far-off quality to them. And as I discreetly looked down over her naked body I could not have been happier.

She smiled. "I think I'm going to join what's left of the party," she told me as we lay there intertwined.

"Good idea," I said, trying to sound as nonchalant as possible.

She kissed me tenderly, almost, I thought, wistfully, and got out of bed. She located her knickers on the floor and pulled them gently over her cute little heart-shaped bottom. You can tell a lot about a woman by the kind of underwear she chooses to wear. Sabina's were small, tight and white, and had tiny red blossom prints over them.

Fleetingly, a feeling of sadness and guilt rose in me. It was the first time I had been unfaithful to Rosio. Was it possible to be unfaithful to a memory of a former time? I wasn't sure. I quickly told myself it was a ridiculous thought and in no small part disrespectful to Sabina.

I watched as Sabina lifted one foot after the other onto the chair to do up the laces on her boots. She picked up her dress from the floor and let it fall down over her head and body. She wasn't wearing a bra. This I took to be due to a combination of her firm, petite breasts and a certain inclination she might have towards feminism. This was no more than guesswork, however. I liked to guess; I liked to make up stories.

She turned as she reached the door and gave me a wave. She winked and opened her mouth as if preparing to say something. Before the space between her lips had a chance to emit a sound, however, I interrupted by declaring, "My head feels a lot better now."

She smiled and nodded and said, "Yes, mine, too." Then she turned towards the door but almost instantly snapped back to look at me once again. So sudden and severe was her upper body's swivel and her subsequent expression that I thought something grave had happened. "Do you think", she began earnestly, "you'll soon be ready to begin on your next book?

"Erm, I, err," I spluttered somewhat stupefied. Then she smiled, coaxing an answer out of me with her eyes. "What a bizarre question," I said.

"Is it?"

"Well..."

"I was... er... just wondering, you know." She looked unsure.

"Oh."

"You don't mind my asking?"

"No, no," I said. "It's just... But, yes – once I've got an idea for a story I'll..."

"That's great," she interrupted. "I'm just excited to..." Her sentence trailed off as she disappeared out of the door.

Or at least I thought she had disappeared out of the door. What I should say is that Sabina was halfway through the doorway when I stopped watching her, having stuck my head under the covers to look for my underpants. Another second or two and she *would* have completely vanished, door shut behind her on her way back to join the party.

But once I had located my pants, pulled them on and lifted my head back from under the bedclothes I was somewhat taken aback to see that Sabina hadn't gone after all. She was gingerly stepping backwards back into the room and closing the door with surgical precision behind her.

"Couldn't leave me after all, eh?" was the sentence that fumbled its way out of my mouth and which I instantaneously regretted. She raised her index finger up to her lips as she'd done when I was sick. She looked anxious.

"What's the matter?" I half wanted to suffix my question with '…this time?'. Just for fun, slightly sarcastically, but didn't think I knew her well enough to know how she'd take it. So I didn't.

"Get dressed." She seemed worried.

"Why? What's…?"

"Please get dressed as quickly and as quietly as you can," she whispered.

"What's the matter?"

"Do it! Please!" she implored.

I jumped out of bed to comfort her and to try to get some information from her. She pushed me away, telling me to hurry up. I pushed past her to get to the door to see what the problem was. She tried to hold me back. She was strong. She had the strength of a desperate person. I was determined though, and she soon realised it was a battle she was going to lose.

"Alright, then, if you must." Tears were beginning to appear. "But please be quiet," she said with a cracked voice.

Then, as I had my hand on the door, she implored me not to open it wide. From the little I knew about Sabina I knew she wasn't the kind of person to over-react to situations. This was why, as I stood there with my hand outstretched, I could feel that everything was about to change.

Dawn was rising on both the beauty and the horror... It was only a crack, but that was all that was required to see five men in uniforms. Makeshift, army surplus, cobbled-together uniforms. Guns strapped across their chests or held out erect in front of them. Penis extensions to rape the defenceless because of deep-rooted inadequacy anxieties; fear and control down the barrel of a gun.

The thin strip of forest green and vermilion daylight I had exposed was a scene of chaos and carnage. The fire had been kicked over. The embers and half-burnt logs were still glowing on the ground. A guitar had been smashed and thrown on top – the neck was beginning to smoke. One of the five held a long knife; its blade was the colour of the morning sky.

Three men lay awkwardly overlapping each other next to the fire. I hoped they were drunk, but didn't think they were. There was a regular beat, a measured dull pound. The march of time... The marching of time running out was being played on a drum by a man with a gun held to his head.

As the bile and revulsion surged within me I caught a glimpse of the face of their leader, giving orders and waving his arms around. His uniform was different. It was not like the others'. His uniform was precision-creased, shiny and professional; a replica of something or other. Just seeing him you could tell he was a hardened campaigner, the chief, the unchallenged authority figure – the man with the idea, the intellect behind the brute force. Gone were his safari suit, matted hair, eccentric spectacles and amiably contrived quirkiness. In their place was someone who was dangerously fucked-up.

Without any recognisable precursor his head cranked up the thirty-five or so degrees required to stare in my direction. He bared his teeth in a late-night black-and-white Eastern European film kind of way. Something was happening that was too vast, too illusory, too *Ride of the Valkyries*. It was all like a flashback of some kind.

Logic told me that in this early morning shadow-land there was no way he could see me through such a sliver of a gap, especially at this distance. He was definitely looking my way, though, with his head motionless, slightly tilted as if ready to pounce.

I didn't close the door, fearing that the slightest of movements could alert his attention. Sabina was already halfway out of the back window. "Come on!" she called. I pulled my jeans on and scrambled into my boots, leaving the laces undone. I grabbed my bag from under the bed and t-shirt from off the bedside table. I stuffed my t-shirt into the bag and made my way to the back window. As I was climbing through I heard a bang. The drumming stopped.

We moved stealthily at first, not wishing to snap branches or make the leaves crackle underfoot. Once we were far enough away we speeded up. I was getting scratched and cut as we careered through the undergrowth. Sabina's dress was shredded and hanging in torn strands. I snatched out my t-shirt from my bag and pulled it over my head. I left it around my neck for a moment like a limp neckerchief.

At the next clearing I shouted for Sabina to hold on.

"Hurry up!" she screamed back at me. I stopped anyway. I threw my bag from around my neck and stuck my arms through the sleeves of my t-shirt. At the opposite edge of the clearing Sabina turned, saw what I was doing and also stopped. She began tearing her dress at about knee height so the loose strands of material would no longer trip her up and get caught on branches.

With my t-shirt on properly I dashed the twenty-odd metres to catch up with her. After the final uneven tearing away of her dress, she instructed me to remain where I was. She headed to the left of the clearing, climbing over roots and between thick vines – Tarzan would have felt comfortable swinging from them. She draped some of her dress material haphazardly over the undergrowth, and some more she left snagged on a branch. This was I presumed to misdirect any would-be pursuers.

In our zigzag and extremely roundabout way, after what must have been twenty to thirty minutes we eventually reached the base of the cliff and followed it along to the right. Along most of it there was a small gap between the edge of the forest and the rock face. This, and the fact that Sabina appeared to know what she was doing, made the going a lot easier.

I hurried along behind her, occasionally pushing against the cliff to keep my balance or to help me squeeze through an especially narrow space. Nonetheless, this natural pathway meant that I had time to consider those we'd left behind.

I hoped Boudewijn and Thomas were alright. If they'd been around the fire or near the stage, I reflected, they'd have had little chance of getting away; they were probably lying in a pool of blood. The tears that came made me rub my eyes at the thought. I considered how fortunate we were that Sabina and I had been holed up in her room, in our own little world.

A tree, gnarled and twisted, blocked our way. Its branches were grotesquely contorted, pressing hard against the cliff's wall. Like a serpent on a samurai's wall one of the tree's thick arms bent down so as to touch the ground, then curved straight up again against the rock's vertical surface. Its enormity meant we had to clamber up then roll over the massive branch on our bellies. Sabina tucked what was now her skirt into her knickers and with a helping leg-up managed to slide over. I threw my bag after her and followed.

Directly behind where the bough made contact with the earth, a coarse bush hugged the crag. By the time I had dropped down the far side Sabina was on her knees, reaching her arm in behind the bush. After a few seconds of feeling around she pulled out a flat piece of wood. She placed the plank at an angle against the bush and instructed me to put one of my feet on it so as to squash down the bush.

I gradually applied my full weight to the board and the thicket was pushed downwards; an opening in the rock face began to reveal itself. Sabina edged her way delicately between the cliff and the bush. She instructed me to slide the piece of wood through to her. As I judiciously stepped off the plank the bush sprang back into place. Sabina was completely hidden. I could hear her voice yet even from such close proximity it was impossible to see that anyone was in there. She pushed down hard on the plank and I sidled my way in to join her.

Once inside Sabina instructed me to stay put. Several shards of light managed to find their way in through the obstacles of vegetation, not enough to make much difference. I could hear sounds of Sabina from the innards of the cave, treading carefully and feeling her way. She swore as she hit her leg against something hard. Then a cinematic fade-in occurred and the cave was illuminated by an oil lamp which hung from the middle of the ceiling. The jaundiced glow allowed me to examine my new surroundings.

A double bed with a single camp bed by its side was situated to the back of the cave. Four bookcases lined the walls. Thirty or forty books and magazines filled the shelves, which were mainly stacked with tin after tin of food. A Dutch dresser full of crockery with several tools hanging from nails was against the opposite wall. To my left was a battered old wooden chest locked with a padlock, on top of which was a navy blue plastic washing-up bowl.

I stood there, incredulous, attempting to make some sense out of what was going on. Sabina was lighting candles that looked fresh out of the box. Some were on a circular table that had a stool either side of it; they were made from cross-sections of a tree trunk. There were some candles on the dresser, and two tea lights were on a small foldaway table that also had a gas camping stove on it.

With a smile and worried eyes she told me to make myself at home. "I'll make us a coffee," she said. After a short pause while she lit the last of the candles she added, "We'll be safe here."

"Looks as though you were expecting this," I said, indicating I was referring to the well-stocked cave. Sabina smiled and nodded. "And what are we going to do about the others?" I asked.

"Yes, we were. Look, let's get comfortable, shall we? Sit down and have our coffees, umm?" She indicated where I should sit with a waiter's wave of an open palm. "Then," she nodded several times to herself, "I think there are a few things you ought to know..."

CHAPTER XX

Renney stood admiring his new house. It was late morning and the sky's scarred beginnings had given way to a perfect, cloudless blue day. Marcus tramped up the incline, sweating profusely, a saw in one hand.

As Marcus approached, Renney, without redirecting his gaze, cited William Clough-Ellis to him: "We need a comfort that is more than that of the animals, and that includes that of the eye and of the spirit."

He turned to Marcus to see his reaction. Marcus' eyebrows were raised, more because he was awaiting an explanation than anything else.

"Never mind," said Renney. "Was your mission successful last night?"

"Yes."

"Good, good… No problems?"

"None to speak of. Everything's on course."

"Well done, Marcus. Well done."

"Yes," said Marcus and headed back down the slope to complete his sawing.

PART IV

CHAPTER XXI

That was the last time Renney saw his mother: as he was carrying some of the remnants of his father's life out of the house and down the garden path. He looked back as his mother was turning to close the door. A wave or a smile or a nod would have been something. Instead, all he saw was his mother looking a little like the woman from Grant Wood's painting *American Gothic* as she turned and shut the door with more conviction than he thought necessary.

Four weeks later he flew to Holland. He arrived at Amsterdam's Schiphol airport on the 18th of December. He booked a mid-range hotel at the airport's tourist desk, went out to the rain-sodden street and hailed a taxi.

The porter carried Renney's luggage up to his room. He hung around trying to appear nonchalant whilst being ill at ease until Renney gave him a generous tip. Once showered and in his grey-with-salmon-trim dressing gown Renney rang down for scrambled eggs on toast and three bottles of beer. The same porter, who doubled up as a waiter, was in his mid-twenties and shared a passing resemblance to Michael X, knocked three times on Renney's door.

Acting as if he were serving in a stately home the waiter ceremonially transferred everything from the trolley onto the table. All the while he was unwaveringly obsequious in his dealings with Renney, anticipating that he might be able to charm a constant stream of hefty tips out of him... After his meal Renney switched on the television and within five minutes was fast asleep.

Renney was a quick operator. In only two days he'd found himself a partially-stocked antiques shop with an apartment above it. And by the middle of January he was purchasing pieces of art from final-year art students and as-yet-undiscovereds. His intention was to sell antiques and art pieces to tourists, foreign art dealers and stupid rich art collectors who wouldn't know a piece of art if it jumped up behind them and bit off one of their ears.

Those who were interested in art, or thought they were interested in art, or, for whatever reason, thought they ought to be interested in art – and had the money – came to Amsterdam and shopped. They stayed in expensive hotels, patronised expensive restaurants, visited the theatre or the opera, purchased some jewellery and some art and felt culturally cleansed.

Two or three nights a week Renney played in a 9-ball pool bar and became friendly with the four regulars who always seemed to be perched at the counter. The two whose company, however, he most enjoyed were Odaline, the barmaid, and Stefano.

Odaline had an Irish mother and an Algerian father. She was both a good listener (a prerequisite, one would have thought, for any bar-worker worth their salt) and a good talker.

She'd moved to Amsterdam from Cork after the death of her grandmother who brought her up and who Odaline looked after until her death. When Renney met her she'd been in Amsterdam for almost six years, and consequently was a great source of information. If Renney needed to know something about the surroundings or where to find someone to do some work for him, Odaline could usually help. Renney could easily have found what he needed to know by other means, but where was the fun in that? Odaline would always spin a good yarn and made even the simplest of activities sound cloak and dagger.

All of which was fine with Renney. He liked a mystery and liked to think of his life as mysterious. The truth, however, was that his life was less of an enigma than he either perceived or wanted it to be, and yet somewhat more of a mystery than people would have thought.

Stefano was the other person Renney had the most time for. He told Renney very little about himself in those early days, but Renney could tell he was down on his luck. He was in his early twenties, had a clipped English accent and could make a glass of beer last most of the evening. Not that he needed to, because Renney would usually buy him a few beers – as on occasion would Odaline.

Within several months Renney's shop was making a not inconsiderable profit. Accordingly, Renney decided he wanted to work less. He therefore employed a thirty-five-year-old Australian woman by the name of Nancy. She was a great find, looked like a Pan Am air stewardess and if anything increased the profits from when Renney had been in the shop on his own.

Feeling confident with his first shop running so well Renney decided to open a second shop. After several days of searching for something suitable he found premises opposite the central train station. That evening, in his favourite bar, having come directly from viewing the new premises, over a game of pool Renney asked Stefano if he'd like to manage the new shop. He agreed instantly. And Renney was soon surprised by how enthusiastic and how much of an asset Stefano proved to be, by far exceeding any expectations Renney had of his capabilities. As if to reinforce this fact within several weeks of working there Stefano had the second shop, *Objets Elégants*, turning a healthy profit...

-------• • •-------

The antiques world was fine, so far as it went. Even the art world was acceptable, if somewhat pretentious. But art, art itself, was Renney's real passion. He'd dabbled in oils himself, but soon came to realise he was no artist. He had the imagination and could see the beautiful and strange images in his head; it was simply that he was unable to reproduce them on canvas.

He enjoyed the company of artists – or any kind of free-thinker, really. He would enthusiastically engage in the types of conversations that inevitably ensued when eccentrics and original thinkers gathered together. He appreciated art and enjoyed being in the presence of the types of minds that created art – but that wasn't enough for him. He wanted to be involved in a manner that demanded more than mere social interaction.

-------• • •-------

One Sunday morning Renney went to buy a loaf of bread, a litre of milk and a Danish pastry for his breakfast. On returning he let himself back in through the shop instead of going around to the back of the building and up the metal staircase that led directly to his apartment. He decided to sit down in his shop and eat his Danish pastry from one of the antique plates on display in the oak cabinet.

The cabinet had been left in the shop when the previous tenants, who'd also been antiques dealers, had hurriedly fled. This was according to the proprietor, who had a wooden cane and a deceitful smile. As Renney bent down to pick out one of the French porcelain plates from a lower shelf he noticed an iron ring attached to the floor. It was half covered by a rug which had crept along into a small scrunched-up mound at one end, under a corner leg of the oak cabinet.

Renney reached under the cabinet to pull back some more of the rug so as to reveal the ring fully. In doing so he saw that it was attached to a trapdoor. He tried for a couple of minutes, but it was impossible to shift the rug any further since the cabinet was too heavy for him. He considered this for a moment before stretching his foot underneath the cabinet and flicking the curled-back carpet over the ring.

That afternoon he telephoned Stefano. Along with his half-brother Marcus, who'd been helping out with any heavy lifting jobs around the shops, he came over an hour later. Between the three of them they managed to lift and slide the oak cabinet out of the way. But the instant that was done and the dishevelled-looking Marcus thought he was no longer required he left, somewhat abruptly, they thought, citing a prior engagement.

By sticking an iron poker through the ring and levering it up Renney and Stefano prised the trapdoor open. They didn't have a torch so they lit two brass ship's oil lanterns. Renney went first. The air smelt musty, damp, foreboding like a tomb, Stefano thought, as he reached the bottom of the steep wooden steps. Now they stood a little above canal level. Five metres in front of them was a thick metal door with a prison-bar grill at eye level, rusty rivets up and down its length. The grill let in the undulating sunlight from the ripples on the canal just outside. In former times, Renney surmised, it would have been the entrance leading to and from the house owner's moored boat.

They turned to the left along the enclosed passageway. Fifteen or so steps along on their left they came to a door. They stopped and considered it before turning to each other as if about to say something, but nothing came. Stefano looked earnest. Without saying anything, each could tell that the other wanted to see where the passageway led before doing anything else.

At that moment, as it happened, the doorbell in the shop rang. Stefano grimaced and, signalled by a nod of the head, left Renney to go on without him while he went back up to the shop to see who was at the door.

The whitewashed passageway turned to the left. The walls were intermittently daubed with caricatures, images and Dutch slogans. Once around the corner Renney saw a wooden door thirty feet in front of him. The closer he got to it, the denser the graffiti became. Some of the Dutch words were still too difficult for him to grasp. His Dutch had become quite proficient, but the writing he didn't understand was, he assumed, written in slang; or referred to Dutch political movements of which he had no knowledge.

Renney pushed hard at the door. It gave way and slammed open. His flame flickered before faithfully returning to its upright position. Due more to habit than to reflection, he turned the light switch on and was somewhat surprised when it worked.

Renney stood in the entrance. As he scanned the room from left to right and back again he blew his puffy, slightly blotchy cheeks out. A hippy cave of '60s and '70s ephemera and memorabilia splashed before his eyes. He'd travelled back and released an airlock on a time capsule. And what looked like the years and years of cobwebs festooning the walls and ceiling only added to the sense of strangeness.

He blew out the flame and placed the lamp on the floor. Waving one arm after the other to prevent the cobwebs from brushing against his face he moved judiciously forwards. In the centre of the room was a bubble chair. It resembled a giant plastic egg on a plinth cut open at a jaunty angle, white on the outside with red corduroy upholstering the inside.

The needle on the record player was stuck a third of the way into playing a Bert Jansch LP. There was a Jimi Hendrix poster on one of the walls and the ubiquitous Ché Guevara picture taped to the back of the door. Books upon books were stacked randomly and haphazardly along the floors and up the walls. They ranged from works on Heidegger and Sartre through Joseph Heller's *Catch 22* to possibly the most philosophical work of them all: *Asterix in Britain*.

Renney knelt down to take a closer look at some of the titles. In addition to the authors who had transcended time and would still be read in several hundred years, there were the books with titles Renney had never heard of: *The Sound of One Hand Clapping*; *Proper Tea and Property*; *Communes: A Study*; *Ist, Ism, Y*; *Life On Pluto*…

About seventy per cent of the titles were in English with the other thirty per cent being in Dutch. To the right of the books was a precariously balanced stack of magazines. A thirty-page pamphlet on Surrealism and Dadaism, for example, he placed to one side to take with him when he left. More abundant than all the other forms of reading matter put together were the newspapers. Pile upon pile of Dutch, British and American newspapers comprising old articles of stories long since played out.

As Renney read over one headline after another he realised how utterly transportable news was from one era to the next. Alarmingly so. Change a name and a date and you have the headline of tomorrow… of today. A politician caught with his trousers down, an American invasion and a starving child. Exploitation, indiscretion and mass destruction were at the fulcrum of everything; also there was the ubiquitous famous person doing something or other that we were supposed to be interested in. Ultimately, Renney thought, people were locked into a cycle of never-ending repetition... repeating the same mistakes ad infinitum. Or at least repeating them to such an extent that mankind eventually spiralled in upon himself and went phut, the end! Renney sighed at this gloomy – yet nevertheless what he thought to be insightful – prognosis.

As his attention moved from the piles of torn, scrunched up and musty smelling Harold Wilsons, Buzz Aldrins, Bobby Moores, Vietnams, Civil Rights Demonstrations and Inaugural Speeches he spied a magazine with a 7″ single attached to its cover. The label on the centre of the record read: Loop – *The Velvet Underground*. He lightly ran his finger over the flexi disc and took a few moments to gaze at it with solemnity and awe. His stare was almost sideways-on, out of the corner of his eye, so to speak, for his subconscious fear was that to challenge it with anything as vulgar and disrespectful as a direct gaze could precipitate its disappearance. It was the respect that someone discovering a lost Picasso or a lost gospel might convey.

When the hypnotic pull had finally subsided Renney delicately placed the magazine with its attached disc on top of the other reading material he wished to take with him.

He got to his feet and looked around. There was a door in the far left-hand corner at the back of the room. Renney made his way over, wiping the clinging cobwebs from his face as he went. The door pushed only a quarter of its way open, enough for him to reach round and discover that the light switch didn't work. He collected his lamp, lit it, and put it on the floor in the entrance of the room. The lamplight made dancing shadow puppets of formless ghosts on the dark walls inside.

The space was approximately a third of the size of the main living space. But there was no feel of psychedelia or revolution in there. As far as he could tell it was a room consisting of nothing save for a mattress in the middle of the floor. Almost as an afterthought he half-heartedly held the lamp above his head to get a final good look at the entire room. There, high up on the walls all the way around the room, was painting after painting; over twenty of them.

He raised his lamp higher and passed his gaze over the pictures hanging around the dank, windowless room. Splashes, dots, cubes and characters greeted Renney's eyes, incorporating a mix of vibrant colours, abstract shapes and gothic scenes. As he moved in closer he could make out a sunset over a medieval city in one and Christ staring down upon Mary Magdalene, curled up naked at his feet, in another.

Some were surrealist, some fauvist, some were verging on the impressionistic and, appropriate for those times, some were unequivocally Pop Art in style. But there was something about them, something about the feeling Renney was getting from them. Even the Pop Art one made him feel uneasy. It was part collage, with the chosen newspaper clippings being about Charlie Manson and Jimmy Jones.

Renney leaned in close with an involuntary look of disgust on his face. He stayed in that position for several moments with his bearded chin cupped in his left hand, considering both what the viewer was supposed to think of it and what he himself did in fact think of it. He moved on and noted how each piece had the identical squiggle in its bottom right hand corner: the indecipherable identity of the creator, of someone long since gone: the territorial piss of a deranged mind.

Holding up the lamp beside his head at eye level he considered one picture after another. There was damage, considerable in some cases. Nothing that care, dry air and a little loving restoration couldn't fix. Some of the paintings were as beautiful as some were bizarre and unsettling. And quite possibly, Renney reflected, he was the first to have seen these works since they had been created...

Next to each picture, in tiny lettering, written onto a piece of black oblong card about the size of a playing card, was a short sentence or two painted in silver grey. Next to each card was written a number between 1 and 23 – representing the number of the picture with which the writing was associated.

The first inscription was to the left of the first picture. Some of the words, and on at least two occasions virtually a whole sentence, had lost their battles with time and flaking paint.

Renney made his way back to what at least numerically was the first painting. He held his lamp close to the wall and began moving from one painting to the next, reading the messages as he went:

1. *I am beginning now and shall do everything in my power to reach the desired end.*
2. *I am pleased. It has taken longer, much longer* [words missing] *but I am pleased, exhausted but pleased.*

[In the gap between pictures 2 and 3 there is no writing and no number. Although a fair assumption would be that at one time there must have been something.]

4. *I feel closer, but these are mere games.*
5. *The flower seller's last wish.*
6. *Do* [missing words] *the fin* [missing letters, presumably making up the word 'final'.] *analysis.*

7. Green I
8. Green II
9. Green III.

[Canvases 7, 8, and 9 were green in colour. They varied slightly in their shading, but all nevertheless were of a murky jungle green colour. And they had a disturbing quality to them if stared at for too long... Number 9 was the most disturbing.]

10. Classic still life (1 of 1): Fruit in a fruit bowl with sun streaming in.

11. [Here only the number was present, the assumption being that time had eroded the accompanying sentence. Though the wall in this section of the room was neither flaking nor damp.]

12. I don't think I can finish. It's too difficult.

13. [No words remained.]

14. I call you laughing for hours. I call this [Most of these words had been crossed out but were still legible. Only the last three words of the first sentence had been left alone: 'laughing for hours'.]

15. Only my name. Only my name. Only my name. [These nine words were suffixed with a similar appellation to that which appeared on the paintings. Here also it was unintelligible.]

Renney was absorbed both by what he saw and by the possible explanations for what he saw. His mind was both in the moment – enthralled by the extraordinary artwork in front of him – and floating some way away from his cognisant considerations, trying to picture the person who created this dark exhibition.

He'd move in close so as to read the appropriate scrawled thoughts or titles or whatever they were. Then he'd back up; back up as far as the light source permitted, to appreciate the picture in its entirety.

16. Jesus and the whore. [Needless to say, this was the inscription that corresponded to the deranged masterpiece of Jesus and Mary Magdalene... The sky was deep and brooding and the translucent quality and tones of the skin were truly accomplished. The naked Jesus was impaled upon a distortedly short moss-covered cross with blood dripping from his open wounds, semi-aroused, and gazing down over Mary Magdalene, who was hugging his feet. Serpent-like, one breast fully exposed and streaked with blood, she was imploring him with her stare.]

Renney spent longer studying this painting than any of the others. Who had created those formidable images down there in that cellar, Renney wondered? Then, as he edged himself on to the next picture and the next and the next one after that, his mind skipped.

Renney thought that for this unknown artist to have produced this art he must have been one of two things: he was either insane, or involved in heavy drug use.

------• • •------

The mind is a creative beast that resides in a fictional world. Sometimes the input it receives becomes stagnant and predictable. On occasion the truly imaginative mind needs to be teased out of itself with the ceaseless bombardment of perpetual distortion (whether that distortion comes from without or within). It struck Renney that if the senses are relentlessly stimulated with the incomprehensible and the bizarre they have no option but to create great works of art. Manipulate reality until the manipulation becomes reality, leaving no crack for rationality or predictability to seep in. Only then can the imagination soar to touch the face of god.

All of the greatest works of man-made beauty, so Renney convinced himself at that moment, were produced by the distorted mind. Occasionally via meditation, more frequently via the means of mind-altering drugs, but the minds that unlocked the most unearthly of thoughts and visions were by far those fed with insanity. Feed what is laughingly called the sane mind with droplets of madness and even the most routine of artists will see through the thin film and eventually create works of beauty. Renney's eyes widened – intense and far-away – as slowly the corners of his mouth curled faintly upwards. There, with the paintings surrounding him and the lamplight in his hand, he felt he was beginning to formulate an idea for a future business.

------• • •------

As Renney advanced he could see that both the colours used and the subject matter (when they weren't abstracts) had become darker, more unhinged possibly. The exuberant and more colourful oeuvres had all been at the beginning. Admittedly that wasn't exclusively the case and dollops of colour did sporadically reappear in the later pieces, but it became markedly rarer. Certainly, after the picture of Christ there was very little joy to extract from any of the remaining paintings. Renney surmised that this was due to the artist's ever-decreasing grip on reality.

Probably the feeling one got from the final paintings was as much due to how physically draining the painting of Christ must have been for the artist as it was to his mood.

20. Lavender Blue dilly dilly.
21. Look out.
22. Always expect the unexpected.

The final canvas – numbered 22 – hanging next to the penultimate inscription was disappointing. To have finished on a high after such outstanding pieces, however, would possibly have been asking too much. This last offering was a blank canvas save for the customary signature in the bottom right corner. Uninspired and anti-climactic though in Renney's opinion it was, it took nothing away from the other twenty-one pictures, a good eight or nine of which he thought were excellent.

Renney wondered what had happened to Stefano as he sidestepped over to the final inscription. This one had no painting next to it, only an empty wall space. The narrative for what he assumed was a missing painting was by far the smallest yet. He held the lamp up above his head and moved in to read card number 23. The digits of the number twenty-three had been written about an eighth of the size of the previous numbers. And the number had this time been separated from its associated wording…

Renney moved in even closer and adjusted his gaze to several centimetres to the right of card number 23 so that he was virtually touching the wall with his nose…

The card where logically a twenty-third painting should have been read:

23. Renney Van der Stratten.

"What the…?" Bang! – Renney fell to the ground.

CHAPTER XXII

Renney awoke in hospital… Marcus had found him when he returned to collect his jacket. Marcus was stocky, unlike Stefano, who was lithe with a swimmer's physique. Marcus had a rather flat, unremarkable face, which had a slight yet permanent look of disappointment to it. His key, that Renney had lent him and he hadn't got round to returning, he kept on a key ring with Alcatraz State Penitentiary engraved onto its bronze coloured surface. He was wearing a black t-shirt he'd bought that week, which he was pretty pleased with, it had multi-coloured writing on it that read: Peace, Trees and Frogs.

On shouting out 'Hello?' and there being no reply Marcus had gone down through the open trapdoor to take a look. He'd found Renney unconscious on the floor with a canvas smashed over his head as though it was Renney himself who was being framed. Later, in the hospital, the doctors had said it was something other than the canvas that had caused his concussion.

The doorbell rang as Marcus was replacing the receiver after ringing for an ambulance. "Where the hell were you?" Marcus demanded as he opened the door.

Stefano explained that he'd given directions to someone who'd come to the shop. He'd taken the gentleman to the corner of the street, then, on returning, had found himself locked out. He'd rung the doorbell repeatedly, but assumed Renney wasn't able to hear it from the basement. Consequently, he'd gone to the café across the bridge, bought himself a coffee and sat in the window seat and waited.

Two days after being admitted to hospital, Renney was allowed to return home. Stefano and Marcus went back to the shop with him in a taxi. He thanked them and, despite their protestations, told them he would rather be left alone. They looked concerned, but he told them he'd be fine and would telephone them both that evening.

Renney unlocked the shop as the taxi pulled away. He turned a knocked-over chair upright, sat down and began to contemplate what had occurred. Before, he'd hardly had a moment to delve into the absurdities of his underground expedition. There was a knock at the door. Renney pushed himself up with a groan. He looked pale, with dark sunken eyes like those on a Halloween mask. His flushed, rounded cheeks were diminished. And his electric-shock curls were concealed by the pristine hospital-white bandage.

It was a gentleman in his mid to late fifties at the door. He had white hair and a pointed white beard with grey flecks, and a white moustache that wanted to join up with its colleagues on the chin, but wasn't quite able to make it. The man spoke with a middle-American accent; occasionally a Manhattan twang seeped through which, thought Stefano, possibly indicated a place where the man had resided at some time.

It was Friday afternoon and the gentleman wished to know if the shop was open for business. Renney told him he was closed "due to unforeseen circumstances". The man closely scrutinised Renney's bandage. And with a smile that involved only the outer reaches of the man's mouth and seemed to have nothing to do with his eyes, said, "Have *we* been in the wars then?"

Renney brushing the stranger's enquiry aside said it was "nothing… just a slight knock."

"I see, I see… A knock, you say?"

"Umm," deliberated Renney, "I fell over… Look, I'd love to stay here chatting with you, but I'd really better go and, er, do some tidying up."

"Look, why not let me…" But before he was able to finish a shout came from the bridge.

Stefano was hurriedly approaching with an old-style shopping basket in his hand. "Hey," he called. "I know you wanted to be alone, but I thought some shopping might come in handy."

"Well, that's very kind, but you needn't have."

"Hello," said Stefano coldly, as he realised who Renney was talking to.

"Ah, yes indeed, how lovely to see you again."

"What are you doing here?" asked Stefano.

"Well," he began, before almost immediately changing tack, "…Listen, maybe I should introduce myself. My name is Alfonso de la Grange, I…"

"You two know each other?" interrupted Renney.

"May I…" he tried again, but was thwarted for a second time as Stefano answered Renney's question.

"Yes, well, not exactly *know*… This was the guy I was giving directions to on the day of your accident… when I got locked out."

"I see."

"So why have you come back?" enquired Stefano.

"Er… as I'm sure you will recall," said the stranger. "You gave me directions to a similar establishment since this particular merchant was closed on the day in question. You helpfully escorted me to the corner of the street where you pointed me in the right direction… But in truth *this* is the place I really wish to patronise since, er, it was recommended to me by a friend. And... well... I was in the café over there," he pointed to the other side of the canal.

Renney and Stefano idly followed the direction of his finger although they knew the café well. "And I saw the gentleman return," he nodded at Renney, "and..."

"*And* you thought I might be opening up," said Renney.

"Quite so."

"So where's your friend today?" Stefano asked abruptly, trying to catch Alfonso out. For Stefano wasn't sure that the man who'd been a little distance away fidgeting near the railing by the canal was the stranger's friend at all. Stefano had hardly noticed the man at the time; only in hindsight, after all that had happened, did Stefano wonder if the man's presence was significant.

"Friend?"

Stefano knew he shouldn't waver if he wanted the truth. And if the man denied any knowledge of the person loitering on the water's edge, nothing had been lost. "Yes, the scruffy-looking chap that was with you."

"Yes, well... he's off somewhere. I don't know, looking in other antique shops, I believe," said Alfonso.

"Look, instead of us standing here on the sidewalk why don't we go inside and I'll make coffee..." said Renney, before adding: "I'll clear up later... After you, Alfonso," he added after Alfonso had nodded his head, half closed his eyes and smiled.

Stefano felt uneasy about Alfonso. A white-haired squid of a man, he thought, somewhat resembling an old-time cape and tricks and snake blood elixir illusionist. If this were a crime thriller, he thought, Alfonso would certainly be a prime suspect – turning up twice like that with no real apparent justification.

Stefano followed Renney into the back room of the shop, leaving Alfonso admiring the antique jewellery.

Renney put the coffee on and Stefano tried without success to telephone Marcus.

The coffee signalled its readiness with a gurgling sound and a Brazilian aroma. Renney put some biscuits on a tray next to the coffee and he and Stefano made their way back through the thick jade-coloured velvet curtain.

Alfonso was bending over a painting. "Anything take your fancy?" enquired Renney.

"Well…" began Alfonso as he stood upright, "lots of interesting pieces, but I'll have a proper look after my coffee."

"Uh-huh. And of course you know we have a second shop, don't you?"

"No – er, no, I didn't."

"Oh yes," continued Renney rather grandly. "It's not far from the Central Station."

"Ah, very good."

Stefano had drifted off into considering what *had* happened and what *was* happening and where, if at all, the two intersected. He took a swig of coffee and headed to the trapdoor.

He switched on his torch and descended into the basement. He crossed the '60s and '70s time capsule, heading for the room where the canvasses had been hung. He directed his beam up from the floor to the walls. All of the paintings had been removed, all except for the most important one.

Mary Magdalene looked seductive and forlorn. Jesus was a vision of sexual holiness. Renney, Stefano smiled to himself, would be pleased when he heard that at least that painting was still there. He lifted it gently, carried it out and propped it against the wall outside the first door in the corridor. He then shoved the door to that room open – the room Renney hadn't made it into.

It was similar to the other room in its feel. It was a '60s-cum-'70s student pad or squat. Books on radical politics were mixed with modern and avant-garde art hangings. The Monks and Faust LPs were piled on top of Dutch, U.S. and U.K. folk albums. The Rolling Stones' *Their Satanic Majesties Request* LP had on its face three cigarette papers and some tousles of tobacco awaiting a pair of sensitive hands. There were anarchist and left-wing slogans on the wall. There was a picture of Nico, a C.N.D. poster, and books about perception, political concepts and drug experimentation.

The room was a museum piece. It felt as though it had been transposed, transported, even, into the present day from a previous time. Stefano shook his head; it was a stage set, a backdrop... a backdrop to some rerun of a seventies sitcom about communal living. So perfect was it that it felt imperfect. It was as if it had been zapped into existence from a period between the late sixties and mid-seventies that had never really existed. It was too perfect – that was the thing. It was too exactly untidy: the posters and books were *too* well chosen.

The room depicted an idealised time: nobody, surely, had such an exclusively good taste in books, or music, or posters. It was very subtle, but, to Stefano, it seemed to be like someone's idea of what a 1972 or 1968, say, student squat should look like.

As he passed a last glance over the room in search of an unequivocal focal point for his doubts he noticed the door in the far corner of the room. He'd probably have seen it sooner except that it was camouflaged. As in those sixties films set in New York or London, the photographic wallpaper, which in that part of the room was looking down on a New York street from a high vantage point, covered the door as well as the wall. It was only the brown wooden doorknob and the tiny gaps surrounding its shape that had eventually signalled the presence of the door to Stefano.

He glanced round to his right at the black and white spiral print of a painting by Mira Schendel which reminded him he was a lot more indifferent to modern art than he probably should have been. He knew it was by Mira Schendel because, coincidentally, Renney was keen on Brazilian Modernism and had tried to introduce Stefano to some of its practitioners on more than one occasion.

Stefano looked back at the door and hoped he didn't find anything as bizarre in there as Renney had encountered in the other back room. As he was about to go across to investigate, he heard a car backfiring, loudly, nearby. It shook him, jolted him suddenly out of his mesmerised search. He decided, on reflection, he should probably return to ensure Renney was alright before exploring another room.

He left the painting at the bottom of the stairs and climbed back up to the trapdoor and into the shop.

CHAPTER XXIII

Sabina placed our coffees on the table and I sat down beside her. I looked her in the eyes and awaited the sentence that would make this entire nightmare at least comprehensible.

I looked at her and she at me and the moment held itself suspended in the cave's hollow light. I was waiting for her to begin, yet I had the feeling she was waiting for me; but *I* had nothing to say. It was her turn to speak. She had promised an explanation, but now she looked doubtful. Promised or not, an explanation is what I required. I needed an explanation, rapidly followed by a plan of action to help our poor stranded colleagues.

I stared, widening my eyes, intimidating her to speak... For god's sake, speak.

This is what she said: "Where to start? Umm... OK then... Umm, well, have you heard of *The Guidebook to Being Strange*?" I shook my head. "No? Well, it's becoming quite a popular read, a cult book if you like. It's as much a story as anything else." She thought for a moment. "Possibly it's a recruiting manual as well. Well, not really a manual, more... an *aid* to recruiting, let's say.

"You see, it's not really a guidebook to being strange at all. We wrote it and chose the title to attract the type of people we want to appeal to, people who we want to *recruit* in other words. It's a story," she paused for a moment, smiled at me, then quickly looked away before continuing, "a strange story that draws certain kinds of people in. They sort of, how to put it… identify, I suppose, yes, identify with the people and surroundings and lifestyle of those in the story…

"Some of them wish it was a true story and would like to be part of it… You know, get to know some of the characters in the story… Well, they can, you see, because it's us here. Clever, huh?" She smiled again, this time, I thought, with a self-mocking air. "It's not just about us, you see, well, it sort of is…" she shook her head and scowled to herself. "What I'm trying to say is we've shrouded it all, the story, in mystery and double meaning.

"Look, let me put it like this: we believe in certain things, certain political things, certain…" she smiled, "psychological things… There are lots of people who don't like what we believe and would like to stop us if they knew where to find us. But they don't – apart from the bastards we've just seen – but I'll get to that later…

"You see, we are in fact *very* secretive, because, as you've seen, we have to be. But if we are ever going to achieve our aims, or even get close to them, we need a constant supply of new recruits. Basically, we need more people. And *there* lies our dilemma. How to get more people to join us?

"You see, it's important for us to let people know about where we live and what we believe in."

The briefest of flutters of a thought entered my head, which went something like: *I've been living with you all this time and I'm not sure what you believe in.*

"Yet, and here's the big problem," she continued. "We have to ensure that those who would do us harm have no way of knowing our whereabouts." She paused, it seemed to me for emphasis as much as because she necessarily had to. "Which, as you have seen," she said, "we've failed to do…"

I thought she was labouring the point somewhat and wanted her to get on with it. "Look, I don't wish to hurry you," I said sarcastically, "but there *are* people dying."

"Yes, not much longer. I promise. It's important that you know this. Really, trust me."

"This is complete madness… Look I'll get the police myself if you tell me which way I should go."

"Yes, look, honestly, just a little bit longer and you'll see why this explanation I'm giving you is so important. And it could even," she stated, I thought, as an afterthought, "help save some lives. So bear with me, please."

What could I do? "Get on with it, then."

"Alright," she gave me a feeble smile, which I didn't return. "Where was I? Umm, yes… So then, the whole thing of letting people know about us, subtly, if you like, is where our book came in.

"We wrote it in the style of a novel. And the story has many strands to it, that can be followed or not. I suppose by 'followed' I mean thought about more; you know… *followed* intellectually.

"We wanted the, I don't know… 'message', I guess, to be extremely well hidden. So that most people reading it would see it as merely a fictional story. Why would they believe it to be anything else – it's a novel, right? But some – possibly those most attracted by the title – would have an inkling that if you read between the lines there is possibly something else going on. Something more than just a story.

"So that's that, really," she said with a sigh of completion. "*The Guide Book to Being Strange* is, we hope, a well written story, written by us for like-minded people to tell them… well… not to worry, really, that we *are* out here, and to come and find us!"

She shrugged and was quiet for a moment. Her lips moved very slightly as her eyes focused up to the left at nothing in particular. Then her head gave a slight tilt as her demeanour changed and she smiled. "Actually," she giggled, "quite a funny thing happened, oh, I don't know… quite some time ago now…" She sniggered. "I won't say where it was for reasons that will become clear. Anyway, these three people – two men and a woman – bizarrely, within three or four days of each other – turned up on a beautiful secluded beach on an island a very long way from here.

"You see, all three of them had gone through the exact same process everyone has to go through. They read the story, read it again and wondered if there could possibly be anything more to what they were reading. They began almost to question their sanity when they began seeing meanings in the text that *surely* couldn't possibly be there.

"They most probably would have left the book untouched for some time, trying not to think about it. Then much later – this is how I see things as happening, anyway – they'd have returned to it. And when they still saw the same encryptions, for want of a better word, they'd have begun the lengthy process of finding all the ciphers and signals hidden in the story. And tried to work out what they meant."

"Listen!" I yelled. "I'm not…"

"Hold on – stay with me…"

"No!" I slammed my fist on the table and stood up. But I must have risen too quickly, for I instantly felt light-headed and unsteady. I sat, using my hands on the table to gently lower myself back into a sitting position and continued, this time with less urgency. A slight bilious feeling rose from my stomach as I began. "There are people who need..." I belched and then swallowed a couple of times to try to rid my mouth of the unpleasant taste. "Who need," I continued, "our help. And we're having a fairy's tea party?" I stopped and swallowed another couple of times before leaning back in my chair.

"Just trust me when I tell you that I haven't got much more that I want to tell you. But I do think it's important for you to hear this. And as for helping our," she thought for a moment before settling on the word 'friends'. "As for helping our *friends*... what I'm telling you now will greatly increase their chances of release. You can't see how – but please just listen and then when I've finished we'll do whatever we think... *you* think is for the best." She nodded while scrutinising me for at least a reluctant sign of complicity. I frowned.

"So anyway..." she sighed. "These three went through all of this. They calculated everything, checked it and re-checked it. And once they were finally happy with their conclusions they set off to join us. Trouble was, all three of them worked the clues out wrongly and ended up on a deserted island..."

She guffawed and shook her head presumably at the ridiculousness of the idea. I noticed how she furtively tried to catch my reaction out of the corner of her eye. "All three of them," she started again, still with trace elements of a chuckle at the back of her throat, "had worked it all out wrongly in exactly the same way."

With a breathy exhalation accompanied by a juddery shaking of her head, she asked: "And do you know what they did?" I shook my head. "They stayed exactly where they were and began their own group... or *branch* really. There are now eleven of them; it's the branch for the *ones who got it wrong*. They're sort of our dim cousins." She smiled at me. "No, no, I'm only joking... In fact it was something we'd done, you know, clue-wise, which was being interpreted differently from how we'd intended. Um – some of the relevant passages were *too* ambiguous.

"Anyway, once we'd realised how the mistake had occurred we told these new colleagues of ours that we'd amend all future copies of the book. But you know what? They wouldn't have any of it. Changing the book, they argued, would prevent *them* from getting any new recruits. And then *their* numbers would never increase.

"Fair enough, we thought… So now we are left with the bizarre situation where the book recruits for both groups… It's surreal, really," she shook her head, gave four derisory snorts, then shook her head again, this time accompanied by a look of dismay.

"Once a new recruit arrives at the second group's location," she continued, "they are weary and hungry. Of course they're elated as well to have finally made it. But it appears to be a common factor that they're struck by two dominant feelings. The first is that they're shocked: shocked to have been right all along; they aren't mad, there *is* a community waiting for them. Then, when these initial thoughts have subsided, they become a little disappointed. Disappointed that it isn't exactly what they'd hoped for: three huts and a fishing rod seem hardly worth writing a novel about, do they?" She grinned. "I'm exaggerating, of course," she said, to which I nodded blankly.

"Then when they're sitting down to eat they're told the whole situation, their mistake and everything. And once their miscalculations have been gone through with them, usually their reaction is something along the lines of *of course – how bloody stupid!* They see it straight away, their error, once it's explained to them. It's quite droll to see really… This realisation just comes over them. You can't help but laugh; they do, too – *in the end.*"

Sabina got up and went over to the cabinet. I saw her take a flask out of one of the drawers. "I thought we could do with something a little stronger in our coffees," she said with her back to me. "To calm our nerves... a kind of brandy; we make it ourselves."

I involuntarily nodded in the direction of her back, but felt blank, sick, sucked of emotion. As though I was in a movie, large, large-scale, my head taking up most of the screen: every line, every despondent worn out minuscule semblance of an expression blown up and exaggerated, to be gawped at like a beast in a zoo. Sack of bones, jelly spine, slouched over awaiting the sound of the helicopters...

Sabina's turning with cups in her hand transported me away from my thoughts. I considered saying something. Then I thought about something else. I thought about Rosio and how I wished I was in her arms. I contemplated shouting something, something about madness, the madness... but the inclination was weak – and nothing came of it.

"Anyway," she said, "*now* they've become an integral part of the whole project. The ones on the wrong island, I mean... One year we do the journey to go and visit them – for a holiday as much as anything else – then the following year it's the other way around. That's what the party was about – they came over to celebrate our anniversary with us."

For no discernable reason she fell silent. The gentle echo in the cave was gone. The pools of light were overlapping on the ceiling, the walls and on the floor, creating shade and a dark yellowy-white. I stared at the wall and focused on one of these patches of overlain light. As I scrutinised it more closely it appeared to hone in on me, just as theatre spotlights do moving in on the central performer... And my thoughts didn't seem to be completely my own.

She sipped her coffee brandy mix. As I sipped mine. Almost as suddenly as she had stopped, she asked "Anything else, then?" But before I was able to reply she continued, "It's probably self-evident that this hiding place is here because we feared one day the game might be up. And we made damn sure that we had contingency plans..." She looked at me, holding my gaze for longer than was comfortable; indeed, I had to look away as I felt a wave of nausea flow through me. "Have you got any questions?" she enquired in a sympathetic tone.

"I havvve, actualllllllyyyyyyy," I slurred.

It was at this point the room began to swim. The walls of the cave swayed gently back and forth. The light became more intense as the candles pulsed and throbbed as though made of bright green mercury pounding to a heavy bass. I looked at Sabina for reassurance. As I did so her nose grew very long, which I thought looked very silly and I burst out laughing. Then her eyes began to bulge and I got scared. She leaned over and kissed me on the cheek. Then I passed out...

CHAPTER XXIV

I woke in a predominantly white room, curled up on the end of a comfortable bed. I felt groggy. My mind was vaguely aware it was no longer asleep. The facets of daylight consciousness came slowly, my brain preferring to remain in the realm of bizarre battles, incongruous links and the superhuman powers of the night.

For some time I drifted in and out of what was a delicious multi-coloured daze. As the light eventually began to win over the dark (as it always should) I heaved myself to the top of the bed like a drained commando who'd been on an assault course and plonked my head heavily down onto the pillows.

The daylight was tipping in from the oblong window along the top of the wall opposite me. After about ten minutes of staring at the light coming through the window and splattering onto the ceiling I pushed myself up. I sat on the edge of the bed for a moment, my head hung low, peering down at the tiled flooring.

I looked up once again at the brilliant sun-filled window. With remnants of strange colours still floating around inside and outside of my head I stood on a chair and peered out over the bay and the crystal waters so far below. I blinked several times because of the light and, I suppose, because it was an outward manifestation of my disorientation...

There were shelves full of art books and books on architecture. There were many novels by the likes of Jean-Paul Sartre, Albert Camus and Agatha Christie. To the right of the bed a motel-style wooden door with a shiny aluminium knob led to a motel-style bathroom. A rather gory print of Christ on the cross with a desperate woman at his feet was situated to the right of and slightly lower than the window. There was neither TV, radio, nor telephone.

I had the feeling I was being watched, although could not see a camera or a peephole. As the colours were fading fast and I was beginning to truly come round I went over and rattled the door. It was locked (as it was always bound to be). I wondered how accurate my memories were. The exit door was made of glass, predominantly glass, clearly reinforced. On the other side of it was a space about four times the size of a red telephone kiosk. It was an empty space: a space that had another door, a solid-looking door at the other end of it. Pressurised, airtight, vacuum-packed – maybe I was a sardine in a tin.

I noticed on one of the shelves – the tall wooden one in the corner – there was a pile of my belongings. Not all of them. Not my clothes. More the items concerned with my literary activities. My pens and pencils; books I was going to read, and some I already had. And three blank pads...

Whatever it was that I hadn't up to then understood had just been given a very large twist. I took a long run at the door and shoulder-barged it screaming out the banshee's wail. It was like running into a brick wall – as the crack of pain split through my brain.

CHAPTER XXV

"I can't say I noticed any paint on him," said Alfonso, a little too quickly for Stefano's liking. It wouldn't have made any difference how Alfonso answered, Stefano wouldn't have trusted him whatever he'd said. There were too many coincidences piling up, he thought, for Alfonso not to have been involved in Renney's attack.

Renney returned from the back room and caught the tail end of Stefano's questioning of Alfonso. Alfonso was standing with his back to Renney in the middle of the shop. Stefano glanced at Renney as he approached. He looked pale, upset, and was gesticulating for Stefano to cease.

Alfonso heard Renney re-emerge; he concluded his exchange with Stefano by saying: "We'll leave it like that then, shall we?" and giving an uninterpretable, as far as Stefano was concerned, nod of the head he made his way to the exit door. He had hoped that Alfonso would have given him a dirty look prior to leaving, or at least some indication he'd been riled by Stefano's interrogation. But there was nothing, not an inkling that Stefano had got to him in any way. It didn't mean he wasn't shady – to

Stefano's mind it simply meant that he was well versed in the art of deception.

"I'll be in touch," Alfonso called to Renney as he waved from the doorway.

"What's the matter with you?" asked Stefano once Alfonso had left and was out of sight. Renney shook his head, said nothing and scribbled a number down onto a piece of paper.

"Ring this for me will you?" he said, handing Stefano the scrap of paper.

"Sure, but..." the concern in Renney's eyes indicated to Stefano that he should just get on with it.

"You can phone from upstairs."

Stefano headed up the stairs to Renney's living quarters. Renney followed. Stefano picked up the receiver and dialled. As he waited to be connected he watched as Renney lifted the television from what one would have assumed was a low table draped with a red and white Japanese-print sarong. As he whipped it off, however, unaware that he resembled a conjurer revealing the conclusion to a final trick, a metal trunk was unveiled.

Stefano handed him the phone. "Hello, Mr Van der Stratten?" the voice asked.

"Uh-huh," said Renney.

"Did you like the paintings?" The man asked before laughing in a somewhat contrived demonic fashion before hanging up.

"What's going on?" demanded Stefano.

Renney returned from taking keys from a chain hidden in a false compartment in his underpants drawer and said: "Help me search through all of this, will you?" He flipped open the trunk's lid. Inside was a chaotic mix of differently shaped and sized pieces of paper. Some appeared to be typed sheets of a manuscript; others were torn-off slips of paper containing hardly legible scrawled messages. Still others had neatly written names and numbers on them. "Alfonso and his cohort want something they say I have in my possession... which they say belongs to them."

"What do you have?"

"I don't know."

"I don't understand."

"Nor do I," said Renney. "Nor do I. I just don't know what to think, Stef... Look, it seems that my father was a gambling man."

"...Down in New Orleans?" suggested Stefano with an ill-judged air of mock solemnity.

"This is definitely not funny, *OK*?"

Stefano nodded. "What... and he... what, lost a bet to these people? Owes them money or something?"

"Well..." began Renney, "whatever it is they want..." He momentarily trailed off. "You see," he said as he played with his bottom lip. "That was my parents' house you just rang... My *dead* parent's *empty* house... Whatever it is they want, we have to find it before they do... before they return.

"Give Marcus a call, will you? We need him here."

Stefano picked up the phone. "There's no answer," he said after leaving it to ring for a couple of minutes.

"Shouldn't he..." began Renney.

"Yes, but, you know... It's Friday afternoon, he probably shut up early."

The two of them sat down on the floor in front of the trunk, the trunk that contained all of Renney's father's papers.

Stefano sat cross-legged and Renney knelt. Steafano glanced across at Renney's expression, then beyond and through the window. The bright metallic-grey sheen light of the day sailed in through both the open window and the closed window and lit up the room in a manner a photographer would have liked to have captured.

They were in a hurry; they had to be. They also had to be methodical otherwise they could easily miss something crucial.

Once a piece of paper had been read it was placed onto a specific pile… There was a pile for the pieces of paper that appeared to have nothing to do with anything – this consisted of Chinese laundry bills, taxi receipts and the like. There was also a 'I don't know what it means' pile – this comprised scraps of paper with telephone numbers and sometimes with names on them, too. Also thrown onto this pile were business cards.

It was onto the final pile they threw the most mysterious and puzzling of all the pieces of paper. Anything that could have been referring to something other than the everyday, or appeared somehow cryptic, or which they thought could have some connection to gambling or debts, was put onto this pile.

They sat there on the floor and the hours rolled on. They scrutinised each scrap of paper, occasionally shifting from one buttock to the other or changing from kneeling to a cross-legged position.

Occasionally, Stefano went into the kitchen and made them both a coffee or a sandwich. They'd pause to drink their drinks and eat their fare and allow their tired eyes a few minutes' rest. They'd talk about what they were looking for and what had happened; or they'd talk about nothing at all. Most of the time they simply sat and read in silence.

Renney's apartment was in a building which was the second block from the end. To the left – as you looked out of the window onto the canal and the buildings opposite – and three doors away was the corner building occupied by an elderly couple with a Chihuahua. Several doors down to the right, after the coffee shop, on the corner was the small road that crossed the canal and penetrated further into the outskirts of the city.

The coffee shop was open only at night. It was very discreet; no signs. Well, only one: there was a long fluorescent green tube in the window that spelt out the word *Shamballah*. Since the sign was off in the daytime there was nothing to suggest it was anything other than a private house.

Shamballah was run by a couple, Maria and Johan. Maria was about 5ft 5ins tall, of Spanish extraction, with long black curly hair that she kept in a loose low-tied ponytail. She was always on the go, buzzing around from project to project. She was attractive in that strong, dark southern European peasant woman kind of way. She had perfectly straight white teeth, a thunderous laugh that she'd launch given the minimum of excuses. And she was generous beyond what one might have considered conducive to survival in the modern world.

Johan, Renney thought, looked a little like Serge Gainsbourg. The hair was spikier, the clothes more loose-fitting hippy-Boho, and he had earrings, a nose ring and a pendant of a red and silver star; but with a makeover he could quite feasibly have earned some guilders as a look-a-like. He spoke softly, in a measured way: his eyes seemingly considering his next utterance at the same time as appraising the person he was addressing.

He treated Renney no differently from anyone else he and Maria were fond of, but he had his reservations about him. Things he'd heard, things he'd felt. He was unable to formulate exactly what it was that gave him this sense of unease; but he was convinced Renney van der Stratten wasn't all he professed to be.

Maria and Johan would pass by Renney's shop most afternoons and, if he was there, they'd always give him a friendly wave. Or they'd stick their heads round the door to announce they were about to brew up a fresh pot of coffee. Renney was welcome to join them if he fancied it. Sometimes he went with them and sometimes he didn't. Either way, he felt it was good to keep them on side. In his experience, when life got complicated it was essential to have people you could call on.

Indeed, Renney would always smile to himself when he recalled how a colleague of his used to define how to differentiate between a friend and a good friend. It was when Renney had been sludging for gold in the north west of the States on the Canadian border. "A friend," he'd say, "is someone who will help you hide. A *good* friend," he continued, stroking his beard with a distinct air of sagesse, "is someone who'll help you hide a body."

Johan and Maria ostensibly had two sets of friends. One was a group made up of former and present drama students. This was because Maria had been an aspiring actress herself for a while. She'd dropped out during her second year after she'd hooked up with Johan. This wasn't a regret, although she still enjoyed the company of people who aspired to tread the boards and appreciated theatre. Johan, in contrast, found some of them pretentious.

They were also good friends with people who were politically active to one extent or another. Indeed, they themselves were vocal members of the peace movement, had links to squatters' associations, had strong environmental beliefs and were avidly pro cycling... Some of these friends of theirs, however, advocated the more radical means of getting messages across. They discussed, for example, kidnapping bankers or industrialists, either with a view to extracting ransoms, or – and this was the influence of an American who'd moved to Holland several years earlier and who'd been a member of the Symbionese Liberation Army – to force supermarkets to give away free food to the poor.

Maria and Johan would sway between being in favour of or against the more radical approaches to social and cultural change. Despite these nuances of ideological strategy it was important that their friends held at least similar overarching values to them. As a consequence, with what they thought was adequately subtle circumnavigation, they tried to ascertain whether Renney was also *one of them*. Maria more so than Johan grew to believe that he was. Without directly revealing his beliefs – apart from verbalising his abhorrence of racism – Maria felt sure he had a non-conformist radical core to him.

They were a sweet couple, Maria and Johan. They knew Renney was single and once they had established his sexuality they made clumsy attempts to introduce him to some of their single female friends. These pre-arranged 'chance' meetings manifested themselves in one of two ways. Either their friend would be sent around to Renney's shop to borrow some sugar or coffee or tea bags or the newspaper, or Renney would be invited around for a drink and introduced to their single friend.

On one occasion when a female friend of theirs had been sent around to Renney's to borrow something or other, on entering his shop the woman had said: "Look, I've been sent around here to borrow some sugar. I'm single, you're single, they don't need sugar and I much prefer finding my own men. Fancy a couple of beers anyway so at least we can give them something to talk about?"

One Friday afternoon Maria popped around to Renney's shop to see if he'd like to join them for a drink. He nodded to her and instantly found himself wondering if it would be rude to take his own bottle of favourite Irish whiskey with him, for he knew they had nothing comparable. On reflection he decided to save it for himself and would settle for a couple of beers instead. He looked at himself in the bathroom mirror and considered how he would spend the remainder of his Friday evening once he'd left Shamballah. He'd do what he always did: go out for his few frames of pool prior to treating himself, as he did every Friday, to a French meal and a good bottle of wine. On this occasion: a *Château Mouton Rothschild*.

Maria unlocked their main entrance and they descended the stone stairwell. Shamballah was a uniquely subterranean coffee shop; operating out of a converted basement they'd renovated themselves. Faces and swirls and patterns jumped out at them from the walls as they headed down into the light of the underground. An African drum and a jazz piano greeted their arrival. The fluorescent lighting lit up specks of dust on their outer garments. Johan got up from his metal stool, leaving his drink on the bar, and approached Renney with his hand held out. Sitting on the next barstool was a woman Renney had never seen before.

Johan had always been uncomfortable with Maria's introducing their friends to Renney. This was mainly because he wanted to be perfectly sure of *who* the real Renney was. This time, however, was different, and he cited the following reason for his concerns: fine in small doses though Maria's friend was, if Renney and she became close she'd end up becoming an increasing part of their lives. And he didn't want that.

Johan proceeded to tell Maria that her friend was a catherine wheel purporting to be a sparkler. He reminded Maria her friend hadn't been out of prison long. Apparently she had been part of a group formulating a plan to hijack a plane in Japan. She'd always declared her innocence. Her friendships with Yasuhiro Shibata and Takamaro Tamiya, as well as her associations with members of the music group Les Rallizes Dénudés, accompanied by the incriminating handwritten notes and radical literature found in her apartment, meant the authorities had enough links to hang some pretty hefty charges around her neck.

Maria insisted that their American friend had nothing to do with the proposed hijacking; that her arrest was dubious and based purely upon circumstantial evidence. And she told Johan she found it despicable of him to even think such things. Johan said he had contacts who, although they couldn't say for absolute certain, were at least eighty per cent sure Maria's friend was involved in the plot.

"Hi," said Johan, standing up from his bar stool to greet Renney. "I'd like to introduce you to our friend Sabina."

CHAPTER XXVI

I lay there for a while thinking. Only half awake. I had had a good night's sleep; undisturbed, deep... I had dreamt, but not in as troubled a way as I might have expected.

There was something to do with a cat; a cat and somebody... A cat that turned into Marcel Duchamp. That was it. First the cat's head morphed into that of Marcel Duchamp's, whilst maintaining its cat body. It cocked its leg – I recall thinking that was more of a dog-like thing to do – and peed in Duchamp's *Fountain*. Then the cat stood on its two back legs and gradually mutated into the normal-looking, as far as a dream can be 'normal', adult Monsieur Duchamp.

I thought about art and madness and pissing in fountains. I dwelt briefly upon the *Manneken Pis* statue in Brussels of the boy peeing into the fountain. I looked upwards and registered the early morning as it flooded in and hit the ceiling and wall above my head with a splash of golden light. The island mornings were so beautiful, my mind reminded me. Singing with the purest of light and steamiest of natural fragrances; the ocean sprays and turquoise waters, and the fish queuing up to be caught and grilled and flaked off into the mouth with a little freshly squeezed juice.

I turned to lie at an angle so as to stare more directly at the patch of sunlight above my bed. I allowed my waking brain to become immersed in the warm yellow light... I began to understand the true genius of Duchamp.

Not only was he mould-breaking, but his *readymade* managed to irritate both the established art world and the establishment itself. I recalled some of the criticisms directed at him and his piece, which I had read in one of Rosio's art books. Some had called his urinal immoral and vulgar, stating that it was no more than an object of mass-produced plumbing. At best, it was said to be plagiarism.

I considered this as I watched the dust particles dance in the delight of their freedom. It was as if they were thumbing their noses at my situation. I yawned and as I turned my neck slowly from side to side, heard it unclick its night-time stiffness...

Those who condemned Duchamp in such a manner were, I thought, missing the point, clearly missing it by miles. These people were unable to see beyond function. I paused over the words *beyond function*, metaphorically rolling them around in my head. I wondered whether the sounds the words made had any connection to their meaning. I mulled over *beyond* then *yonder*... and then I wondered if the word *meaning* had anything to do with *mean*. I idly concluded that it did not.

My mind soon became bored with these asides and eagerly jumped back to Duchamp and his critics. Unable, as they were, to see any value other than that of function, his critics were therefore incapable of grafting an appreciation of artistic merit onto anything that had once performed another duty.

The true genius of Duchamp's *Fountain*, my waking mind relayed to me, was that you couldn't piss on art. That was the genius and the joke…

Those idiots, those blinkered, anally-retentive fools could piss on what they liked. They could condemn, fear, moralise about whatever they wished, but *this* time – at *least* this time – they could not piss on art. Not *this* art, at any rate.

I smiled as my focus left the wall and ceiling and moved over to the small window from where the sunshine came…

A urinal you cannot urinate in… I wondered if I could get anything close to that in literature. What could I do with my writing that got anywhere close to Duchamp's achievement in art?

------• • •------

Once the anger had subsided – once the locks had been rattled and rattled again, once the door had been barged several times, and kicked and kicked and kicked again, once the screams had been screamed and objects had been thrown, there was nothing left but to wait. Wait. Calm down and wait; or pretend to calm down and accept that there was nothing else to do but to wait. I was a prisoner. For some reason that I was grappling with and failing to comprehend, I was a prisoner.

I had spent most of the previous day bored. There was nothing to do. I had studied the rather vulgar print of Jesus and a naked woman entwined, which was no doubt supposed to depict the whole pain and pleasure, sex and death, dichotomy. But there's only so much time one can spend doing that. For the rest of the day, which was most of the day, I had sat lost in my thoughts.

I realised that this unreality in which I found myself had come about following a sequence of episodes; episodes and events that seemed distant and dreamlike now. And yet, despite occasional instants of what I presumed to be advancements in my understanding of my situation I was unable to fathom what was chance and what was design.

I briefly considered whether I had been drugged by religious nutters. What was that amusing piece of graffiti I saw somewhere? Something... oh yes: 'Nietzsche is dead, (signed) God.' Funny what people come up with to write on a wall. It's a very honourable exercise, blighted in these slipshod snipped snapshot days. It used to be the traditional manner through which to reflect the thoughts and activities of a community: from a bison and a spear to a philosophical idea. From food to thought. I wonder what our next cave depiction will be, in a few hundred years' time. From food to thought to... I don't know – it might not be good.

I sort of rolled and dipped out of bed. I wished I could go for a swim, so took a shower instead. The towel was motel-fluffy and bits stuck to my skin. With it wrapped around my waist I went into the kitchen and put some water on the stove.

As I went over to sit at the table and wait for the water to boil I noticed that food had been left in the enclosed passageway outside my door. I went to see if the door would open today. It did; easily. I stepped over the tray of food and tried the other door, the one that no doubt led to freedom. It was locked.

I took the tray into the kitchen. I put the tins and bread in the cupboards and the milk, eggs, fish and cheese in the fridge.

I stood on a chair and looked out of the window down onto the bay and the wisp of beach that wasn't cut off from my eyes by the edge of the cliff. I surmised that I must have been more or less above where the encampment was, right at the end of the bay. I was unaware of any houses as far along as that, that close to the cliff's edge. Still, there was no reason why I should have known about such a dwelling. From the encampment, even if I had looked up, the forest's canopy would have hidden anything on the cliff. Only from the beach at the very edge of the water would I possibly have seen a construction; but how often had I been to the water since my accident?

There was a note on the tray under all the food. It read:

Please return your tray to the partitioning cubicle. Any rubbish please leave in the waste bags provided and also leave this in the partitioning cubicle. Any special requests you may have concerning dietary requirements, or materials for activities, please leave on the tray.
Thank you.
PS No harm will come to you! But please be aware that you are in a completely isolated world. Nothing will escape without our approval; no sound, no fire, no light.

The one thing that did perturb me was how my possessions from the camp had turned up in my white prison. There was collusion going on, of this there was no doubt. I figured that the crux was to establish whether Sabina was in on everything. Once that was clear I felt that lots of other issues would be resolved. To have any chance of getting to resolving that, or any of it, I needed to have contact. I needed to ask questions; ideally, I needed to look into people's eyes…

A brief flash of thought, accompanied by an image, passed through my mind as I tried to recall the name of the music group that wore giant circular head-masks of eyeballs.

I felt as if something was going to happen. To my mind there was no other course of action than for them to begin talking to me. Logic dictated that I was there for a reason. They had me where they wanted me; at some stage soon communication, dialogue, negotiation, had to occur. Communication other than a piece of paper instructing me what I should do with my rubbish.

Time went on. The days rolled on, one much the same as the next. I got to know every square centimetre of my cell. For, despite pretensions to the contrary, that is what it was. I knew the time of the sunset and the time of the sunrise. I knew that once a week I would get clean bedclothes and towels. I knew the sound of the extractor fan. I knew everything... What I didn't know was why I was there and who had put me there. I'd written them a note, a polite note, with several questions. There had been no reply.

Every so often I'd get angry and shout and scream, or I'd leave a much nastier note for them; or I'd smash eggs everywhere in the partitioning cubicle. I thought that if I stayed awake long enough, or pretended to be asleep, I would catch someone in the cubicle leaving me something or picking up my rubbish. I never did. On one occasion, one desperate maniacal occasion, I left a turd under an upturned bowl. But I don't wish to say any more about this.

I became convinced I was being watched twenty-four hours a day. I never did find a camera, though. For a time I fixated on the ventilation grill. After not being able to take it any longer I broke off its outer casing. But there was nothing in there, only air.

None of it made sense. And it was boring – so tediously boring. I spent hours peering out of that little window. I hoped that one day I would see someone. A little moving speck on the beach far below. Or even catch someone walking around the back of the building – between the window and the cliff's edge. But there was never a single sign of life. You'd think, wouldn't you, that some damn person would walk across that narrow strip of beach, or swim in the bloody sea?

I would torment myself by imagining dozens of people just out of view playing beach volleyball, having barbecues and running around laughing and smiling and enjoying the warmth of the sun on their bodies. Some of them I imagined naked; cavorting around and throwing Frisbees and smacking each other's bottoms playfully.

I would spend ages standing on that chair. Then I would have to lie down. It took a lot out of me; my back would begin to hurt. Either I'd lie down or I would have a fried egg butty. The olive oil was delicious and glutinous and the sandwich would momentarily cheer me up.

Time began to steal my mind. It stole my playfulness and accentuated the bad. Any desire I'd had to 'draw lines under things' or 'turn pages' or 'begin new chapters' *or* better still, the desire I'd had to avoid such clichés altogether and just clear my head and start again, any such wish had deserted me. The claustrophobia of my soul had turned into a cage. At times I queried whether I had become a metaphor in someone else's imagination.

There were periods, increasing periods, when I couldn't care less how healthy I was – mentally or otherwise. Then other times I'd have these manic obsessive spells of working out. I'd engage in a strict fitness régime: push-ups, step-ups, running on the spot and lifting the end of the bed up and down. But this was a madness – I don't think it stemmed from any real desire to get fit. A hamster on a wheel or a tiger padding around a pit is all it was.

When it all got too much – when the boredom, and the staring out of the window, and the using the bed as dumbbells, and the scrutinising to the nth degree the picture on the wall, and the fruitless game of trying to catch somebody in the corridor, when all of that and more had got too much – I began to write. I took my pen and my pad from the shelves in the corner and I began to write.

I wrote beautifully and poetically, and sometimes not so beautifully. No more press-ups and striking bodybuilding poses in front of the mirror. Writing was my new obsession. It had always been my obsession – I'd merely rediscovered it. I wrote page after page. Great sheaves would pile up on the edge of my table, and then every so often I would get great pleasure from giving them the lightest of prods and watching them cascade to the ground. A waterfall of words. It was most beautiful really.

It felt as though words had been queuing up for an eternity; waiting for a red light to change at a deviation in the route. Conceivably all these words had been there all along and had just required the green light to let them out. Not in London; surely they had not been there then. No, they cannot have been. But sitting at that table, surrounded by walls, they flew out. It got to the stage where I couldn't pull myself away from my flowing words; from my pad on the table and the pen in my hand.

I can't recall eating during this period. If I did, it would have been on autopilot. It matters not. I had a few days like that. It is incredible how much you can write in a twelve-hour virtually non-stop binge.

By this time it was established practice that if I wanted anything I would place my request on a piece of paper in the airlock (at least that was how I referred to it in my mind: the airlock). If, say, I don't know, I wanted fish on Friday, I would leave a note for them on Wednesday.

Not that I was religious or anything, I wasn't. I certainly wouldn't want to give the impression that I had 'seen the light' or felt the hand of the almighty or any other similar metaphor. I believed in aliens more than in fatalism. So, anyway, I don't know why I said *fish on Friday* – it was just an example, I suppose. I should have said *crab on Tuesday* or something like that to save any chance of misunderstanding.

Anyway, I digress. Usually whatever I asked for within reason I got. I learned pretty quickly that if my note was accompanied by questions concerning all the Whys? and Wherefores? I got nothing. That was my punishment, I suppose. So I soon learned to stop asking. I accepted – for what else could I do? – that when they were ready they would tell me what I wanted to know. And there was nothing I could do to hurry them along. So when my paper ran out or my pen ran dry, that would be the focus of my request. Clear and simple. No adjunctions that might put them on the spot, nothing they wouldn't be prepared to answer.

Then within a couple of days I'd get what I needed. I couldn't quite understand how they managed to find what I required each time at such short notice. As far as I was aware there were no shops around selling the kind of stationery I told them I needed. I supposed they were watching and anticipating when I was about to run out of something.

One time I asked for a pen with green ink. In truth the idea of writing in green had appealed to me. But the principal reason for my request was to see how they'd manage with a more out-of-the-ordinary demand. The following day when I awoke and went to the dividing doors, there it was. My request hadn't foxed them – which foxed me. Green pen, green ink.

I found it astonishing at first. Then I rationalised it by telling myself it wasn't such an unconventional demand after all. And I vaguely planned to come up with something really far-fetched; something which there was no way they'd be able to provide – not unless they had a stationer's shop above my head. A quill and inkwell had popped into my head, but I never got round to testing my theory. It would have been fun, but I had bigger issues to address…

I soon became fed up with writing in green and reverted to my usual black ink… The days slipped seamlessly into each other. In very little time the paper began to take up most of the floor space. From the table over to the bed; it had even reached the edge of the kitchen floor. Almost wherever I walked I heard the crinkle-crunch of twisted storylines and strange characters reaching up to grab me by the ankles. The more space that became filled the happier I was. I was surrounded by words, *silent words* – except in my mind.

I numbered the pages. But then, usually around a period of intense scribbling, I'd forget that small yet vital detail. And when I remembered again it was too late to find and put into order all the pages that had slid onto the floor. Too many sheets had fallen and got mixed up; and so I'd begin numbering again – from page number one.

I was never really sure why I bothered to number them at all. In a way, their out-of-orderness created its own meaning. On occasion I would indiscriminately pick up six or seven sheets on my way to or from the toilet. As I read through them I could see how they formed their own random beauty. Why, I thought, attempt to create order out of haphazardness? In a random universe it would be a crime to attempt to construct constraints.

There were little sequences of order here or there at the times I'd remembered to squiggle a number in the top left-hand corner of the page. Since the numbers were duplicated many times over (as I'd sporadically begun at number one again every so often) there was even a strong potential for randomness within these otherwise seemingly ordered air pockets. 'One' necessarily came before 'two', and 'four' followed 'three' – but was this 'one' the right *one*, and that 'two' the correct *two* for this *one*? There was no way of knowing.

A wondrously bizarre, and often – at least to me – meaningful construction (of words) could be built. A certain page number 'two' – any number two – could follow any number 'one'. The pages, as far as I was concerned, were in the right order – page five followed page four. It began to become irrelevant whether page five, for example, followed its original predecessor or not.

The one exception to the new meaning that my words were creating without me was the pages I had written in green ink. Pages one to fifty-nine in green were always destined to be joined at the hip. And as such I saw them as being of inferior significance. They somehow didn't sit comfortably with the new random world that was being augmented around me.

Once patterns and routines had developed, Sabina and the identity of my captors passed into the back of my mind. Later still my writing frenzy calmed down, and eventually the compulsion subsided. From having to spew my present and former madness onto paper I eased through into a more tranquil realm. I developed a less urgent working day for myself. Or more accurately: that is what evolved.

At first, I recorded everything – everything that had been piling up since London and Rosio. Every conversation and every action that had stuck in my mind as being significant, I put down on paper, even if it was far from easy to retrace my steps and distinguish which decisions had led me to where I'd ended up.

As time shifted, so inevitably had my perspective. Once the desperation and the madness had finally burnt out and cluttered themselves onto a thousand different sheets and more, a new approach was born...

CHAPTER XXVII

"Pleased to meet you," said Renney, extending his hand towards Sabina, who was visiting Maria and Johan for a few days from Rotterdam.

Renney sat down on the stool next to her. Soon they were chatting away as if continuing a conversation they hadn't quite finished from a previous encounter. They talked about where they were from and how they'd both ended up where they had. Sabina lied. She would have done so in any case, but Maria's firm instructions not to discuss her erstwhile Japanese exploits made her even more circumspect.

Realising it was later than they'd thought, Maria and Johan gradually retreated. They set about getting Shamballah ready for the evening. As they were pottering around they fleetingly caught each other's eye and smiled.

An hour after the bar opened to the public and groups of twos and threes began to arrive, Sabina and Renney announced they were off for a bite to eat. They walked under the archway that led to the exit stairs; Maria beamed and winked at Johan. She took a little skip towards him behind the bar and tried to slap a resounding high five on him. Johan caught her hand mid-air, pulled her gently towards him and kissed her on the cheek.

They went for Malaysian food: Sabina's suggestion. Renney hated it. Sabina loved it. Renney pretended he liked it. On their way back they walked some of the way past the formidable-looking *Westergasfabriek*, a gasworks built in 1883. Sabina explained that it had shut down in the 1960s, but there were vague plans to reopen it as a cultural centre.

Renney allowed her to do most of the talking. He found her to be an energetic and somewhat scatty, slightly nervous character for most of the time. She'd dart from one subject to another without warning. Her eyes, he noticed, were similarly predisposed: jumping around, as they did, from one location to another. And yet sometimes, as though a calming warm summer's breeze had enveloped her, he noticed, there were moments when she became utterly relaxed.

He rather liked her. He was rooted enough in reality to know that, at his age and with his dimensions, if a woman he didn't have to pay showed interest in him it was a reason in itself to spend some time with her.

She told him she was drawn to barren and industrial post-apocalyptic-looking architecture. Metal grinding its rusting tentacles into smog-engorged skies were the kinds of images Sabina had always found provocative. "An apprehensive attraction to factory wastelands" is how she described it. She equally loved the sounds that fabrication made: the clunks, scrapes and grinding of the regular metallic beats of industrial noise.

Renney was impressed by *Westergasfabriek* and told Sabina it would make an atmospheric location for a music concert. As he was saying this as they walked side by side down the darkened streets he was thinking of the unsurpassable, in his opinion, performance at Pompeii by Pink Floyd.

They arrived back in front of Renney's shop. Renney courteously proposed that Sabina might possibly like to go out for Mexican food the following evening; this time on him. She agreed – marginally too eagerly, she thought when she recalled that moment the following day.

Sabina was eager to grasp a slice of normality for herself, even if that meant she'd have to play a role. Naturally, judiciously, she'd continue to remain in contact with her comrades. She'd just keep her head down and try to be less gung-ho until the heat was off.

She hadn't mentioned it to Maria, she wouldn't be so crass, but it seemed as though Renney might have money. If he did, she reckoned, it was possible he owned another property, a second home, in, say, the south of France or Italy. Somewhere where there was sunshine and a discreet underworld – mainly fascists, most probably. Nevertheless, she mused, he might have some place somewhere where she could relax and decide what to do next. Opportunities like this, assuming he was wealthy, she knew wouldn't present themselves to her more than once or twice in a lifetime.

The following evening Renney spruced himself up, splashed on aftershave and even trimmed his beard. He opted to wear jeans and a white granddad shirt with an old black denim jacket slung over the top. The loose collarless shirt hanging over his jeans lessened the effect of his paunch. He looked at himself in the full length mirror and was quite pleased with the result. He now looked a little more university lecturer or social worker, and a little less roadie for the Grateful Dead.

As with the previous evening they began by drinking a few drinks with Maria and Johan before going for their meal.

Early the following morning as they returned from their evening out, under the neon glow of the Shamballah sign, they kissed. It was a long kiss and to both of them, for their differing reasons, it felt right.

-------• •-------

"I've found it!" shouted Renney, waving several stapled-together pieces of paper in Stefano's direction. Stefano was in the kitchen grinding coffee beans with the old wooden machine that had belonged to Renney's grandmother. He hurried over to where Renney was smiling and swaying backwards and forwards on his haunches. "Here," he said thrusting the document at Stefano. "See what you think." Stefano read the pages. As he did so Renney finished making the coffee. Stefano reread them; then Renney read over them yet again.

Renney moved over onto the burnt sienna-coloured settee and armchair to drink his coffee and stare out of the window. He found it difficult to believe his father's connections to such insalubrious worlds.

Possibly, Renney considered, his father had been acting out of character for the duration of his marriage. From what he'd discovered over the preceding hours, below the surface his father wasn't remotely similar to the person Renney thought he was. That man had been gambling and making shady deals. Why his father pretended to be an upstanding pillar of the community at the same time as frequenting backstreet bars and strip joints, smoke-filled, with a shady deal on the table next to a pack of cards sitting patiently waiting beside an ice-filled glass of bourbon, he had no idea.

The only thing Renney really had to consider was what to do next. Those shysters would soon be back for what they thought belonged to them. And if Renney didn't come up with a way of avoiding them he was sure they'd get even nastier.

After several moments contemplating his predicament Renney jumped to his feet. "Right," he said, "you give Marcus another ring."

"But he's…"

"Look, it's… What time is it? He should be home by now."

"Well…" began Stefano doubtfully.

"OK, look," said Renney, "you go home and pack instead. Two cases each – no more! Pack as much of Marcus' stuff as you can as well. And then wait for him to come home."

"– But?"

"I'm sorry, but we *all* have to be gone by morning. They'd do some nasty things to both of you if you stayed… to try to discover my whereabouts, even if you had no idea where I was. I'm sorry, but you'd be in very serious danger if you remained here. So let's do this as smoothly and stealthily as we can, shall we?" Renney nodded to Stefano. "Ring me the second Marcus comes home, OK?"

"– But, surely…"

"Look," said Renney raising his voice. "I'm knocked unconscious, they're in my childhood home, they're threatening me and they're going to be back soon. What other choice is there? Now, will you *please* just go?"

Stefano inclined his head solemnly, finally accepting that things did appear bleak. "See you soon," he said and turned to head for the stairs.

"See you soon. Hey," shouted Renney as Stefano was already making his way down the stairs, "Thanks! Thanks a lot… I'll be round later with a taxi… Ring me, OK?"

"As soon as Marcus stumbles in," Stefano called from the bottom of the stairs.

Renney folded the crucial document and put it in his pocket. The rest of his father's papers he scooped up and threw back into the trunk and locked it. He slid two of his cases out from under his bed and began to pack. His diaries, clothes and a few toiletries were all slung into the large suitcase. Into the small one he put some books and all his official documents – passport, driving licence, deeds to property, share certificates and signed photos of Jim Morrison and Janice Joplin. He carried his luggage down the stairs and left it in the shop before going round to see Johan and Maria.

The Shamballah sign was turned off, but Renney could see the glow of the lights down the stairs. It was close to the end of Johan and Maria's evening and the last of the customers were being encouraged to leave.

"Hi, Johan."

"Hey hey, hi… Wow, it's the late bird that catches the worm," said Johan with a smile on his face and an ashtray in his hand.

"Yes, I certainly hope so, Johan. Listen, I have to leave." Renney took hold of Johan's arm and gently coaxed him over to the wall out of earshot of the last five customers.

"What? … Why?"

"I just do… Sorry, Johan, I mean it's maybe better I don't tell you."

Johan nodded, and somewhat smugly – and yet not completely accurately – thought to himself that he always knew this moment was going to happen. "When do you have to go?"

"Now."

"Wow, that's sudden, huh?"

"I'm afraid so, but there's nothing else I can do."

"Is it something to do with Sabina?" he enquired just on the off-chance Renney had discovered Sabina's true identity. The instant he'd heard the words leave his mouth, however, he knew it was a daft question and wasn't likely to be the cause of this sudden action of Renney's.

"No, no, nothing like that."

Johan nodded. "You want me to tell her something?"

Renney thought for a moment. "Yes, tell her I'm really sorry and I'll contact her when things are a little less crazy..."

"No problem."

"Look, I need a favour."

"Name it," said Johan. Half meaning it – although not wishing to get directly entangled with anything too dodgy.

"Can you hide my father's trunk somewhere until I collect it?"

"Sure thing. I'll get rid of these last few night owls and then Maria and I'll get it. I've got a, what shall we say, *secret*," he winked, "lock-up outside – far outside – the city. I'll take it there in the morning."

"Are you sure you don't mind? Some people might come by asking questions."

"No sweat, Renney. I know nothing." He winked as he said this.

Renney placed a set of keys in Johan's hand. They exchanged a doleful look and a final handshake as Renney indicated that he should be getting a move on. "Kiss Maria for me," he said as he nodded to himself, turned and parted. Johan watched as Renney's legs then feet disappeared up the stairs to the street. He wondered what trouble Renney was in and if he'd ever see him again. And he told himself that if there was even a slight whiff of him or Maria getting embroiled in Renney's subterfuge, he'd dump the trunk.

Renney let himself back into the shop and locked the door. He phoned Stefano, who told him that Marcus had just returned very drunk. He ran his finger over the numbers of restaurants, dealers and friends pinned to his corkboard, found the taxi firm's number and dialled.

The cab driver wheeled the larger case to the car. Renney carried the other one himself. He turned and took a moment to look back. His time there had been a happy one, in the main. To his regret it was time to move on.

He left his case on the edge of the pavement for the driver to lift into the boot. He went back to turn the lights off and lock the door. As he did so he spied the painting of Jesus. He placed it up on the cabinet, stood back and admired it. He placed it on his desk, bound it in some material, removed some brown paper and a roll of sticky tape from the drawer and wrapped it up. Cumbersome though it was he couldn't permit himself not to take it with him. With it in his hands he looked for a last time over his shop and shut the door.

Ten minutes after leaving the shop the taxi pulled up in front of Stefano's apartment. Stefano had been watching the road and was already coming through the front door as the taxi arrived. By this time Marcus was already in a slightly better state than how Stefano had described him. Thirty minutes of black coffee and water splashing on his face had helped.

The three of them remained silent during the journey, each lost in his own thoughts. They watched the concrete and the urban ballet of those finally seeking refuge from the night. Street lights, the occasional blast of a passing car's stereo, the flashing of a nightclub's lights, the aroma of the city's night air. This was the city by night: party people getting ready for bed, a final beer and some street food before catching the night bus home. Amsterdam by night; Amsterdam on a Friday night; Amsterdam on *this* Friday night.

The three of them slept for most of the plane journey. Marcus had a loud snore. Every so often Stefano would give him a swift dig to the ribs with his elbow. Eventually they landed and transferred to an internal flight. It was approximately another hour's journey before they arrived at a ramshackle airport. It was mid-morning. The sun was rising in the eastern skies. As they descended onto the runway and walked across towards the terminal they were all sweating profusely.

Marcus was feeling terrible. He made sure his travelling companions were aware of his condition. He needed to drink a lot of water quickly, he told them, or he'd pass out. Stefano reproached him for moaning and being melodramatic; and in any case it was his own fault for drinking so much. Marcus tried to protest, but the moment had gone as Stefano had walked on ahead.

It took them an hour and a half to buy an old banger. So, in a pale blue truck coloured with a multitude of rust spots they headed northwards. Renney gave the directions to Stefano, who was driving, based on the information in his father's document. Through the midday heat they meandered their way along the potholed lanes. Finally they bumped their way along a single car-width route until they reached the brow of a hill. Stefano turned the engine off and they sat there, silently perspiring, looking down over the sun-drenched, plunging depths of the ocean.

There, off to the right, just before the cliff's edge, was the bizarre sight of the brilliantly white and impossibly balanced building of which Braque would have been proud, known, to those who knew it, as the Cubist's House.

CHAPTER XXVIII

I'd been obsessed, possessed. Taken over by an out-of-body insanity. And whether it was the whole Rosio thing, or my head injury, or the idea of my having been drugged and imprisoned, I was now ready to write my fourth book.

I woke up early, excited. I strode over the mass of A4 paper carpeting I'd created. Some pieces momentarily stuck to my sweaty morning feet before falling off again as I made my way to the door-less entrance to the kitchen to put some coffee on. I paced for a moment in front of the stove, then went and stood on a chair to look through the window at the inky blacky-blueness of the undecided skies. I stared, reflected; considered what the opening line to my book was going to be.

I heard the coffee machine blurble. I jumped down from the chair and replaced it under the table. I took the coffee off the stove and poured myself a cup. I took a mouthful and placed the cup on the table. Constantly thinking about the writing I was about to do, I somewhat absent-mindedly walked over to the other side of the room, around the corner from the bathroom.

Behind a heavy worn rusty-orange coloured settee was a cream curtain. The curtain matched the colour of the wall. It concealed a narrow, barely two persons'-width, recess. I'd peered in there before, held the curtain back and peered. But I'd found the space to be just full of rubbish, in any case nothing that had caught my eye.

This time, however, just while I was drinking my coffee and awaiting my opening line I decided to clamber in, just to make sure. Some broken garden furniture, pots of paint (that if I'd found in my first few days there I'd probably have daubed all over the walls. Possibly I'd have written something Situationist, something that I remembered from one of Rosio's art books. I don't know, maybe: *La beauté est dans la rue*.) Some rusted and bent tools: a screwdriver that had been used to stir paint, a hammer whose head looked as though it was about to come off.

I pulled things out, dragged cardboard boxes out, piled the settee with what was there. I scraped my shin against a bracket and grazed my elbow against the rough wall. It didn't matter; I was curious. I think *that* was my true motivation: curiosity. Curiosity in the sense that anything, of course, that enlightened me about my situation would be welcome. But, in truth, by this time I'd pretty much resigned myself to accepting my lot. Or I'd accepted that there was little I could do to get out of there, and as a consequence had to bide my time until whoever it was deemed it time for me to be released… I'd become sort of institutionalised – although that wasn't quite it, and so, later, much later (once I'd read everything), I came up with the term *Cubealised*.

I judiciously un-contorted myself and climbed backwards out of the recess with a paint pot in one hand and a bag of nails in the other. I placed these items in a wooden fruit box full of old newspapers I'd already put on the settee. The alcove was only about six metres deep, but it was nearly as high as the ceiling, and was mainly rammed with objects associated with labouring, carpentry, painting and decorating, that sort of thing.

In an asserted attempt to unveil all that was there, at the back under a ripped-up tarpaulin I found four trunks. Old-time cruise liner Agatha Christie mystery guests at a Mediterranean hotel type of trunks. They were locked and they were old, but now I had tools. It took me some time and considerable sweat to pull out everything that was left, drag the trunks out, and then chuck the rubbish and uninteresting stuff back in. They were heavy and the padlocks were sturdy and looked new. The hinges, however, were original and partially rusted. After a rest to catch my breath, have a drink of water, and wipe myself down with one of the towels from the bathroom, it was easy enough to open each trunk in turn. A jimmy and a jostle with a chisel and they were open.

In the first two were tins of food. That was it, just tin after tin of food. Corned beef, soup, spinach, quite a lot had labels in Russian, so they could have been anything. I found it disconcerting, the Cyrillic labelling, I mean, I don't know why; but at least I wasn't going to go hungry, I supposed.

In the third trunk, which had several splendid old shipping labels stuck over it, were books. Lovely lovely books. I couldn't comprehend why my captors hadn't stacked the shelves with them. It wasn't as though they were trying to make my stay as uncomfortable as they could. The food was good, the accommodation was comfortable, surely they should have provided me with more than the eight books that had been on the all-but-bare bookshelves. Possibly they'd forgotten.

Once I'd arranged the three hundred and sixty (I counted them) books in neat rows on the shelves I went back and opened the final trunk. Inside was bottle upon bottle of I didn't know what. Little glass bottles, some transparent, some opaque, some brown, some jade-coloured and some blue. On closer inspection, bending over and reaching in, I saw that almost all were bottles containing toxic and dangerous chemicals. They had those chemistry danger symbols on them, but somehow old-looking ones. Perhaps they were foreign, hence the sense I got of unfamiliarity (I'd done 'A' Level Chemistry, then I'd gone on and done the first year of an undergraduate Chemistry degree before dropping out to go travelling for a year. The following September, I'd enrolled on an English Lit. Degree – the point being that my knowledge of Chemistry meant I was familiar with the symbols and signage of the subject). Skulls, pictures of corrosive drops of liquid falling, and red crosses indicating something shouldn't be done – shouldn't be done without goggles or gloves.

All this made me feel uneasy and momentarily shook my otherwise quite determinedly upbeat beginning to the day. It was clear that my state was fragile. Certainly, in the early days of my incarceration, even up until very shortly before discovering the trunks, I had been existing on the edge of something or other. I was determined, finally, not to be a madman in a seemingly normal environment. I was going to be a sane man in a crazy situation. Salvador Dali, I recalled, said – *La seul différence entre moi et un fou c'est que je ne suis pas fou*: the only difference between me and a madman is that I'm not mad.

I closed the bizarre mobile chemistry lab and returned to my neatly arranged books. How beautiful they looked…

The first book I picked up was on psychology. I sat on the edge of my bed and read about the *Karpman Drama Triangle*. This, I learnt, is concerned with the three habitual psychological roles that people adopt: there is the person who plays the *victim*; the person who coerces or persecutes the victim, *the persecutor*; and the *rescuer* who, supposedly out of a desire to help, intervenes to alleviate the problem of the victim.

Of these, apparently, it is the rescuer who has the least obvious role. He or she is someone who has a mixed motive and is benefitting somehow psychologically from taking on the role of the perceived rescuer. Superficially it appears as though the rescuer is trying to help the victim. Indeed, so I read, that may well be the case. At a deeper level, though, the rescuer also has a desire for the victim not to be redeemed. In one way or another the rescuer benefits by the victim remaining a victim: the rescuer gains self-esteem by supposedly aiding the victim, and in truth it is of benefit to the rescuer if the victim continues to perceive himself as a victim.

The covert motivation for each of the players is to have their psychological needs fulfilled in a manner that benefits them, without their having to deal with or even acknowledge the greater harm that is being done. Interestingly, according to the piece, each of the role-players acts in their own selfish interests – even the so-called victim does.

After ten minutes' reading I put the book on the bed beside me and allowed myself to fall backwards. I settled on my back, knees bent over the end of the bed and my feet still on the ground. I thought about what I'd read and wondered whether it had any relevance to me. I mulled it over and tried to apply it to my situation. But despite how interesting I found the article I couldn't see any lessons to be gleaned from it.

The next book I picked up was ostensibly about avant-garde music. Its cover had the picture of a piano being played, if played is the right term, by two feet. Its title, which had been what had attracted me to it, was *Avant-garde Music, Dadaism and the Left*.

I opened it and began to read. I read a bit about a group called Amon Düül II, who, according to the book, had close ties with ultra-left-wing activists such as the Baader-Meinhof Gang. Then I flicked a little further and read a long piece about The Velvet Underground and Andy Warhol, and how, the author claimed, many believed that Lou Reed was an alien who would live forever.

I was about to close the book, irritated, reckoning I'd heard all I could take about alien beings, when I spotted something about John Cage. I was still on the verge of closing the book however, having mixed up John Cage with John Cale in my mind and figuring I'd read enough about The Velvet Underground for one day... But as I allowed my gaze to slide over the page I realised my mistake. Instead of shutting its pages and moving on to another book I read on. Pretty quickly I became fascinated by the piece of music being discussed. The composition in question by John Cage was entitled 4'33".

It was a silent piece, all four minutes thirty-three seconds of it. I was struck by its brilliance: an opus where the orchestra were instructed not to play their instruments. The idea to me was mind-boggling. How fantastic, how innovative, how ground-breaking – wow, this was really something. Of course, it was no longer as *ground-breaking*, composed as it was in 1952. But to me it was new and exciting and... well, *and*... it would be clichéd to say it was a eureka moment, but it was certainly something that made me appreciate I had to begin to look at things differently. If I really wanted to achieve exceptionalness (in part by not using such words as 'exceptionalness'), merely writing a new book, a good book, was not enough. I had to creep up around the back of literature and grab it by the throat. Throttle it and wring it out.

A piece of music that could not be heard, my mind reeled. How could my new novel completely break the mould of that which had gone before? Not just a story but a statement: a statement about art... about art and confinement; about expression and secrecy. About words and non-words and the missed meanings and intentions oh-so-briefly glimpsed in the spaces between the lines.

I racked my brain and squirmed with convoluted mental gymnastics. But I couldn't see it. Not at that moment, not quite.

I flicked to a section in the last third of the book. There was a heading entitled *Avant-Garde and Dadaist Records and Record Sleeves*. I vaguely ran my eyes over the text while my mind was still coming to terms with the enormity of the John Cage piece. Until, that is, I came across a 7″ single by a group called *The Gender-shifting Seventeenth Planetary Project and the Disc-eye Conspiracists*. The cover of their record was quite intriguing: bright green with the picture of a distorted head, which was complemented by a cuboid typescript. But none of that was what drew my attention. The remarkable thing was that the inside of the sleeve was made out of sandpaper. Sandpaper! Each time the listener pulled the record out or placed it back in its cover – so the accompanying text stated – the disc became more and more scratched, to the extent that the record would eventually become unplayable.

I went over to the table, gently shaking my head from side to side. I felt as though somehow everything was converging... I idly noticed the splash of sunlight on the kitchen floor. I slowly reached up to touch my head and realised my hair was greasy and long. I'd wash it and chop a couple of inches off it later on, I told myself. I picked up the remnants of the by then cold cup of coffee. I returned to the bed, sat down and sipped the black coffee.

I shook my head and felt defiant, revolutionary in a sense – how... how to break literary conventions? How could I break the conventions in literature as these artists I was encountering had broken the conventions in their own fields? What on earth could I do? Was it possible even: a thought that hadn't been thought, an idea that hadn't been had before? When even 'originality' had become clichéd and when the new was retro or yesterday's fashion, how could you give birth to something in a vacuum? And indeed how could you pinprick the long-accepted boundaries when all the vacuums had been appropriated by those who thought that nothingness was the next big somethingness?

I stretched over for another book, then another and another. Eventually I came across a book called *Dadaist and Surrealist Poetry and Aphorisms*. I read poems by Paul Éluard, René Crevel and Malcolm de Chazal. In the notes accompanying the work of each writer I learned that Salvador Dalí said that René Crevel, who'd committed suicide shortly before his thirty-fifth birthday, was the only serious communist out of all of the surrealists.

I also read a piece by Jacques Rigaut who, according to the accompanying commentary, perceived suicide to be the ultimate act of Dadaism. Hence, at the age of thirty, as he'd said he would, he killed himself.

All of this fed into my growing acceptance that I was on the verge of destroying convention. Destroying perceived bourgeois definitions of worthiness, or quality or intellectual piety. Destroying any preconceptions of what I thought I should write, or more fundamentally how I should write it.

A moment of clarity, realisation even, of the direction I should take struck me. As my mind was spiralling and contorting with thoughts of music and yet no music, words and yet no words, I came across and read two poems. It was as if everything had been leading to this moment. One was a poem by Hugo Ball entitled *Karawane*. And the other was *Paloo Paloo* by Alain de Sournier, the great Dada-Chef:

Lapa loola lapa lila lapa loola li
Fala foola fala feela fala moola ki
Jaka jaka waka waka mass-de doodi da
Hama harma hama hoola hamer poola pa
Paloo paloo paloo pyjama weeeeeeeee

Those two poems, accompanied by one of Alain de Sournier's inedible yet aesthetically and sensually pleasing recipes, helped formulate the new ideas that were bubbling up to my psychological surface.

I felt that although I wasn't, or at least hadn't been, a fatalist a number of apparently separate experiences appeared to be shadowing each other. Here, for example, I was struck by the two poems in that they had no meaning. Just as earlier I'd been taken by music that you couldn't hear.

It made perfect sense to me. All of it. As did the footnote to the first poem that quoted Hugo Ball as saying: "We should burn all libraries and allow to remain only that which everyone knows by heart. A beautiful age of the legend would then begin."

I found that to be such a beautiful idea. To will the epoch of the legend and the folktale to return seemed to me to be an honourable pursuit. I vowed to aid its return by the method I adopted for my fourth novel…

Unbeknownst to me at that time I had still not yet had my epiphany moment. I was close – everything was in place. All that was left was to figure out how. How to break through the barriers of conventional writing?

CHAPTER XXIX

Renney stood a little way up the slope observing Marcus busy on the second house. The sound of Stefano's motorbike approaching prompted him to turn. He watched as Stefano pulled up, dismounted and went to have a few words with Marcus before going up to chat to Renney.

"Good morning, Stefano. How are things?" asked Renney.

"Good, thank you. I've just been talking to Sabina."

"Great. How are they getting on down there in the bay?"

"Not bad. They're pretty busy... They completed their third hut yesterday. At least they've all got a roof above their heads now."

"They're not stopping at three, though, are they?"

"No, no; but their next priority is to make a clearing. A living space, tables and chairs, that sort of thing."

Renney nodded thoughtfully. "How long 'til the house is complete?"

"The Tetragon House," Stefano volunteered as nonchalantly as he could.

"The – what?"

"Well, I just thought… You were saying the other day that you were trying to think up a name for the new building."

"Yes, but…"

"I just thought that this had a similar ring to it."

"Umm," said Renney who didn't care for Stefano's suggestion, but couldn't be bothered to object. "We'll mull it over, OK?" he said, to which Stefano nodded. "And –?"

"Hmm?"

"How long until we think the… the" Renney couldn't bring himself to say 'The Tetragon House', "new house will be ready?"

Stefano concealed his disappointment at Renney's obvious avoidance of using the name. "I would say at a rough guess," he began. "Oh, I don't know, four or five weeks should definitely do it."

"And you're sure about that?"

"Well, as long as there are no unforeseen problems."

"Why so long?"

"I don't think that's long."

"Well…"

"There have been issues… you know this, getting the materials over here. And, well, a few other bits and pieces."

"Mm."

"And we want the bay commune completed as well before…"

"Yes, yes," interrupted Renney. "I suppose so. Well, anyway, tell Marcus to work as quickly as he can, will you?"

Stefano nodded, but he wouldn't do anything of the sort. That would only irritate Marcus; things would take even longer.

"It's just," added Renney, realising that he'd sounded somewhat petulant, "time is m-," his voice petered out aware that he was about to utter a cliché. "You know." Stefano nodded and smiled.

"How are the Americans doing?"

"I think they're beginning to realise what's expected of them."

"They're comfortable enough, huh?"

"Certainly. There's everything they need in the basement of the Cubist's House. Of course," said Renney, "once this is complete," he nodded at the construction Marcus was working on, "our future guests will have more room and -."

"Mmm," said Stefano thoughtfully. "And…"

"And as it happens I've got a Londoner booked in for, I don't know exactly… six weeks, two months' time, I think."

"Mm-huh…"

"It all depends upon whether his woman can get him here without his knowing…"

"Right… Another artist?"

"No, an author this time."

"Oh?"

"Yes, a writer who's been suffering from depression, I believe, depression and self-doubt; possibly a little schizophrenia as well… I'm not really sure yet."

"That's interesting."

"Yes, I want us to help the whole gamut of creative types."

"Mmm."

"I really think we could make a go of this, you know."

"Uh-huh… Hopefully. And you'll…?"

"Well, that's why Marcus *has* to get a move on."

"You could always put the writer in the Cubist's House."

"No," said Renney defiantly. "The Americans are the first and last in the Cubist's House… We move… it's time to move over to the, er…"

"The Tetragon House," ventured Stefano, a cheeky glint in his eye.

"Hmmph… The point is… Oh well, anyway… What have you on your agenda this afternoon?"

"I've got Sabina's final two friends to pick up from the airport. I'll be leaving in about an hour in case the flight's early."

"Could you fill the car up when you get to town?"

"Yes, I was going to anyway… And what about you?"

"Sorry?"

"I mean what's next for…?"

"For me? Mmm… I get the feeling I'm going to be on the phone for quite some time trying to get a date out of that East German guy for when all of this surveillance equipment is going to… well, and those bloody thick doors for the basement…" Renney shook his head, "are going to arrive."

Stefano went off in the direction of the jeep and Renney headed for his recently completed office in the new building. It was through the front door and first on the left, as in the Cubist's House. He'd wanted to keep as much of the layout of the Cubist's House as possible. It was the clients' basement that would be the innovative built-for-purpose part of the building.

He sat in his black swivel armchair, unlocked the top drawer of the army green metal filing cabinet, extracted his diary and began to write. He wrote for about twenty minutes, as he tried to do on most days. Once he'd finished his entry he checked his watch, picked up the phone that had been connected two days earlier and dialled.

It took him a while to get through. Then: "Hello...
hello? Helmut? Helmut? Are you...? Yes, yes – it's Renney.
Uh-huh? Renney... yes, yes. You're... it's a bad... yes,
yes... now I can... that's better. What did you...? You're in
West Berlin for... OK, listen. Fine, fine... The cameras
and... yes, that's great. And the... Sorry? The security
doors? Yes... It's gone bad ag... No that's... yes, the doors.
Is there...? Uh-huh, the... uh-huh... Well, why... Oh,
alright... but, the... well, why? Yes, yes – the price. And
you're sure...? OK – so when? Two to three weeks? In the
port of...? Alright..." Just then there was a knock at
Renney's door. "Come in! No, no Helmut... Somebody at
the... Listen, you're sure... I know, I know... I'll transfer...
Fine – no, no, that's OK. Alright. Yes, you ring me next
time. When it's all left. Alright... Yes, yes... and you
Helmut. Uh-huh, yes – bye. Bye, Helmut... Yes!"
Pheeeewwww. Renney slumped back in his chair and
sighed.

"Ahem." A cough came from the doorway. Renney
swivelled round from facing out of the window.

"Hello, Marcus. Yes... sorry. Yes?"

"Problems?" asked Marcus.

"What? Oh, well... not rea... Well, the doors, you
know, the security doors." Marcus raised his eyebrows.
"Well, there's something wrong with them," said Renney.

"Yes?"

"Their release is – it's... but, of course I should have
known because the price is so..."

"What?"

"Yes, sorry, Marcus. Listen, the doors for the
basement have a built-in release system. So that... Well,
anyway, the doors apparently if left un-touched open
automatically after ninety-nine days. So... my supplier tells
me that – well, naturally he says it's no problem. He says
that we'll just have to reset the timer every so often. Before
the ninety-nine days are up."

"Yes, no problem – if you're getting them cheaply. I might be able to repair them anyway. I'll take a look when they arrive."

"Thank you, Marcus."

"And anyway – ninety-nine days?"

"What?"

"Well, it's such a long time. It doesn't matter, does it?"

"I suppose not. Silly really?"

"I'd say."

"Mmm," Renney nodded his head. "It's just I like everything to be working the way it should… You know?"

"Mmm… So, anyway," said Marcus somewhat abruptly, wanting to move the conversation on. "I actually came to ask about the roofing."

"What about it?"

"Well, do you want a thatched circular section and a giant egg up there like on the Cubist's House?"

"Mmm…" Renney scrunched up his eyes and ran his hand down from his forehead over his nose and left it to rest on his beard and chin. He was tired. And with Marco having initiated the notion he thought it a good idea to go over to the Cubist's House for a siesta. He had a hammock on the roof over there in the shade of the thatched canopy. "Why not? Make them match, eh?" he said while pinching and then releasing his chin.

"Uh-huh," Marcus muttered while turning to leave.

"Thanks," Renney shouted after him. He wondered if that would have been a good moment to talk to him about the speed of the build.

Renney got up and left his office. He went along the corridor to the kitchen, shaking his head slightly in thought as he went. There were still lots of loose wires, but at least all the white goods were in. He stared out of the window down over the drop to the slither of beach visible and the sapphire sea. He reflected upon how quickly the time was passing and how everything had to be finished and in place for the arrival of their second paying 'guest'.

PART V

CHAPTER XXX

"Hello, yes?" said Renney.

"Hello... hello?"

"Yes?"

"Oh, hello. This is Rosio... Rosio Carmichael," said Rosio.

"Yes, of course. How are you?"

"Oh, fine, thank you... Well, actually I... er... I was a little concerned."

"You want to know how your Jethro is doing?"

"Well, er, yes... I..."

"Of course you do, of course you do, Mrs Carmichael. Well, let me tell you he's absolutely fine. More than fine – he's excellent."

"It's just..."

"Yes?"

"Well..."

"Yes?"

"Well..." she hesitated. "It's just that I'm not sure I did the right thing."

"Now, now, Mrs Carmichael."

"Yes, but… I'm not sure… I mean it might have been a bit extreme… You know…"

"Yes, I do know what you mean and your reactions are perfectly normal. You're feeling guilty. Of course you are. Who wouldn't? But let me tell you you have absolutely nothing to worry about."

"I was wondering if maybe you could tell me where *exactly* you are so I could maybe visit him."

"I'm sorry?"

"Well, I was wondering… No, look, actually now I come to think of it I think possibly the best thing is if we just call a halt to it all. He's been there long enough to… he's probably…"

"What exactly are you trying to say, Mrs Carmichael?"

"I think it's been *long enough*. I'd like him to come home now."

"Mrs Carmichael! Please be strong! You know that's not possible."

"Wha…?"

"Of course I don't have to remind you of the contract you signed, do I?"

"Yes, yes… I thought we could maybe come to some arrangement… You know… I mean I'd be prepared to pay," she said while trying to maintain her composure.

"I'm sorry, Mrs Carmichael, there is no arrangement possible. I *really*," he barked, "*am* sorry. This is not a two-way road, Madam. There are no revolving doors. I… *We* are not exclusively here for the benefit of you and your husband. In a way I suppose we are. But you are two of our first clients, hence the special price – I hope you haven't forgotten *that*, Mrs Carmichael – so we are also learning. And I don't wish that to be interr-," Renney chose not to complete his sentence. He paused, trying to ignore the stuttered, breathless sobbing on the other end, before continuing on a different tack.

"Hmmph. I really sincerely hope you appreciate what we're trying to do here... This is an experiment. An experiment in art and creativity, yes; but it's more than that. Oh, Mrs Carmichael," his voice soared, "so, *so* much more. This, Mrs Carmichael, is an experiment in life, for a better life: to engage those who are disengaged, and to refocus those whose clear talents have been nudged off course by... by *life*, Mrs Carmichael. By life."

Renney gazed out of the window to gather himself and to take a moment to clear his mouth which had filled with saliva. It didn't do to frighten the patrons. "But I can tell you", he went on, with a decidedly more conciliatory tone, "– which may allay your fears somewhat – you'll be happy to hear that recently your husband has begun writing again. I shouldn't really be telling you this, but since you're upset I can make an exception. Yes, he has begun, just begun, but begun he has, writing... and indeed at a *truly* ferocious pace. Really! He undoubtedly has a story in him that he needs to put onto paper..."

"I just... I just thought... you know... I just, oh god, what have I done? ...I just just thought, you know..."

"Not possible."

"Oh, God," she cried. "Well, er... oh, God... er, well, is he thin... is he eating properly?"

"Yes, Mrs Carmichael I can assure you our chef is providing him with the very best of fare."

She spluttered something through her anguished weeping.

"I'm sorry, Mrs Carmichael, I didn't quite catch..."

"Is he alright? Er, has he got lots to read?"

"Yes, of course, Mrs Carmichael..." As he said this he was switching cameras on his monitor so as to view Jethro's quarters. "He's a writer, Mrs Carmichael, of some talent. We naturally presumed that as a writer he would also be a reader. Do not worry. We have provided him with hundreds of books. Certainly do not concern yourself on that score…"

Apart from possibly a dozen books, maybe less, Renney couldn't see any other reading material in Jethro's living quarters. He wondered what the hell Marcus had done with all the books with which he should have lined the bookshelves. He made a mental note to remember to have a word with him about that.

"Well… well," blubbed Mrs Carmichael, "how… how much longer?"

"Oh," his voice deepened and slowed, "it could be quite some time yet I'm afraid…"

After a "Good day, Mrs Carmichael" Renney hung up. Almost immediately he took the receiver back off its cradle and gently put it down on his desk.

He looked out of his window and wondered what was for lunch.

CHAPTER XXXI

I wrote and I wrote. I wrote the story of my life, my immediate life. Everything that had resulted in my being in a prison on the edge of a cliff.

Necessarily I had to invent portions of *my* story. Clearly, there were episodes that eluded me. But that was OK; I was a writer, after all. And the getting down onto paper what I did know – the whole Rosio episode, for example – was cathartic.

I was finally beginning to know who I was. It sounds clichéd, doesn't it? But it was true; I could feel it – purpose without doubt. A strange experience, to be without the eyes of others. An odd phenomenon indeed not to be deafened by the thoughts of a thousand surrounding discontented souls.

I was, I felt, purely me. A pure version of me. Yes, I wanted to run and stroke the warm sun with my pale body, but it was superfluous. I didn't require it for sustenance, for life, nor for well-being. All I required was solitude and a pen. That was all I needed, and that was all I had… And food. I also required food.

Other than these things I was a self-contained writing machine. Reluctant as I would have been to admit it – and I certainly wouldn't have said it out loud to anyone else – incarceration had provided me with what I had ultimately been pursuing: peace and quiet, and peace of mind.

So there I was, happily – if happy is the correct term… well, I suppose, happy in my way – anyway, there I was absorbed with the ritual of my everyday writing routine when: bang, bang, bang, bang. Gunshots.

They rang out about late morning. Four of them, one after another. A ricocheted sound with a slightly delayed echo. Probably bouncing off the mountains or the building I was in, or both… I had just come out of the shower and was wrapped in the fluffy cerulean towel.

Bang, bang, bang, bang: shit, what was that? I'd thought and dived immediately under the bed. Shit, shit… What was going on? The shots sounded so close. Just above ground, to the front of the building, it seemed to me.

I was under the bed for over an hour. It could have been nearer to two hours. In that time I completely expected someone, some people, with a gun, guns, to come through my airtight prison passageway, hold a revolver up to my temple and say "bye, bye". And then 'pop', blackness, the end.

But that wasn't what happened. I waited, as I said, and nothing happened. At last I crawled out. I rather pointlessly and somewhat stagily looked around. Like a man appearing from the trenches, looking to see if the war was really over. But I couldn't know if the *war* was over or not. Or even if there had been a war. Shit – I knew nothing.

I stood on a chair, as I did every day, and peered out of my only outlet to the outside world. I held myself as far out of sight as I could, gazing out only from the edge of the window. Just in case a person came into view. But nothing happened.

It was possibly another half an hour after coming out from under the bed that I thought – only thought – that I heard another two or three shots in the far distance. But maybe it was nothing, or something else, or my imagination playing tricks with me...

And that was that – excitement over...

------ • • • ------

Life continued. Almost as if nothing had occurred. After that one day of pacing around and keeping quiet – I didn't heat up any water, or cook anything – I returned to normal. *My* normal: I wrote.

But not quite *everything* returned to normal. Within a few days it became apparent that there was no one left to send down food to me anymore. The natural conclusion I arrived at was that whoever he or she or they were who had imprisoned me had been killed. I had no proof of this. But it was the most obvious explanation for my requests from that point on being ignored.

I did try every so often after that time to put in an order, but it was always to no avail. Thereafter, once my cupboards were becoming depleted, I slowly began making my way through the tins of food I'd found in the trunks.

It wasn't so bad. I paced myself. I ate less. I figured that so long as I remained disciplined, I could probably last on the food I had for maybe half a year, just – at a push. I hoped, needless to say, that I'd be discovered before then.

Once I'd decided upon my new regime I put it all out of my mind. My main objective was to write... to write my partly fictional account of the last several months of my life.

And it went well, it flowed nicely. I wrote about how we'd met, Rosio and I. I wrote about the terrible depression I'd experienced. A depression that on the surface seemed to be wholly due to my sense of lack of self-worth and inability to write. Probably, too, it had elements of work-related stress and relationship anxiety mixed in with it. Not forgetting a genetic predisposition towards the darker way of looking at things.

I wrote about the Preacher, the ransacked apartment and all the rest of it. My last weeks in work, coming to the island, meeting the woman in the bar and talking about alien conspiracies or whatever it was, and then I wrote about my head injury, Sabina, the fascists, the cave and waking up in my prison apartment.

Of course, I made it more interesting than that sounds. I added completely invented elements to *my* story. About Rosio having been abducted and taken to the island and my having to rescue her from this strange alien-worshipping end-of-the-world cult.

Renney I cast as the puppet master, the Charles Manson figure. Recruiting young, unsuspecting, forlorn, wayward types from cities around Holland. He would bring them to the island, ply them with drugs, apply a little of the Sirhan Sirhan or the Patty Hearst treatment on them, and do with them as he saw fit.

Just as my tale was developing into a more and more twisted Reverend Jimmy Jones kind of story, two things changed everything.

One morning for breakfast I made some heated up and squished-with-a-fork kidney beans with cumin powder, to have with my last two crackers. I put my plate of food on the table, and then made a cup of tea with the same tealeaves I'd used for five previous cups. When I'd done that I put the cup on the table next to my plate and went over to my bookshelf. I wanted something to look at while I was eating.

I passed my eyes over the spines of several books. Nothing took my fancy. I didn't want to begin reading a novel. A bit of poetry would have been fine. I didn't want to look for too long, either, or my beans would get cold. Then, squeezed between two of the larger hardcovers, I spotted a magazine. An art magazine. It was from the early 1970s, from New York, called *Plexus Art*.

I sat back down, put my fork in my right hand and slow-shovelled the beans into my mouth. As I did this my left hand was thumbing through the pages of the magazine. Its cover was of a semi-naked woman caught in that serpentine flames-of-a-fire dancing pose so typical of the era. It struck me that she looked slightly like Lena Nyman from the film *I am Curious Yellow*. And this in turn led me to consider the pre-summer release of The Fall's eleventh studio album: *I Am Kurious Oranj*.

Surrounding the woman, whoever she was, and thus taking up most of the cover page, was an egg shape consisting of numerous coloured lines. Each line made up the egg shape, each one inside the other. They went from an oxidised orange colour to a pale buttery colour on the innermost circles. Behind the young woman were green and blue thicker lined spirals. It looked like a still from a psychedelic version of some Alfred Hitchcock adaptation where someone is falling into an abyss.

I flicked through the pages of art and comments from another time. The magazine clearly wanted to stay open at the centrefold. The spine had been broken by someone who had pressed down on those centre pages, in my mind so as to look at them without using his hands.

I wondered who that person had been. Whose hands had flattened those pages while possibly he was eating *his* meal? Maybe a croissant in a Paris café, or a doughnut in a coffee bar in Prague staring out at the bright lights and the red East western sunset. Or possibly, I considered at the time, those pages were flattened by a previous prisoner.

Where the magazine fell open was at two pages of pictures and descriptions of a young London artist who'd made books that, according to the subtitle of the piece, could not be read. He'd made a series of them. Books that were so well sealed that it was impossible to lever their pages apart, either that or how the action of attempting to open them destroyed them.

The first book described, for example, had a lead cover. It was a book that if you managed to heave it apart, which is what you had to do, according to the accompanying article, the spikes running through the book's pages with their tips bent back into the paper would rip the text like some medieval shredding machine.

According to the article the artist's choice of lead was significant for two reasons: firstly, it is the base metal of alchemy, and secondly, the earliest known lead objects apparently date from 6500 BCE – approximately three to four thousand years earlier than the construction of Stonehenge. And this, so the article explained, was of particular importance to the artist; especially since time, and notions of time, he saw as being important concepts in his work.

I pushed my plate to the side and took a big swig of coffee.

I read on. Another of the books consisted of undeveloped photographs of images and text. Apparently the instant the pages were parted, the photographs would be exposed to the light and hence rendered useless.

This was fantastic.

Another had phials of acid concealed within the book. Once the cover, which was bound with bandages, was cut the spring-loaded spine would flip open thus breaking the phials and burning away the folios… Another was a tome in the form of a lead-covered bear trap; yet another still had jagged broken glass for a cover.

I found this all to be astonishing. I was almost shaking with the excitement of what I'd unearthed. My thoughts raced as they tried to formulate a coherent structure, as they attempted to mould these ideas into a relevant structure for *me*.

Books that couldn't be read. Stories that could never be seen. Stories that could have been the most beautiful in the English language. They probably weren't, but they could have been. The point was they could have been anything...

This was it. I shook my head in disbelief. This was what I'd been looking for. I wanted this for myself; something along these lines. But something that was more me. Something of course that had less to do with art and more to do with literature. That was it. This artist had used books as his artistic piece. But I didn't want to create an art piece. I wasn't an artist. I wanted to create literature.

What I'd read had been about a phenomenal and completely original piece of work. The only slight similarity that leaped from my memory was of an artist Rosio and I had once seen a film about in that little cinema we used to go to. I seemed to recollect that his name was Gustav Metzger and he'd invented something called auto-destructive art. The music lover in me had probably remembered the guy since he was the one who had influenced Pete Townsend in his guitar-smashing escapades... This was better than that, though, like the leaves of a book, here meaning was layered upon meaning.

I wanted my words to be read, though. Well, I did and I didn't. I wanted them to be read, but I wanted there to be some futility to the exercise. An emptiness, a hopelessness had to permeate the reader's essence somehow; in the same way that such feelings had taken hold of me in the long lead up to their creation...

Once I'd finished my drink I put the crockery in the sink. I'd have a real problem if the water stopped running, I thought, as I absent-mindedly turned both taps on and off in turn. I returned to my place and tried to continue with my story. But my heart wasn't in it any longer. Not then – not after having read about the unreadable books. So I went over to my bed and lay down. And reflected on what possible slant I could put on the young artist's wonderful oeuvre.

I worked at my story for a little over another week, maybe eight or nine days. I didn't do what all films tell you a prisoner should do, namely, keep track of time by crossing off those little lines and grouping them into fives. And so the hours passed into the days, which in turn passed into weeks, which themselves turned into ever increasing chunks of my life. How large the chunks were I couldn't tell, not exactly.

Then, and I consider myself to be extremely fortunate that this happened during the day – during the day when I was not making a noise – I heard a restrained clunk. Had I been cooking, if I can call heating up the contents of tins cooking, I wouldn't have noticed a thing. Had I been taking a siesta, or asleep, or pulling the chain of the toilet, or even been in the bathroom at all, I would have been oblivious to what turned out to be the noise that signalled my liberty. For the clunk was the sound of my doors releasing.

And so I got up from where I'd been sitting at the time and went over to where I thought, correctly as it turned out, the sound had originated.

I tried the first door: open. I walked along the transparent tunnel where they used to leave my food and tried the second door. This *too* was open... I was hesitant: a trepidatious man who'd been institutionalised. But it wasn't quite that; it was more disbelief than anything else.

And for some inexplicable reason this manifested itself in my turning to see I don't know what. Just turning I guess. Maybe turning to be sure there wasn't a version of me still sitting at the table, and that I was imagining all of this.

I wasn't imagining it. The doors were open. I rushed back to pick up the sharpest knife I could find in the drawer and then returned to the passageway. I advanced through the second door, turned the corner and stealthily mounted the stairs.

At the top of the stairs was another door. I silently turned the handle with my left hand, gripping onto the knife with my right. I pushed the door gently to. I waited and listened. Nothing. I edged forwards from the top of the staircase into a hallway. I looked to the right, which I could see led into a kitchen, approximately above where I'd been kept.

I turned left towards what looked like the front door. I quickened my step. Then, just as I had my hand on the front door I glanced to my right, through an open doorway. It was an office; an office with dried blood on the desk and office chair, and with splayed red markings over the floor.

I slowly eased my head around the corner of the door. There was nobody there. Then I went back along the hallway into the kitchen. Nobody there, either. I briefly looked out of the large expanse of window, above the sleek black cooker and the double sink made of pure white porcelain, that looked down over the bay. I went back along the hallway and climbed the stairs. No one up there, either. Three bedrooms, each with a bathroom. Up a couple more stone steps and through a door onto the roof. An outside stone counter in the shape of a 'C' was surrounded by concrete seating and hammocks; it had a thatched roof, held up on poles, which covered the centre of the building's flat rooftop.

I helped myself to a beer from the fridge under the counter and sat looking out at the turquoise waters. I could see I was above the end of the bay; the opposite end to my farmhouse... The sun on my body and the fresh air entering my lungs made me relax. I nearly fell asleep, but just managed to catch myself. I finished my beer, grabbed another one and walked around the roof. I looked over the landscape, rugged, mountainous in the distance; not a single soul in sight.

I descended. At the bottom of the stairs next to the door that led down to my pristine dungeon were two other doors. I tried them both, but they were locked. I went along to the office and placed my beer bottle on the desk.

There was a switched off or broken monitor above the desk. Next to this was a metal filing cabinet. And figuring it was time to find something out about the bastards who'd incarcerated me I tried to open it. It was locked. There was also a set of wooden drawers in the far corner of the room so I went over to see if they were open.

Just then the thought struck me that possibly Sabina was imprisoned behind one of the other two doors in the hallway. I rushed back and tried their handles once again. Then I tried kicking at them. I shouted her name, two, three, four times. I ran outside, looking for a garage, a workshop, a toolbox. Eventually, around to the side of this oblong construction I found a sturdy thin flat piece of metal, approximately three feet in length. Whatever its original purpose it had at some point been used to stir red paint.

I tore back inside and within several moments had levered the doors away from their frames. Both doors led to virtually the same sized areas: both led to stairways that led to floor space that in turn led to a security passageway, a locked security passageway, behind which was an apartment almost identical to the one in which I'd been confined. Somewhat flabbergasted at what I was seeing, I concluded that these people were professional incarcerators. Whatever they were, there was no sign anyone had been imprisoned in *these* cells, only metres away from where *I'd* been forced to reside.

I went back to the office and prised open the metal cabinet. I riffled through papers that didn't tell me much. I was becoming frustrated. I got to the bottom drawer and as with the rest of the drawers I pulled out a pile of papers and dumped them on the desk to have a look through. This time, however, as I was lifting the papers out I spotted the corner of a piece of paper jutting up from under the metal flooring of the drawer.

I pulled at it, but it wouldn't come. I looked at where the bottom of the drawer was in relation to the bottom of the cabinet. The heights didn't match: the drawer evidently had a false bottom. I smiled, knowing that finally I was on to something.

I soon discovered that each drawer, all the way up, had a false bottom. And once I'd dismantled the cabinet I was left with thirty-six A4 sized notebooks, each of which had 'from' and 'to' dates on its cover. Above the dates on each of the notebooks was a name. It was a shock to see it there. Later, however, I considered myself to have been idiotic not to have realised that this person *must* have had something to do with my imprisonment. It was the only possible explanation.

On the cover of each notebook were written the words: *Renney's Diary*.

CHAPTER XXXII

I piled all of the diaries into an empty cardboard box I found in a store cupboard along the hall from Renney's office. I carried them onto the roof and put them on the floor next to a wooden table. I went back downstairs into the kitchen and prepared myself a plate of spaghetti with tomato paste, garlic, parmesan and some dried oregano. I opened up a bottle of white wine and took both back upstairs. I placed my dish and the bottle on the table and went behind the bar and took a glass.

I sat down, took a forkful of my meal… then five or six more shovels into my mouth for it tasted so good and I realised I was *starving*, possibly literally as much as anything else. Thinking about it I was probably a little emaciated.

After that initial burst of feeding frenzy I calmed down. I took a long swig of wine straight from the bottle at first, before pouring myself a glass. I put another fork's worth of spaghetti into my mouth; I looked down at the cardboard box and reached for the notebooks.

I began with the earliest one. I read; I ate and I read. Then I drank and I read. Then I just read. And I read... I read about his life, his business ventures, his opinions and attitudes. I began to comprehend his mischievousness and even his outright underhandedness.

I read about some of the women he'd loved and the women he'd used, and about the women and men that he'd paid for. I comprehended the relationships he'd had with his father and his mother. I understood his love of art and artists. I sort of gathered his insecurities and his desire to make a mark, as I kind of grasped his need to be around creative and original people.

As soon as the sun went down it got very cold. I picked up the box containing Renney's diaries and took it inside. I left my plate and glass and empty bottle on the table. I left the box on the floor inside the roof door and descended the stairs.

Bizarre though it may seem I went down the next flight of stairs as well, back down to my quarters... I knew about Stockholm Syndrome, where a detainee develops a fondness and understanding for his captor. And I'd even heard of Lima Syndrome, in which kidnappers develop warm feelings toward their hostages. What I'd never come across was a syndrome that described the irrational affection a person can develop for the environment in which they'd been held.

In my mind, as I wedged securely open the final of the three doors that led down from the hallway through to my cell, I decided to call such a phenomenon *Confinement Syndrome*. It seemed to fit. Not that that was what I suffered from. It was merely, as I saw it, that I had a job to do, and the bed I'd been sleeping in for all that time was actually quite comfortable. And there was zero chance of anyone coming back to imprison me. I knew that from the blood and from what I was reading in the diaries.

I took a hot shower and went to bed... The next day, after breakfast, I went back onto the roof terrace and began reading again. What a complex character this Renney was, I thought, full of contradictions. It wasn't exactly that he was leading a double life; it was more that he wasn't really fully a part of the life he was leading. It struck me that he was always in the future, well, his mind was, that is. Always looking to the next thing, the step ahead, the future move... He was running both away from something and towards something. I suppose simple psychology would claim he was running from his past, his upbringing and his childhood. And he was trying to run towards success. Both in financial terms, which was important to him, and in his desire to be looked at as an intellectual or at least an individual thinker. As with the artists he so admired, yet was unable to emulate due to his lack of talent, he wanted to be respected for something unique. Something unique that somehow left the world with more beauty in it than it took away.

Then I got to Renney's father's (it wasn't clear from the diary) secret stash of winnings from gambling I suppose. Then after reading on for some time I got to the night-time escape to the island. And then... then... I got to his 'big idea'. Wow, what complete and utter lunacy! There was an insanity I then realised that lay just below the surface, which his diaries hadn't up to that point even come close to revealing.

I read about the setting up of the camp, the imprisonment of the American couple, and the leftist radicals and would-be actors on the beach. And Sabina? Lovely, lovely Sabina. That's what I thought. That's what I had thought. But clearly she was as good at keeping her own counsel as were the rest of them.

That night I slept badly. Restless from all the madness in my head; perturbed by what I'd been part of and how inept I'd been at spotting any of it.

I woke early, weary from tossing and turning; I felt anxious, unable to halt my mind. I figured I may as well get up. Apart from anything else I needed to read on. Read on deeper into the private thoughts and spirals of Mr Renney van der Stratten. I climbed the stairs to the roof. The sun had just risen. It was early.

I took a juice up with me from the well-stocked storeroom in the kitchen. I took the box from inside the roof door at the top of the stairs and put it down next to the table. I was wearing a black jumper with the sleeves a little too long. It was cool at that time of the year, at that time of the morning when out of the sun. In less than an hour the sun would have risen, and if there wasn't a strong breeze, my usual shorts and t-shirt would suffice.

I opened the diary I'd been reading the previous evening – I'd kept my place with a paper napkin – and read on...

After reading for two and a half hours, just before I was going to go down to make a coffee I came across Rosio's name. What the...? What the hell was...? There's no way there were two Rosios. What was going...? Rosio, my goddamn... My... my... Rosio... I cried. I cried for the days and the weeks and the months and the weariness I had felt for my existence. I cried; and I didn't have to hold back, not the slightest bit – for it was only the sky and the ocean that were my witnesses.

I read about me and my depression, let's call it that, shall we? And about how I apparently kept complaining about my worthlessness. I would have shouting spells about my inability to write. I threw objects; a glass ashtray against the wall was mentioned.

Most of these bouts I couldn't recall. But I can't state with any certainty that anything I read about myself on that day was untrue. It mentioned how often these spells of anger were followed by periods of introspection. I'd lock myself away. For days on end I wouldn't talk, or I'd sulk and snap.

This was all incredible to me. I was reading about my life… *my* life, mind you, nestled amongst the pages of a stranger's memoirs.

And then the dénouement of what was bound to come, what had to come, what had been floating overhead just out of grasp for some time: Rosio had paid Renney to imprison me. That's it! That sentence there. Nothing more needs to be said. The one person, the only person, you fully trust in the whole world does that to you!

Numb, punch drunk, with a sledgehammered brain, I went down and made a coffee. I took my jumper off and tied it around my waist while I was waiting for the coffee to percolate. I poured it and took my cup out of the front door and went and sat on a rock the other side of the levelled-off parking area. I looked up at the white oblong building framed, as it was, by the blue of the sky that hung above the waters.

Once I'd finished my coffee I got up and walked. I just walked. I walked along the cliff in the direction of the hamlet where I'd arrived all that time ago. My mind I allowed to wander at its own pace. I peered over the cliff's edge every so often. But mainly I walked onwards.

Eventually I saw the top of the Cubist's House. With its small circular Roman tiled crown perched on top of its flat roof terrace, its large white egg thumbing its nose at convention. I strolled towards it. I suppose I should have been circumspect, cautious, but no such thoughts entered my head.

I approached the structure and entered with an easy push of the front door. To the left, as with the oblong house, was what had clearly been an office. The chair was overturned, papers were all over the floor, the painting of the print I had in my quarters of Christ had a broken frame and lay contorted on the desk. Glass was on the floor from a smashed clock, part of which still clung to the wall.

I made my way down some stairs at the end of the hallway, into the basement. It was a more amateurish operation down there, but had obviously still been a prison. A couple of dozen or so paintings were leaning against a wall. I thought of the American couple. I wondered what had happened to them.

I left. I was a shell. I couldn't process the reams of information which had bulldozed my truth. I'd had enough. Everything I came across reinforced that which was inexplicable and indefensible. And I didn't know what I was doing there, doing anywhere. I was just searching, sort of verifying, killing time until I felt I knew what someone in this kind of situation should do... What *was* standard procedure?

I left the Cubist's House and continued in the direction of the cluster of buildings where I'd first got off the bus. I hugged the cliff line as much as I could. The gentle breeze and the view of the waves helped. Occasionally I'd have to veer inland to avoid the fragile cliff's edge or the boulders or the coarse scrubland.

Within half an hour of leaving the Cubist's House I was at the farmhouse; 'my' farmhouse. The door was locked. I could have forced it, but what would have been the point? I peered in through the window to the left of the front door. I spied on a wall shelf by the side of the double bed a few of my folded clothes. Traces of the life of a man so far away now.

It was similar to returning to a school many years after leaving. Not to a reunion, but surreptitiously, clandestinely, maybe during the holidays or at a weekend... Feeling like a ghost listening out for the echoes of one's past. That's how I felt: as if someone else, someone less tainted, had trodden these steps. Someone who wasn't quite the same person. Someone who'd had part of himself destroyed and re-created with a darker edge. That was it: I was darker now. Not the darkness of before, not the self-doubt and the black dog. This was slowly developing into a different kind of darkness: a calculated darkness.

I descended the winding path and went along the beach. I wanted to see the encampment one last time.

It was more or less how I'd remembered it. There were a few small virtually faded red patches here and there. But I now knew they were spots of tomato ketchup or fake blood of some sort or another; certainly not real blood.

I thought about the strange storyteller recounting his anecdote about Stalin. He, I reflected, was the best actor of the lot of them. His story, as I recalled, standing there surveying the site of where I'd last felt happy, reminded me of the story of Vladimír Clementis and Klement Gottwald...

Vladimír Clementis, author and a prominent member of the Czechoslovak Communist Party, was standing next to Klement Gottwald (leader of the Communist Party of Czechoslovakia) on the balcony of the Palace in the Old Town Square in Prague. He was delivering a speech. Clementis saw that Gottwald was cold on that February in 1948. It was snowing and Gottwald was bareheaded. Clementis placed his warm fur hat on Gottwald's head.

The moment was captured by the photographer Karel Hájek. In its small way, for a short moment in time, it was as iconic a photograph as that taken of Jack Ruby shooting Lee Harvey Oswald.

The Czech Communist Party propaganda machine made up thousands of these photographs to be distributed. It was soon in school books all over the country. Everyone knew the image of when the fur hat had been placed on comrade Gottwald's head. What finer example, after all, was there of the spirit of communism?

Until, that is, in 1952, when Clementis was charged with being a bourgeois nationalist, a 'deviationist' and being part of a Trotskyite-Titoite-Zionist conspiracy, and was convicted in the Slánský show trial and subsequently hanged.

After which, *á la* Orwell, that balcony moment was erased from history. Clementis was airbrushed out of existence. Gottwald stood alone delivering his speech to the masses – with a warm head... Where *did* he get that hat?

I allowed myself a trace of a smile as I about-turned and headed back along the beach. *That* was a fine example of the re-writing of history... Who the hell are we at war with now, I asked myself?

As I walked and climbed and walked again, clarity progressively came to me. I finally knew what I was going to do. I hadn't quite been able to see it before. But returning to the encampment and being reminded of what at the time I'd thought had been death and destruction on a terrifying scale had been the catalyst.

It had taken a while: music you couldn't hear, poetry that couldn't be understood, unplayable records, inedible food, and books you couldn't read. And finally, conclusively, the comprehension of the significance of the Gottwald and Clementis recollection: it was the rewriting of history; the rewriting of history with a photograph of a person you couldn't see. A photograph of a person who was there, but who you couldn't see... Nobody should be permitted to rewrite history, to make lies become truth. That was the ultimate crime, surely.

And stupidly, perversely, unfathomably – yes, all that and more – I headed back to my oblong edifice. For, never in my life had I been more motivated to write, to actually *tell* a story.

I made myself a mushroom omelette on toast, with tinned mushrooms and frozen bread. I even had a large mug of tea with UHT milk. I had my meal on the terrace before descending to my living quarters and beginning to write...

I wrote the story of my life, my recent life. I knew it now; *all* of it. I knew about the different strands that had culminated in my sitting there in an empty house on a small island. Renney had provided me with the complete story. And the complete story was what I was going to write.

I wrote for hours at a time, without pause. Until my back hurt, my wrist ached and my neck was knotted. Then when I'd eventually finished my story I cut it up into neat pages, bound it as best I could, and made a cover by cutting out a picture of the Cubist's House I'd found in one of Renney's drawers. I went to Renney's office and photocopied it for myself.

That done, I went back downstairs to the trunk filled with the chemicals. I put on the protective gloves and painstakingly painted a thin strip of Batrachatoxin along the outer edge of each page of the original copy. Batrachatoxin is a chemical that seeps through the skin and results in eventual death.

I had created the story of my life. It wasn't quite a book you couldn't read, unlike those created by the artist I'd been enamoured of in that magazine from the 1970s. Because I wanted my story and my feelings to be known and understood: I wanted *my* words to be read.

I had created a book that you *could* read. But in so doing it would kill you. It was perfect. It was some kind of Dadaist dénouement: "Should I kill myself, or have a cup of coffee?" as Albert Camus once said.

------ • • • ------

A couple of days later I phoned Rosio from the small port on the other side of the island. I told her where I was – or rather, I told her I was in the house along the cliff from the Cubist's House, the oblong house, and how she could get there. I told her to come and get me. I'd broken my leg and was in bed recuperating, I said, and could hardly move and no one was around… She wouldn't stop apologising. I told her it was fine; such a good idea!

She'd be pleased to hear, I told her, that I'd finally written my fourth book. So it had all been worth it. And the instant I said that I sensed the relief in her voice. I said that I couldn't wait for her to come and get me and read my new novel. I also mentioned a lot about us and our relationship together. There was a hush at the end of the line when I was talking about us, us together, us as an entity.

"Yes… I've left my new novel on my desk in my apartment. It's the third door on the right, then down the stairs… Don't let me forget it," I feigned a laugh, "not after all this."

An almost inaudible, slightly pained laugh was her response. "I can't wait to see you," she stuttered.

After we'd said our goodbyes I went downstairs, reset the timer on the doors and wedged them a few inches open with bent cardboard. As soon as the doors were pulled open and the person had walked through they would close behind. Clunk – for ninety-nine days.

I had a backpack with me. Once off the boat I took a coastal train to the first medium-sized town, went to the bank and emptied Renney's accounts. I wouldn't have to think about money again for many years.

I walked from the bank to the outskirts of town. I took the coastal road winding up and around the edge of the mountain. The water glistened and sparkled below me. After an hour's walk I came to a lay-by on a bend. I went to the edge of this parking area to the knee-high wall and stared out over the ocean. In the distance I could just make out the island. I stood there for a while contemplating the madness that had been my life. And I thought about the changed person I'd become.

I returned to the roadside and prepared to thumb a ride. After forty minutes a woman in a red 1960s Triumph TR3A pulled up. The roof was off and I could see her pencil skirt was hitched up high. The car model aside, I felt I could have been in an Italian film.

"You want a lift?" she asked in an East European accent. I nodded. "Where you want to go?"

I shook my head. "Surprise me." She lifted her sunglasses slightly up and raised a quizzical eyebrow in my direction. She then nodded, smiled and gestured for me to get in. I opened the door, took my bag from my shoulder and patted it. I'd taken the Batrachatoxin with me – just in case. Just in case I decided to write another story.

I turned to the woman and smiled as she opened up the throttle…

THE END

NOTES AND ACKNOWLEDGEMENTS

Thanks to Lynn Bonnin for advice, help and encouragement. Thanks to Paddy Long for all her help on this manuscript. Invaluable help which has made this book a much smoother read than would otherwise have been the case. Thanks to Dave Eure, and thanks to Nick Pope.

Reality is subjective… I hope this life reads like a film and you, as I, can easily see the pictures in your head.

Jean Bonnin
La Charente, France
22nd October 2015

V5

This was my fourth manuscript.

www.redeggpublishing.com

Lightning Source UK Ltd.
Milton Keynes UK
UKOW04f0952180716

278420UK00020BA/535/P